WHAT THE NANNY SAID

LARA FINCH

Ebook ISBN: 978-1-83700-098-2
Paperback ISBN: 978-1-83700-100-2

Cover design: Ghost
Cover images: Alamy

Published by Storm Publishing.
For further information, visit:
www.stormpublishing.co

For Tom, with love

ONE

EVIE

NOW

Evie Segura's beautiful life will burn down today. Before the week is over, almost everything she knows about herself and her family will prove false. There will be an agonising death and a terrible discovery; an ending and an unimaginable beginning. But Evie doesn't know any of that yet and she listens happily to music on her AirPods, picks up her keys and leaves Antonio's apartment, skipping down the concrete steps. She's in the street now, in the warm dusk of Mexico City, off to visit her mother, Mia, for an early supper and a chat.

The traffic on the highway is loud and crazy, but she looks past it, across four lanes of chaos, to the purple blooms of the jacaranda trees on the far side. With an intake of breath, she steps onto the road, dodging trucks and bikes and cars, moving coolly, like a fish slipping through reeds in a river, ignoring the gratuitous honks that she attracts, this tall self-assured girl with sharp shoulders and short blonde hair. Her composed and airy look is unusual, at odds with the vivid, overheated neighbourhood.

She pauses on the central reservation, humming along to the music, then weaves her way to the far pavement and, turning right, walks carefree under shimmering clouds of petals. A neighbour, a skinny, sloe-eyed youth, sitting at a table outside a café, drinking Corona from the bottle, raises his hand and she raises hers back; her mind wanders, making connections – street cafés and outside tables, an open book, a single espresso. She's drifting into a familiar dream – Europe, Paris, the Louvre. She'll go there one day with Antonio. Or without Antonio. She has a decision to make and she wants Mia's advice.

She bears left into a cobbled street, a fifty-metre walk, and there is Mia's gate in the high stone wall, left ajar. She removes her AirPods and, for a second, watches her mother tending plants in the courtyard at the side of the house – her precious tomatoes, chilis and peppers in raised beds under the branches of an oleander tree. Mia, as always, is wearing a practical, roomy linen dress – today's is deep blue. On her head, she wears a straw hat with a wavy wayward brim. Evie's heart warms as Mia looks up quizzically, surprised out of her reverie. 'Lost in gardening again!' Evie says, not noticing an unusual dullness in her mother's eyes.

'You know me so well.' Mia lays down her trowel, a slight uncertainty and weakness in the movement of her arms as she rubs her hands down her dress and hugs her daughter.

'So... Shakespeare,' Evie says, still oblivious. 'I was thinking about a line just now; I was reminded by the jacarandas, a famous line about violets. We studied it at school, but I can't remember the play...'

'*Twelfth Night*,' Mia replies, removing her hat and running her fingers through her long fringe. '*The sweet sound that breathes upon a bank of violets...*' Mia knows such things, having been raised and educated thousands of miles away, in England. 'It's about fickle love, Evie – don't mistake it for true love, will you?'

Evie smiles, thinking of the decision she must make.

'*Twelfth Night* has an Antonio in it,' Mia adds, as though this bonds Evie's Antonio and the whole of Mexico to Shakespeare. 'What would you like to drink? I have Jarritos, sparkling water – red wine?'

Mia will have the sparkling water – the wine has been bought specially for Evie.

'A glass of wine, thanks. Are we eating outside?'

'I think so, don't you? It's a comfortable temperature. And not too dusty.' It is, in fact, fairly dusty, but not unbearable.

'Good,' Evie says. She has loved this courtyard for as long as she can remember. When she was little, she'd come home from school and sit at the table and sketch whatever she could see, in reality or in her imagination – the snaking branches of the tree, a bony cat that wandered in, a tiger, a goddess, an invented bird. The courtyard is where she learned to draw.

Mia, brushing soil from her dress, goes into the house to fetch the drinks and returns almost immediately with a tray. Wine, sparkling water, Jarritos, bread, olives, olive oil. She sets them down on the table, on a pretty patterned cloth.

'Thank you,' Evie says, only now noticing that Mia looks pale and seems distracted. 'Are you okay?'

'Oh yes. A busy day in the classroom, that's all... Tell me your news.'

At twenty-six years old, Evie is confused about life. Her Fine Arts degree was completed two years ago, but now she's working in the coffee shop near Antonio's apartment, serving endless espressos and lattes. In slow moments, she finds herself sketching on napkins and filling notebooks with ideas for sculptures she never has time to create. Occasionally, she thinks of travelling to Europe and of exploring the art galleries there.

But Antonio has been dropping hints about marriage and putting down roots. She loves him – of course she does – but something else is calling to her, something wild and uncertain that she can't quite name. She needs Mia for this conversation. Needs her mother's steady wisdom. Most of all, she would like her blessing.

'Are you sure you're okay?' Evie says.

Mia is a little slumped on the bench. 'You know, I do have a headache,' she says, picking up her straw hat which has been lying on a chair. 'I'll take a painkiller and go lie down for five minutes. Do you have everything you need?' She surveys the table, the food and the drinks, with a serious expression.

'Oh yes. No problem. I have quite an agenda for you later. A big decision to make.'

Mia smiles. She gets up and goes into the house, and Evie listens to her mother climb the stairs up to bedrooms, then she takes her phone from her bag and sees a message from Antonio about ingredients for dinner. She replies, then clicks on Instagram. Always, every day, there is new artwork to see. Young people making computer art, textile art, multimedia art, political art – and seeming to get by in life. She scrolls past a spherical yellow smiley face mounted on a spike; an intricate piece of weaving; a small boy with a telescope in the middle of a forest fire – on and on past dozens of images, becoming stupidly zoned out and numb and that is why her heart beats twice before she hears an uneven and jagged scream, as violent as metal clashing with metal, and it takes her several seconds to figure out what it is and where it's coming from.

She drops the phone and runs into the house, slamming her thigh against the kitchen table, clumsily running up the stairs and into the bedroom where, in disbelief, she watches Mia's body, tangled up in her blue dress, twisting and arching on the bed like she is possessed, her face contorted and tortured, her eyes fixed in a terrified stare at nothing at all. With all understanding deserting her, Evie falls to her knees and holds her mother's head: 'Look at me, Mama. Please, look at me. Please.' She can't think... What should she do? Why did she leave her phone outside? She should call an ambulance. She stands up, ready to run for her phone. But it's too late. Mia's stare leaves her eyes, as her gaze, her expression, her entire being melt into silence and emptiness.

Evie feels her own body quietly, slowly splinter into a thousand parts and her brain attempts to float away as she realises that this is the moment of her mother's death and she is the witness.

In the following week, Evie is robotic. She sleeps ten hours a night and relies on others to get her through the days. At the apartment, Antonio cradles her, makes comfort food and is kind when she cannot eat it. He brings her tulips and cornflowers and takes them away when Evie asks him to. Grief has crushed the life out of her. Grief and shock. At night, she dreams of Mia: of her mother's wide arms and her last hug, of her long red hair and her kind and loving eyes peering through the strands of that heavy fringe – and then she sees Mia swept up in a black tornado, disappearing into nothingness. Her dreams aren't subtle.

At the house, Mia's old friend Ramona visits and takes care of organisational matters, talking on the phone with Mia's school, registering her death, looking for a will, discovering that there is none, making arrangements for the funeral. Ramona's face is almost expressionless, and she retains a stillness as she works through the tasks, efficient and diligent; but her clothes are as flamboyant as ever – bright reds, yellows and blues – and when she speaks, her voice is loud and expressive. Evie, even in the depths of her distress, appreciates that it's good to have the house filled with a familiar sound.

On the sixth day after Mia's death, just two days before the funeral, she sits in the kitchen while Ramona makes tea. 'Mia always offered me tea. She loved her tea and this little fat teapot,' she says, holding it up. 'Her English days were full of tea, I suppose. Her Melody days.'

'Yes,' says Evie. 'Her Melody days. She became Mia to become properly Mexican.'

'She loved this country. But she was always half-English, don't you think?'

'Definitely. You're right... More than half.'

Ramona brings the tea to the table. 'Evie, mija, when you are ready, you should go through her belongings. Maybe you should do three categories. Things to keep. Things to be given away or sold. And a category for *not sure*... I can take care of the rest for you. You know, the practical side.'

'Thank you.'

On the table in front of them is the pathology report from the hospital, still in its white envelope. Ramona takes it out and passes the papers to Evie, who reads in silence. All is exactly as the doctor had expected, Mia had suffered a catastrophic brain haemorrhage; she was only fifty-two – it was incredibly unusual. Ramona looks briefly at the statement, then returns it to the envelope. 'Shall I look after this for now? It isn't a nice thing to see.'

'Yes, please.'

Ramona drops it into her red raffia bag.

'Actually, Ramona, I'm not ready to get rid of her personal things,' Evie says. 'I think it will be a while. You know, all those linen dresses and the straw hats? When I look at them in the wardrobe, it's like she's almost there – some of the dresses are so old, I've grown up with them. They have sort of formed her shape...' She doesn't mention that as she holds them to her face, she imagines that she can smell the scent of Mia's skin, or that, on one occasion, she took them all from the wardrobe and lay on Mia's bed with dresses all over and around her, wanting to disappear into them.

'I understand,' Ramona says. 'Maybe it's best little by little, starting with silly inconsequential things.'

Evie smiles. At the minute, nothing of Mia's seems silly or inconsequential. Not even her stationery drawer with random paper clips and sticky tape and blunt pencils, or her cooking pots and pans which look like a million other pots and pans, and yet there is a dent here or a scratch there that has been part of their little family forever. As for Mia's books, her gardening books, her Spanish textbooks, the favourite English-language novels that she read when young, Evie will keep those forever.

Ramona says goodbye and Evie goes upstairs to Mia's bedroom, opens the wardrobe doors, and lies once more on the bed – gazing into the wardrobe. Mia had had such simplicity in her life, she'd liked it that way. Those long dresses, all the same, made by Mia herself with practicality in mind. They were wide at the hem, but not flowy – nothing about Mia had been flowy. And she'd picked a limited palette of colours: blues, greens, greys and whites. Then Evie notices a spot of bright red fabric at the back of the shelf above the rail, just a spot sandwiched inside a pile of sweaters. She's never seen Mia wear this colour, a brilliant crimson, and she's moved to get up off the bed and take a small wooden chair over to the wardrobe. Standing on it and reaching in, she discovers that the fabric is a loose-weave cotton, a scarf or shawl, and her hand is surprised by the firm shape of something wrapped inside. She pulls the scarf towards her and peels back the fabric to reveal a lumpy brown envelope. Evie extracts Mia's old, long-expired British passport – Melody Jane King, *her Melody days* – and briefly examines the faded picture of her mother when young, strange but still familiar; she'd continued to line her eyes with smoky kohl, was always peering out from under that long fringe. Then she pulls out several papers, yellow with age, along with a strip of four passport photos of a young woman. A stranger.

Evie climbs down and sits on the bed to examine them,

unfolding press cuttings from British newspapers dated September 1999. Two from the *Daily Telegraph* and a double-page spread in the *Daily Mail*, all reporting the same story. Evie reads of two murders and of three disappearances in a wealthy part of London called Little Venice. At first, she reads idly, vaguely wondering why, of all things English, Mia had kept these news reports. But the switch comes quickly, to a sense of sickness and violation. One of the missing people, she discovers, was a little girl who had just turned three. Her name was Evie Preston-Bliss, the daughter of Sam Preston and Lucy Bliss. Like her, an English Evie. Like her, born in the summer of 1996.

TWO

LUCY

1999

Evie and I were in the communal garden today. My eyes were tearing up from the cold spring air, and my head was numb. I hummed a favourite Bach melody, as though it might warm me up, pausing to blow warmth into my frozen fingers. A child's mitten was lying on the ground by a bush, and I picked it up, sensing that it was a special glove – hand-knitted by someone who'd taken care in choosing a particular shade of apple-green wool and had worked in a single red stripe. I laid it on a bench.

Sam texted to say he'd be home late. More long hours in the edit suite. He didn't know if he'd be back at eight or nine or midnight. His words carried a familiar chill, but I tried not to dwell on it. Self-pity was ugly. Suspicion even worse. I tilted my face to the silver sky instead and surveyed the garden. Our glorious Little Venice private park, framed by grand mansions. A millionaires' paradise, for God's sake, and I told myself: *You live here now, Lucy. Act like you belong.*

I scratched at the patch of eczema on my hand, willing it to go away, and was pleased to be distracted by the sight of a young

Chinese man at the far end of the garden, wrestling with his lively dog, a golden labradoodle. He caught my eye and shrugged helplessly as the dog bounced and twisted. I smiled and waved as he scooped the wriggling mass of fur into his arms and strode off in the direction of his flat.

Evie was now bobbing along merrily from one tree to the next. She sat down with a bump and grabbed a bunch of purple crocuses from the earth, stuffing them into her mouth and looking at me defiantly, one bud hanging out like a cigarette. Oh God, some plants were poisonous, weren't they? I sprinted across the grass, desperate to save her from a crocussy death, but she resisted, vigorously, arching her back and tossing her head from side to side while I attempted to sweep the petals from her mouth. The more I begged her to be still, the more she twisted away.

Mid-struggle, I turned around and found myself facing a young woman, standing five metres away, holding a grey cat. She was pretty, fresh-faced from the icy air.

I'd thought we were alone in the garden and couldn't work out where she'd come from.

'Look,' she said to Evie, her voice full of wonder. 'A cat. Would you like to say hello?'

'I hope you don't mind.' She turned to me. 'I thought the distraction might help.'

I smiled and put on a grateful face. 'Thank you. That's just the thing. My daughter's such a barbarian.'

'You're not a barbarian, are you?' She laughed. 'You're an angel.' Evie was soft and still and snuggly in my arms now – completely transformed. She said: 'Cat,' and reached out to touch its thick fur, but the cat twisted in the woman's arms, and she let it run away.

'I'm Taylor. I live on Sanderson Road.' She looked directly at me with glittering green eyes, and I felt slightly dazed.

'We live on Russell Drive,' I said. 'I'm Lucy and this is Evie.'

Taylor leaned in, tapping Evie's nose and saying 'pop'. Evie laughed and said 'Taylor.' Amazing. She'd never done that before – repeated someone's name first go. And her face was glowing. I mean it was glowing anyway because of the cold, but it seemed to be glowing for Taylor. I wanted to keep the conversation going but couldn't think of anything to say – my head was too thick and foggy. Eventually, I managed, 'Have you lived here long?'

'Only a month. It's all new to me. Isn't the garden lovely?' She looked around, like she was awestruck by its grandeur.

'Yes, it is. And this time of year, so few people in it.'

'Just us!' She shivered a little and stamped her feet to warm them. No wonder she was cold – her legs were bare inside her biker boots, and she was wearing a flimsy skirt that flopped to her knees under a parka that was undone. She seemed carefree and untroubled.

'We're obviously the hardy ones,' I said.

'I like the cold.'

'Me too.' I don't really. I like being in the warm.

'I saw you put that on a bench,' she said casually. 'It might get rained on out here – that would be a shame; it's a nice glove. I'll take it and do some sleuthing, see if I can find its home.' She picked it up and put it in her pocket.

'That's nice of you – I hate to think of someone taking the time to knit a sweet little glove, and then it gets lost.' I paused awkwardly, then I reached into my bag and said, 'I have this little video camera – would you mind filming us, just for a minute or so. It's such a stunning day and the garden looks so spectacular. I thought, maybe Evie would like to see this when she's grown up – how beautiful her life is, I mean.'

'Sure.' Taylor looked delighted and took the little camera from me. 'It's neat!' It was a tiny thing called a Flip. Who thought you'd ever be able to make videos from something so small?

I took Evie's hand and Taylor filmed us. 'Let's go!' I said. 'Let's run as fast as we can! Do you like running?'

'Running,' Evie said excitedly.

I laughed and led her by the hand as we ran at her fastest speed across the grass, round the trees, round the islands of shrubs and back to Taylor. I picked up my little girl and wiped the cold-induced tears from her eyes and turned to Taylor: 'I try to protect her from all the dangers in the world,' I said. 'But she has such a curious soul. I love that.'

Taylor handed back the camera and I felt suddenly self-conscious. 'We should probably head in – it's Evie's teatime,' I mumbled, my face flushed. 'Thanks for the crocus rescue. It was lovely to meet you.'

'You too, Lucy. See you another time, I hope.'

As we walked away, her voice stayed with me. Warm and life-enhancing. You can tell so much about someone by their voice.

I saw her today from the window in Evie's room, in the garden walking alone, her hands in the pockets of her parka. Like last time, a skirt underneath and bare legs, her feet in biker boots. She has a sweet walk – her toes point out and she treads gracefully like a dancer. I dashed down to the kitchen and pretty much shoved Evie into her coat and boots. 'Bobble hat and go!' I said, practically dragging her out of the French doors and into the garden. It was cold again, but this time the sky was heavy with low ponderous clouds. It looked like rain. I didn't care – with my cloudy head and unsteady legs, the weather wasn't my main concern.

Taylor spotted us immediately and came over to talk. I asked her about the glove and whether she had managed to reunite it with its owner. 'I've been worrying about it – it looked so sad without its pair,' I said. 'And I don't know any other families on the garden with such a small child.'

She put her head on one side and did a wonky smile. 'Big coincidence, but I found the owner!' Taylor worked as a live-in housekeeper (which sounded so Victorian!) and she told me that her employers were friendly with their neighbours who'd hosted a cold, wintery barbecue the previous Saturday. The glove belonged to one of the visitors – a little boy called Oliver. A family hand-me-down that had once belonged to a great-uncle.

'Between us, we did a good thing!' I said.

Taylor asked if she could give Evie a ride on her shoulders, and I watched as she was the horse, prancing around, Evie the delighted rider, her arms wrapped around Taylor's head. They cantered to the tennis court and back and Taylor said she had to go in now – she had bathrooms to clean. I wished her luck and hoped there wasn't too much disgusting hair clogging up the plugholes. We made comical yuck faces at each other. I was disappointed that she couldn't spend more time with us.

A chance meeting in the garden today after two long weeks. Evie was thrilled to see her and begged her to be a horse again. But the rain came down – horrible spiky sleet – and I asked Taylor if she'd like to come to Russell Drive for a coffee. Her eyes lit up like I'd asked her to tea at the Ritz, and the three of us ran towards the flat, the sleet slapping our faces, our noses and knuckles red with cold. As she came into the glow of the kitchen, she looked around in wonder. 'Lives of the rich and famous,' she said, making me blush with embarrassment.

'We're extremely lucky.' I took off Evie's outdoor clothes and draped her damp coat on a chair while Taylor walked around the room, stroking the worktops and inspecting the taps over the sink.

'This kitchen is so wow, but it's friendly too,' she said brightly. 'Such a home! Who's this?'

She'd taken a photo from its fridge magnet. My darling Melody nervously holding newborn Evie, her kohled eyes peering up from under her long fringe, blissed out but nervous. 'That's my best friend from childhood.'

'She looks nice. Are you still best friends?'

'Yes. Definitely. But she doesn't live nearby; so I don't see her as much as I'd like.'

She replaced the photo and took another. 'And this one? Is this your husband?'

'Yes, it is. That's Sam – that picture's a favourite of mine.'

She'd picked the one we call 'the sexy hero photo' – Sam in the desert of the Western Sahara. Sand in his hair, making it stand up on end. Wearing reporter's clothes holding his reporter's notebook. A long cotton turban wound round his neck.

'Oh, Lucy. He's handsome – who doesn't love blonde hair and dark eyes? And lucky Evie to inherit them!' She wrestled herself out of her parka and pretended to cover Evie with it, lifting it off straight away. 'Peep po.'

I took two cups to the coffee machine. I loved the way she said the first thing that came into her head.

'Espresso or lungo?'

'Oh, whatever you're having. I'm just excited that it comes out of a machine.'

'Don't you have a machine?'

'Oh sure. But they give you a thrill every time, don't they?'

'Yes, they do! You're right. Two lungos then, with a dash of milk.'

She giggled. 'Yup.'

'Ooo.' She started feeling inside the pockets of her discarded parka. 'I have something in here.' She presented a foil-wrapped package. 'Chocolatey slice. Perfect with our coffee. It's healthy. Mainly oatmeal. Dark chocolate. Dates. I made it last night.'

As she put the parcel on the counter and unwrapped it, I noticed that her fingers moved quickly and delicately, like she was playing something complicated on the piano. She wore silver rings, different styles and shapes. I saw a seahorse and a bee.

I said I'd love some of her chocolate slice – which was actually more of a small chocolatey brick – but first I'd put Evie down for her nap. I told Taylor to make herself at home. I took Evie through to the downstairs playroom, settling her in the cot and, as usual, I sang our favourite Celtic lullaby, feeling a little slow in the head, straining to remember the words. I loved the way Evie responded to that song – when a mother laid her baby down in a field, her eyes would widen. When the mother couldn't find the baby, she often whispered 'poor baby.' Then, of course, the baby was found and Evie was delighted and consoled. That didn't happen today – she fell asleep before the end.

When I returned to the kitchen, I found Taylor sitting on a bar stool, one leg idly swinging, leafing through my Claudia Roden cookbook.

'I love these recipes.'

'Do you know Claudia Roden?'

'Not really. Is she famous?'

'Well... she is in this neck of the woods.'

'Oh, I don't really know this neck of the woods. Being a new arrival.' She held up the book; it was open on a page with a recipe for aubergine slices with pomegranate, yogurt and tahini. 'Have you made this?'

'Well, actually no. I haven't made any of them. I'm from a meat and two veg background and I don't really know what to do with exotic ingredients.'

'You can always learn.'

I wondered whether to confide in her. 'Yeah, but then, not really. Sam's from a sophisticated cuisine sort of world – but I just look at the recipes and... I don't know. Pass me the book.'

She passed it across the kitchen island.

'There we go,' I said. 'Concoction with fifteen ingredients and one of them is pomegranate molasses. First of all, I've no idea what that is or where you buy it. Second of all, fifteen ingredients! I'm getting palpitations just thinking about it.'

She laughed. 'Does Sam cook?'

'No. He works so hard – he's always knackered when he gets home. I cook old school, which he doesn't mind, but I'd like to be able to do sophisticated cooking for when his friends come round.'

'I love cooking. It's one of my things. If ever you need someone to cook for you, I could do it.'

A generous thing for her to say – but kind of strange. She picked up the picture of Sam again. 'What work does he do, your husband?'

'He's in TV. He's a reporter at the BBC.'

'Cool.' She surveyed the room, and I could read her thoughts – *How on earth...? Is TV work that well paid?* I didn't tell her that the flat was bought with money that Sam inherited from his grandfather. Or that I'm not used to wealth and wonder whether I ever will be. I mean, I'm totally grateful. Just not at ease.

'What sort of reporting does he do?'

'Current affairs. He travels a lot. To dangerous places sometimes – scares me to bits. He's covered the wars in Afghanistan and Kosovo. He's on TV a lot. Sam Preston.'

'I've never met anyone as glamorous as you.'

'Honestly, we're not at all glamorous. Well, Sam might be. But I'm just a stay-at-home mum. How about you? What did you do before you came here?'

'Difficult question to answer. I've done a bit of everything.'

I couldn't place her accent. 'Where are you from?'

'Pretty much nowhere. My mum's Portuguese, though, and my dad's Scottish.'

'Nice mix. I'm fairly thoroughly English – grew up in a country village.'

'Opposite of me then,' she said. 'When I was little, we lived in Brazil – then, when I was nine, we moved to Australia for a few years – then Ghana – then two years in Alaska, then Scotland – so…' She sipped her coffee and tipped her head to one side, taking a bite of the chocolate cake and curling her hand to catch the crumbs. She's *very* pretty. That mass of thick hair, those smiling green eyes. 'I think your cosmopolitan background is wonderful,' I said.

'Not really. The middle of nowhere in an Alaskan winter. Not the greatest.'

'Why did your family move so much?' I took my cup over to the sink and ran it under the tap.

'My dad's a mining engineer – we were always in mining towns. Not in Scotland, though. That was an attempt to live somewhere normal – it didn't last.' She popped the last of the chocolatey slice into her mouth.

'Do you speak Portuguese?'

'A bit.'

'And university?'

'Oh, I didn't go. I saw the world instead. I mean, places more fun than Alaska. Working bars mainly, but I'm happiest working with children. I do those holiday kids' clubs sometimes. You know, where the parents dump their children all day long while they knock back the local wine and slob about on the loungers soaking up the sun, kind of taking a vacation from the kids as much as anything. I've done it in Portugal – I'm pretty in demand there, as you can imagine.'

'Oh. We've done that kids' club thing. Evie seemed happy and it's good for them to mix with other children.'

'Oh,' she said. 'I'm sorry. I know most of the parents are brilliant really. You obviously are, Lucy. You're a brilliant mother – I can just tell.'

I turned my back, suddenly overwhelmed by her sympathy and our easy intimacy. That rush of emotion when someone says kindly 'are you all right?' I stood at the sink; pretending that my cup still needed washing.

'Are you feeling okay, Lucy?'

I turned to face her, rubbing my eyes. 'Yes, yes, I'm fine. I was feeling ashamed about the kids' clubs. Stupid of me.' I couldn't think what else to say. 'I'm glad you came in for a coffee,' I murmured. 'Sometimes, I long for a little adult time. I mean, you're obviously much younger than me – but still...'

She jumped down from the bar stool and came and hugged me. I caught her scent – citrussy and fresh; she smelled like summer. Briefly, she touched my hair, then pulled away and went back to her stool, blowing me a kiss.

'Thank you,' I said. 'I'm sorry you've caught me at a strange moment. I've been having bad nights. Insomnia messes with your head.'

'Don't worry about it, everyone has moments. Especially if their sleep is wrecked. I've had loads of them... Come and sit down – tell me about your work. Before Evie.'

'I was a solicitor. Family law.'

'What – you advise people on divorcing? Like how to get tons of dosh out of their cheating husbands?' In an instant, she'd snapped from sweetness to vivacious. 'And custody of the kids? Hang on. Is that how you got all this?'

She made eyes at our kitchen opulence.

'Taylor!'

'Just a joke, Lucy – have you given it all up completely then? The divorce work?'

'Looks like it.'

'It's just – my mother – she's an architect and wherever we

lived, she always had her work. I'm really proud of her. I think it was good for me that she worked.'

'Yeah, I can see that.' There was a pause while we gazed thoughtfully at each other. 'I don't know why,' I said, 'but I feel like I've known you for ages.'

'Perhaps we knew each other in a former life?' She raised an eyebrow, like it was half-joke, half-true. 'You're scratching your hand – I've noticed that you do that a lot.' She gestured with fluttering fingers. 'Show me.'

I held out my palm.

'It looks painful.' Across the kitchen island, she held onto my hand. 'I have something that can help. I have to go now. But can I see you soon?'

'Yes,' I said. 'I'd love that.'

THREE

SEPTEMBER 1999

DI Adra Roy watches as an officer places a knife and other items into bags, ready to go to forensics. 'Is the witness ready?' she asks her colleague Sinead.

'Yes, she's in the interview room.'

'Anything I need to know before we begin?'

'Well, it's a peculiar situation, that's for sure... She turns up here with evidence of murder but says she's completely innocent.'

'Yes, that's a new one,' says Adra briskly. 'Come on in, Sinead. Let's see what she has to say for herself.'

They enter the interview room at Paddington Police Station, where Taylor Love, a pretty young woman wearing an incongruous floaty dress, is messing with her hair. She looks up with big anticipatory eyes. Adra Roy introduces herself and Sinead and starts the tape:

AR – Thank you for coming in Taylor... We appreciate your help. For the record, you are here of your own accord and are free to leave at any time. You have brought us, I understand, a part of a yellow blood-stained T-shirt belonging to Lucy Bliss and several strands of hair from the head of Lucy Bliss. Is that correct?

TL – That's right. And you'll find a knife with her blood on the blade. In a bush in the garden at Russell Drive.

AR – And you have information about the death of Lucy Bliss that you would like to share with us?

TL – Correct. Quite a lot of information.

AR – Let's start at the beginning... Your address is Flat 1, 37 Russell Drive, London W11 2JV.

TL – Yes.

AR – You worked for Sam Preston and Lucy Bliss looking after their daughter Evie Preston-Bliss... correct?

TL – Yes.

AR – Can you tell me how that job came about?

TL – Lucy and I became friends, and I started helping out with her daughter, Evie. It went from there.

AR – You didn't know Sam or Lucy before spring this year?

TL – Correct.

AR – Can you tell us how you came to know them?

TL – Sure. It started in the spring, like you said. I was in the communal garden one day. Back then I was living on Sanderson Road. Anyhow, I spotted Lucy and Evie, and Lucy looked incredibly weird – like she shouldn't be in charge of a small child.

AR – What do you mean by that?

TL – She was unsteady on her legs for a start. She bent down to pick up a kid's lost glove and almost fell over sideways! Her hand was shaking like a jelly, and I thought, *is she actually drunk?*

AR – Go on.

TL – So, Evie started ripping up flowers and Lucy went crazy – screeching and yelling. She lost it completely. I felt sorry for the child, for Evie, and I went over to help. Concerned citizen and all that. Lucy practically fell over herself thanking me. But her eyes were swollen, and she was finding it hard to focus – and she kept glancing over at the glove on the bench like it was going to attack her or something.

I told her not to worry about the glove, I'd see if I could reunite it with its owner. I mean, I knew I wouldn't, but she was so freaked out, and I felt genuinely sorry for her, and that's how I got to know her. One day, she invited me into her house for a coffee and that's when I realised how rich she was. Or Sam was. Whatever. And the weird stuff just kept coming. I found her singing this creepy lullaby to Evie about abandoning babies. Who does that to a little girl? Shocking, right? I didn't think Lucy was doing it *intentionally*. Just that she hadn't a clue.

I mean, she left Evie in a holiday kids' club once and you'd think she'd committed murder when she told me about it. She was crying real tears, big ones. I hugged her and she clung on to me way too long and too desperate. I thought she was having a nervous breakdown…

AR – And yet you continued the relationship?

TL – Well, the coffee was good and I had time to kill. Plus, I was curious. Her crazy neurotics were kind of fascinating. Of course, I didn't know the full story then, about the danger she was in – that all came later.

FOUR

LUCY

1999

Taylor knocked on the French doors, making me jump, and came in cheerfully, carrying a red plastic ladybird on wheels, its handle over her arm like it was a handbag. 'For Evie to ride on,' she said. 'I hope you don't mind. I saw it in a charity shop and couldn't help myself.' She took off her parka. She was wearing a silky dress, blue with tiny white daisies, a bottle-green cardigan, kind of grungy, and bare legs in biker boots. Her big joyful smile made my head flip from mad to sunny in an instant.

'Our second date!' she said.

Evie was eyeing up the ladybird, super excited. Taylor touched my arm gently, then knelt down: 'You can sit on it Evie!' Evie clambered on and whizzed around the kitchen at full speed, bashing into walls and kitchen units like she'd just discovered bumper cars.

'That's a success,' Taylor said.

'Lucky find. It looks new.'

'I know. I just had to grab it.' She flopped onto the sofa,

flipped her hair away from her face, pulled off her boots and tucked her bare feet under her.

'Thank you so much!' The words came out too eager and too bright. In the moment, my new friend made everything seem lighter and easier.

I brought over the coffees and croissants and put them on a table by the sofa and could hardly stop myself from bombarding her with questions. I wanted to hear about Brazil and her terrible time in Alaska. And how come someone like her, not obviously rich, had come to live in our crazy upper-crust celebrity neighbourhood. She changed the subject, and said that she'd been exploring London, looking for casual jobs and seen an ad for a housekeeper in the newsagent's window on Clifton Road. She makes the most unlikely 'housekeeper' – the opposite of Mrs Danvers in *Rebecca*. I didn't know until today that her bosses are called *Orlando* and *Persephone!*

'Well, she calls herself Seph,' Taylor said, 'but Persephone's her real name. I've seen it on her post. And he does the full Orlando. Heavens, they're a mouthful.'

'My goodness. You thought we were glamorous, but I don't think we can compete – plain old Sam and Lucy.'

'No, no, they're the opposite of glamorous! Their names are compensation for being dead boring. They're management consultants. They go into companies and like, turn everything on its head and say Gloria should be sacked from HR and Mo should be demoted, and they think organisations should have a motto like, I don't know – *Imaginators Shape the World* or S*tep out with Boldness* or some shit.'

'Haha! It's a way to earn a crust, I guess. Do they have children?'

'God no. They don't have the time. They leave the house at the crack of dawn and they're often not home till about eight. One morning, I woke up at five, don't know why, but I went downstairs for a change of scenery and Seph was in the kitchen doing squats and lunges in her bra and pants. Huffing and puffing like an old boiler.'

'I can't imagine living like that.'

'Me neither,' she said. 'All work and no play. A balance is best... Oh, it's so nice to have discovered you in the garden. A friendly neighbour! And Evie too, she's adorable – so smiley and sweet-natured.' Evie looked up from the ladybird, calling out 'Taylor!'

She's right about Evie. It's a miracle, given her fucked-up parents.

Taylor twisted the rings on her fingers. 'Anyhow, Orlando and Seph need someone to do all their crap. Like food shopping and cooking and cleaning and laundry. So, yeah, I clean their toilets, make their bed and do all sorts of dreary stuff. I'm supposed to be researching them a holiday. They can't decide between St Lucia and Barbados.'

'And you live with them?'

'Yeah. I'm up at the top, like in the roof. There's a little bedsit up there. With a microwave and a kettle and a shower-room. It's fine. It suits me for now... They have shedloads of money like you do. But their place is, I dunno, lifeless. They don't know how to make it nice like this. Can I see the rest of the flat? When we've finished our coffees?'

'Yes, of course,' I said. 'If you'd like.' But I felt bad about the difference between our lavish circumstances and her restricted ones. 'You'd better prepare yourself for some over-the-top luxury – like real *Homes & Gardens* stuff.'

She wasn't bothered. Not at all. She just nudged me and said, 'I don't do envy, Lucy. I just do nice people.'

I told her that I struggle to take all the expensive 'stuff' seriously, that I'm from a not-quite-poor background and take nothing for granted. 'All the designer knobs and handles and lighting and shelving are kind of ridiculous.'

'Stop it! I *adore* nosing around other people's houses.'

'Me too! While Sam's at work, I'm always looking at property programmes – do you know them? *Changing Rooms* and *DIY SOS*. Have you seen them?'

'I love *Changing Rooms*,' she said. Something about it jarred – this worldly girl settling in for cheesy makeover shows.

'Those programmes are my secret pleasure... So we both love trashy TV?'

'Don't you tell Sam you watch them? Wouldn't he approve?'

'He doesn't really like television,' I confessed. 'You know, tons of people who *work* in TV don't actually watch it. It's not a requirement, apparently.'

'Why not?'

'It's a bit beneath them I guess.' I felt a tiny bit guilty for sharing a secret at Sam's expense, but Taylor enjoyed my cheekiness – she made bright conspiratorial eyes at me, a flash of emerald. 'The tour!' she said, standing and picking up Evie. She carried her on one hip, secured with one arm. She did it naturally, like a mother would, and Evie buried her head in Taylor's neck.

'So, welcome to the grand tour.' I swept my arm across the kitchen, playing tour guide to mask my embarrassment. 'Marvel at our self-opening drawers. Feast your eyes on our Corian worktops. And behold' – I gestured to the French doors – 'our south-facing aspect.'

Taylor grinned as I channelled my inner Carol Smillie.

'The garden's by Charles Fairbrother.' My voice caught. 'Three-time Chelsea gold medallist. Though I'd wanted my friend Melody to design it. She creates these incredible, peaceful spaces. But Sam overruled me.'

'Well, whoever did it, it's beautiful.'

'Yes. Yes, it is.' I moved us along. 'And here's the bathroom – fully electronic and...' I searched for the word. 'Swish.'

She peered in. 'Does the loo swishly flush?'

'Couldn't flush swishlier.'

'You have a funny mummy.' Taylor kissed Evie's head.

'And finally,' I hurried through the designer details – Italian tiles, Farrow & Ball walls, 'Evie's playroom.' Just a cot and some toys, but somehow my favourite space in all this grandeur.

We peeked in. 'Ooo,' said Taylor icily. 'What's that?' She put Evie down on the floor and bent down, reaching under the cot. Carefully, she pulled out a Sabatier kitchen knife and held it up at arm's length, like a priest with a crucifix, her expression hard and alarmed.

My hand shot to my chest. 'Give it to me!'

I marched the knife to the kitchen sink and threw it in, staring at its sharp edge, feeling sick. It happens sometimes. You do something, quite by accident, that could put your child in danger. They were legion – the stories of kids drinking bleach from loose-capped bottles, throttling themselves with curtain ties, crushed by falling furniture. I was hot and sweating at the thought that I must have left the knife where Evie could reach it, and I could feel tears welling up inside. But I'd cried the last time Taylor was here – I couldn't let it happen again. She might never come back. I controlled my breaths. Long and slow.

'Don't worry, Lucy. No harm was done.' She came over to stand with me.

'I don't know how it happened...'

'Come on,' she said kindly. 'Show me the rest of the flat. I'm enjoying myself.'

She picked Evie up again and we went upstairs. I quickly indicated the formal sitting and dining rooms, then we went up again – to the bedrooms. Evie's first. I slumped in the armchair, still thinking about my foggy disturbed mind and the knife, while she took Evie around, picking up her little toys and animals, admiring them with her, but glancing at me, checking that I was okay. 'Oh, this is cute.' She was examining a little frame containing the tiny identity band a nurse had placed around Evie's wrist when she was born. 'Girl Bliss. Is that Evie? What does it mean? Were you going to call her Bliss?'

I relaxed a little. 'Oh no... We wanted her to have a proper name. Evie is short for Eveline. Bliss is my surname. I'm Lucy Bliss.'

'OMG. And I'm Taylor Love. Love and Bliss. We could go into business. What as? A spa resort?'

'Ha. Yes. Or scented candles. Or two lady detectives.'

'Or sex toys.'

'Taylor!' I was pleased – her joke helped me recover myself. I turned the phrase over in my head. Love and Bliss. It sounded so *nice*.

'Okay, and now we will progress to the bathroom,' I said, standing up and leading the way. 'Prepare to be amazed.' I opened the door, and in we went.

'It's a bathroom for dancing in!' She twirled around with Evie, singing to the tune of 'Singing in the Rain'. 'We're dancing in the bathroom, just dancing in the bathroom, what a wonderful feeling...'

I sat on the armchair by the window. 'Nobody has ever had that reaction. Everyone just says, *"Wow. It's huge."*'

'Well, it is huge, Lucy.'

'We converted a double bedroom. It was Sam's idea.'

'Well done, Sam!'

'More lovely Corian,' I joked. 'And such a tasteful colour scheme.' Sam thinks I'm silly to feel guilty about the lavishness – and he's right. It's a mindset thing. I need to work on thinking about the work we gave to skilled craftsmen and the fact that we've made something beautiful.

Thoughts about the knife were almost gone now, and Taylor continued to sing softly and to dance with Evie while I watched. 'Okay,' I said eventually. 'Master bedroom.'

. . .

She and I lay side by side on the bed with Evie snuggled between us, her thumb in her mouth and her head buried in Taylor's side, drifting off to sleep. Taylor mused on the painting on the far wall. Our crazy surreal painting. She liked it, she said, for the way it brought beauty and danger together. I laughed, happy at her perceptiveness. I've never known what to make of it. I like the three beauties – the nude maidens by the pond. But the dead animals in their hair? The fact that the water is actually a tangle of meandering snakes? And the sharp-toothed fish swimming in the meadow? 'I had a nightmare about it,' I told her. 'The snakes' fangs were flicking at my neck, and those fish were biting my fingers and toes.'

'Recently?'

'A month or so ago... The painting is special to Sam; he inherited it from his grandfather. The artist is Mexican. He's famous.'

'I've never seen a famous painting actually in someone's house.'

'Sam's grandfather was a collector.'

We gazed at each other. I noticed that her crimson lipstick had faded and realised I preferred her lips their natural colour. She was wearing practically no other make-up. A little mascara, a flick of eyeliner. I wanted to compliment her on her incredible green eyes – but didn't know how without seeming creepy. Then she said to me: 'You have a lovely face... I mean, I'm not coming on to you! But I love your colouring, grey eyes and red hair. You look somehow regal.'

'Regal!'

'Well, you do... How did you meet? You and Sam?'

I told her how Sam had been staying in Gloucestershire with friends, recovering from a bout of flu. He'd just come back from a trip to Colombia, where he covered the Cali drugs cartel.

'I love Colombia,' she said dreamily. She was so young.

What? Twenty-three or twenty-four? But she had so much experience of the world.

'You've been there?'

'Oh yes. I'll tell you about it another time. Go on with your story.'

I told her that Sam's friends had brought him along to a concert, where I was playing.

'Playing?'

'I should have said – I play the cello. Or I used to. Not so much these days. I was in a string quartet, and we were playing Schubert and some Debussy that evening. Afterwards, Sam said to his friends that he'd enjoyed the concert so much, could they linger and congratulate the players? It turned out that he had been watching me the whole time.'

'That is romantic.'

'It was. We were walking back through the hall – me and the violinist – and Sam intercepted us and told me how fabulous my playing was – which was awkward for the violinist – and he started asking questions: when would I be playing again? what was my favourite music? Before I knew it, he'd taken down my phone number.'

I told her about those first days with Sam – about our long country walks, climbing over stiles and trekking across muddy fields while we asked each other a million questions, weaving an intricate web of connections with our answers, our touches and our glances, taking each other in. My whole being had seemed twice as alive as usual as I registered a thousand small things – the shape of his hands, the tone of his skin, the timbre of his voice. Everything.

'He told me about the lives of foreign correspondents,' I said, 'and how they became hooked by the adrenaline rush from being close to danger, or in extreme situations. Sam said you need it, to return again and again to human suffering without going mad yourself... He knew that, to stay sane, he wanted roots here, at home, in England. He called England his psychological anchor.'

Taylor's eyes narrowed mischievously. 'I've never been seduced by anchor-talk. That's a new one.'

'I was *so* excited by the anchor-talk. I knew right from the beginning, that I wanted to be the person he came home to.'

'You fell in love,' Taylor said.

'Yes, I was sure that women just threw themselves at him. But he fell for me. *A simple country girl, who plays the cello.*' I was putting on an exaggerated west country accent.

'Like *Pride and Prejudice.*'

'I'm no Lizzie Bennet. I'm more shy and quiet, I think, like Fanny Price in *Mansfield Park.*'

Evie wriggled and woke up, and the moment was broken. Taylor sat up and looked at her watch, 'I have to go – but I'll write my phone number down for you. Call me if you're not feeling okay and need a chat, or if you want to meet up. Oh, and I have something for you – in the kitchen.'

I gathered Evie up, and we went downstairs. Taylor reached into her canvas bag. 'This.' She gave me a small brown bottle. 'Tea tree in a base of almond oil. I made it for your eczema... You know eczema is aggravated by stress. We need to look after you.'

'Oh, thank you, that's so kind.' She picked up her coat and bag and left through the French doors, blowing a kiss to Evie.

Ten minutes later, Melody phoned with news – she was coming to London for two days to visit garden centres and see which plants were fashionable in the metropolis and might sell well back in Gloucestershire. I laughed at the idea that gardening had fads and trends. I'd always thought of it as something constant and calming.

'That's brilliant,' I said. 'I can't wait to see you.'

Melody was my dearest friend, the only link to my past, the

one person who truly understood me and knew how the events of my childhood had warped my brain.

FIVE

SEPTEMBER 1999

Adra Roy is puzzled by this girl. She's giving her testimony with more enthusiasm than an average witness and seems to be revelling in the detail in a way that is odd, to say the least. Her manner is mesmerising. She fixes each of the policewomen with quick, intense glances, moves about in her seat with an ease that is practically feline, and constantly gestures with delicate fine-boned hands.

For the moment, Adra thinks, the jury's out. Taylor Love, despite her theatricality, may be a genuine and innocent witness to terrible events. She's intelligent, that's certain. And possibly, she's simply trying to be helpful. Adra tells Taylor to go on, to continue her story:

TL – The second time at Russell Drive, Lucy was just the same, a bag of nerves; half the time she seemed to be on the edge of tears. She was kind of manic, too, quizzing me on the details of my life, where I'd been and the work I'd done, and talking obsessively about her wealth and all the fancy improvements she and Sam had made to the flat. She was obsessed with this stuff Corian – which I've never heard of. Have you? And the garden, she was resentful that her old friend Melody hadn't been allowed to design it and Sam had insisted on some fancy shit-hot famous gardener – and Sam had the money, so he had the control. Anyhow, Lucy was showing me around the flat and this terrible thing happened. When we looked into Evie's little playroom downstairs, there was a kitchen knife on the floor! Right there where Evie could pick it up – a horrendous sharp blade. Oh God – I'm pretty sure it was the same knife that killed Lucy… A Sabatier, right? A long knife, like you'd use for chopping something like a butternut squash?

AR – Carry on with your account, Taylor.

TL – Okay… So I picked the knife up – I feel sick now – and Lucy snatched it out of my hand and threw it in the kitchen sink. She was shaking and turning red, and I thought she was angry that I'd got a glimpse of how out of control she was. I wasn't sure how to react – I said something like 'It's a mistake anyone could make.' I mean, part of me actually thought that could be true… These things do happen I suppose. Then we pretended that everything was normal and went upstairs to look at the other rooms.

She and Sam have this enormous bathroom that cost £75,000. That shocked me. When you think the good that money could do. And in their bedroom, Sam and Lucy's, there was this totally terrifying painting at the end of the bed. Like naked women with dead animals on their heads being engulfed by snakes and fish with pointy little dagger teeth. It was just bizarre – I mean, I knew it had given Lucy nightmares, can you imagine the effect it would have on a small child? And Evie was such a sweetie, it was horrible to think about… I just buried the thought. That's what people do, I guess, when things first seem out of kilter… But I feel so guilty now. Anyway, I think the painting was worth mega-dollars because Lucy said it was famous.

We were lying on the bed, the three of us, at that point and Evie curled herself up into *me.* Not her own mother. Lucy just kept talking. But she definitely noticed, and she didn't like it.

She told me loads about Sam. The first time I went to Russell Drive, she'd been bad-mouthing him – saying he was a snob about these trash TV shows, property programmes, that Lucy liked. The second time she told me how she and Sam met. How she'd been playing her cello in a village hall and he'd appeared out of nowhere to scoop her up and rescue her from nowheresville. Like Prince Charming. At that point, I felt sorry for Sam. Like Sam had given her so much, the perfect daughter, this amazing flat, no need to work… but Lucy was as needy as fuck, a basket case and didn't seem to appreciate her wealth at all, or her husband. It made me wonder what Sam was like, how he coped with it all – that's how it was at the beginning. I saw Lucy as the problem, not Sam.

Taylor leans forward as she says this, her face resting on her knuckles, and Adra is struck by her witness's self-confidence and the certainty in her delivery. It's unusual in a murder case. Witnesses are generally shaken and unsure. Taylor Love's strong narrative may, of course, be borne out of her mission to help – to bring the perpetrator to justice. Or, just maybe, it's a sign of something else entirely.

SIX
EVIE

NOW

The little kitchen at Mia's house has always been cool, a refuge from the sun; the dark wood of the cupboards and furniture suggesting solidity and safety; the rich tones of the Talavera plates and mugs and the bright hand-painted ceramic pots that have occupied the same shelf all of Evie's remembered-life; the heavy glass tumblers and the brown English teapot – until now, all intimating to Evie that her existence is constant and rooted. When Mia died so suddenly, these aspects of the house had brought some comfort. But that is gone. The foundations of her life have collapsed. Nothing seems certain or reliable.

She and Antonio sit in silence at the kitchen table, the limp yellow scraps of newspaper laid out in front of them, along with the passport photos. Even Antonio seems changed to her. The gentle gaze of his dark eyes, the note of optimism and calm in his deep cherry voice, the stillness of him – all disturbed by a confusion that mirrors her own. How many times in the past hour has she said, 'I simply can't believe it... I just don't understand?' And Antonio has looked at her gravely, in quiet astonishment. They have each read the articles over and over, trying to find something between the lines that is the route towards an explanation.

Murders and disappearances at a house in Russell Drive, Little Venice in London. The sort of place inhabited by glamorous, wealthy people, the international sort you might equally find in Upper Manhattan, the Tuscan Hills, or some exclusive private island in the Caribbean. And a list of names, a primary cast: Lucy Bliss, murdered by her husband Sam Preston, who is wanted by the police; their missing daughter Evie Preston-Bliss; a missing nanny, Taylor Love, who may or may not be in hiding with Sam Preston and Evie; and finally, a young man, Jackson Wu, whose body was discovered in the communal garden at the back of the Preston-Bliss home. And there was mention of his missing dog, Rupert. Then two more names, Lucy's mother, Geraldine Bliss and her close friend Melody King, barely mentioned other than through a short comment to a journalist: 'I loved Lucy like a sister... I'm sorry, I'm too shocked to speak.'

The *Mail* story is the most graphic. Blood found in the kitchen of a beautiful home was 'revealed' as belonging to Lucy Bliss and two witnesses had come forward to testify that she was dead. The murder weapon, a bloodied kitchen knife, had been found, along with an item of Lucy's clothing and a part of her body – the article did not state which part; that was left to the imagination of the reader. A grainy photograph showed Lucy and Sam on their wedding day. Evie had looked at the picture for so long, the big smiles, Lucy holding her long thick hair with one hand to stop it flying across her face, her veil caught in a gust of wind and flying into the air; Sam, clearly alive with happiness and amusement, tangled up in his bride and her windblown dress. How on earth can these joyful strangers be her parents? How can it be that such a wonderful moment had ended in murder?

For so many years, Evie has believed that her closeness with

Mia is a bond of blood, that her own quiet character is a genetic thing, the direct reincarnation of her mother's reserve and enjoyment of solitude, that Evie's height and her dark eyes, are reflections of Mia's ancestors. Now what? The core of her very being, the cells of her body and brain, were nothing to do with Mia at all. They were inherited from this alien woman Lucy Bliss and her handsome husband who was tall like Evie, blonde like Evie. And the photos – were they of Lucy Bliss? It was hard to tell from the one grainy wedding photo. 'Maybe they're of the nanny,' Evie says. 'There aren't any photos of her in the press.' The face in the photos, all of them identical, is of a pretty young woman, fine-boned with wide-spaced eyes, a high forehead, full, slightly parted lips, long wavy hair.

'Who knows what Lucy Bliss and Sam Preston were like?' Evie continues. 'I can't find anything online – just a few news cuttings. I guess because the internet wasn't such a huge thing back then. It's impossible to get a sense of them.' She glances at a painting on the wall, a still life of three plump lemons in a deep blue ceramic bowl. Mia had loved it, as had Evie. 'I can't believe it all,' she says. 'I can't believe my mother never told me... I trusted her. Totally. Without question... It's tearing me into pieces. I feel like I don't know who Mia really was, who I really am.' In the past days, her sense of Mia has been reduced to a list of her qualities, her quiet kindness, her conscientious homemaking, her love for her little garden. But they are qualities without context – the completeness of her is gone.

The funeral service is in an hour's time and only two streets away. Mia wasn't Catholic, or even religious, but Ramona thought this church was the right thing. Mia had walked past it most days on her way to work and had occasionally gone inside, just to sit quietly and reflect. Evie had no objection; she did not have the energy to make alternative suggestions and was grateful to her for taking over the arranging and negotiating and dealing with the world, tasks that were beyond Evie's capability.

She had asked Ramona dozens of questions when they'd been together at the house, drinking tea and reminiscing.

'Do you know why she left England and came here?'

'Oh, I remember her so well when you were about five years old, mija. Always so cool and mysterious... The men, oh she was attractive to the men! Some of the teachers at the school were fascinated by her.'

'But Ramona, did she tell you *why* she left England and came here?'

'It's a cold country, Evie. And I believe, very foggy and rainy. Don't you think it natural that she would prefer a warm place? And her Spanish was excellent. At least, it became excellent very quickly. What a talented woman she was.'

Evie tried again: 'Did she tell you anything about her life in England? Anything that might have happened to make her leave?'

'Oh, you know Mia, Evie! She wasn't a chatter, chatter, chatter person like me. More of a listening person like you.'

'Did she mention an English friend of hers called Lucy Bliss?'

'A pretty name – I don't think so, no.'

Cupping a hot mug of tea in her hands, Evie tried a different tack. 'She was distressed when I asked about my father. That was sad for me. Did she tell you anything about him?'

Ramona raised her eyebrows and turned down her scarlet lips. 'My goodness! There's a subject – it would take courage to ask Mia something like that. Something that was a secret in her heart.'

She downed the last of her tea and Evie tried again: 'You understand that, because she died so suddenly, I have all these questions? It upsets me that so much is unknown.'

Ramona leaned over to stroke Evie's hair. 'Oh baby! Of course you feel that way. This is a disaster for you, being left alone without your dear mother. But now you are saying these things, I'm feeling bad. I wish I had asked more forcefully about your father…'

'So you know nothing?'

Ramona's lips stayed downturned, almost comically. 'She didn't like that question. Once, I asked, and she just said, in her Mia way, *I hardly knew the man, Ramona. I slept with him, he disappeared and Evie came along. That's it.*'

This hadn't been the story that Mia had told Evie. When small, she had asked, 'Where's my papa?' and Mia had told her that he lived far away in another country. 'When will he see me?'

Mia had taken Evie in her arms and said, 'I don't know, darling. I don't know where he is. But he always loved you.'

But one day, when Evie was fourteen, she had arrived home in the early evening with the smell of alcohol on her breath – the consequence a bottle of vodka that her best friend Sofia had secretly taken from the drinks cabinet at home. She'd added a slug of pineapple-flavoured Jarritos 'to make it taste better' and filled their water bottles. After school, the friends had sat on a bench in the local park with their 'cocktails,' then Evie had walked home on wobbly legs and fumbled with her key in the front door.

'Evie?' Mia had called out from the kitchen, her expression somewhat startled. 'What's wrong?'

'Nothing wrong, Mama! Everything very right. Very nice time…'

She had dashed up the stairs to her bedroom as Mia called out, 'Come back down here! Right now!'

Evie, deciding to be confident, came down the stairs, breezily. 'Nothing's wrong. I told you. I've just had a nice time with Sofia. In the park.'

Mia approached, a stern look on her face. 'I smell alcohol, Evie. What have you been drinking?'

'Nothing. Just pineapple Jarritos. You can smell pineapple. Now, I want to read my book in my room.'

As she turned towards the stairs, Mia shouted – something that had never happened before. 'Do not lie to me! Do not lie!'

Feeling reckless, Evie snapped back: 'Why not, Mama? Why not? You lie to me!'

Mia sat down hard on a chair, as though her legs had given way. Quietly, she said: 'What about, Evie? Tell me.'

'My father... You never tell me about him. It's the same as lying.'

'I can't, Evie,' Mia whispered. 'I can't.'

Evie felt a surge of anger rise inside. 'Of course you can. You're choosing not to! Why would someone do that to their own child? Why?' She glared down at Mia.

Tears formed in Mia's eyes. 'I can't, darling. It's too difficult.'

'Give me *something*! What is his name? What does he look like? What is he like – his character, his looks?' Her voice was hostile and tinged with disgust. 'Anything. Any little clue...'

Tears ran down Mia's face and she removed them quickly with the palms of her hands. 'He's a clever man,' she said. 'Handsome. Blonde like you. Brown eyes like you. Tall like you... Please don't ask, Evie...'

'Just tell me his name.'

'Please, darling, just think of him as Papa.'

Suddenly overwhelmed by the fact that she was hurting her mother, suddenly ashamed, Evie collapsed into the chair next to Mia. 'I'm sorry, Mama,' she whispered.

'No, Evie. I'm sorry. I'm truly sorry.'

The alcohol was never mentioned again. And Evie had never again asked about her father.

Antonio checks his phone and says gently, 'We should leave soon.' He touches her arm.

She takes Antonio's hand and descends the concrete steps to the busy road. They turn off to the left and wander through cobbled streets in silence and strange formality to the chapel of Santa Catarina. Outside, quietly talking, are Isabella and Sofia, who, smiling solemnly, tell Evie that she looks beautiful in the purple dress she has borrowed from Sofia. It's peculiar to hear her friends speaking normal words in this reverential tone. Little Isabella kisses Evie's cheek and does the same to Antonio, who has to bend low to receive her affection. 'Sara is inside already,' Isabella says. 'Saving us three a space together.'

'Are there many people?' Evie asks. Mia's life had been so quiet. The only regular guests at the house were Ramona and an older neighbour, Enrique, who did handyman jobs and always stayed for a beer (while Mia drank tea), enthusiastically filling her in with neighbourhood gossip and bizarre stories of what was going on inside other people's homes. His big, bearlike presence had been warm and reassuring.

Isabella gazes into the cloudy sky, thinking about Evie's question. 'About forty people I think,' she replies.

Evie and Antonio look at each other, a note of surprise in their eyes, both thinking – *how can that be?*

Antonio squeezes Evie's hand, and they enter the chapel, people looking up as they walk to the front, many sending sympathy with variations of the same serious smile as had been offered by Sofia and Isabella a few moments ago. Mia's coffin is at the front of the church, a small arrangement of white roses on top and a note from Evie saying, *Mama, I will love you and be grateful to you forever, your Evie.* She'd felt a stab in her heart as she wrote the word Mama – and now, as she and Antonio take their seats at the front of the chapel, she's burning up with a kind of desperation born of sorrow, love and confusion. There's also an unwelcome anger inside her, provoked by two dominant thoughts: *Mama, how could you leave me alone?* and *Why did you never tell me?*

She can't look at the coffin for more than a few seconds without feeling that she will lose control and weep, so she grips Antonio's hand and glances over her shoulder to see the congregation, recognising only perhaps fifteen of the forty people. She sees Enrique, wearing a solid frown and looking directly ahead as though left and right do not exist; various teachers from the school; her own friends, a few neighbours; Ramona, swathed in voluminous black cloth and wearing a hat with feathers; and finally, about thirty people who she does not recognise. She watches as a tall man, probably in his fifties and dressed casually in black shirt and jeans, enters from the back of the church, a sudden shard of light from a high window illuminating his silvery hair. For a second, Evie feels a quick burn of recognition. Then the music strikes up – the Pie Jesu from Fauré's requiem. Evie's tears come now; all restraint is hopeless. This movement was a favourite of Mia's, deeply loved by her. Antonio has a cotton handkerchief at the ready and she grasps it with a shaking hand.

As the service continues, Evie drifts away from herself, as though she's sinking into dark water, her body seeming far away and without definition. She can barely feel her own skin now, and Antonio's voice becomes distant and unclear.

Later, at Ramona's house, still in this otherworldly state, she sits silently in the corner of the living room, surrounded by vivid paintings of flowers, dancers, sunsets and in one case, a polar bear.

Drinks are set on tables, flanked by brightly coloured handicrafts, ceramic bowls, vases and figurines. Evie is led to a painted wooden chair in the corner of the room and is provided with a glass of red wine by Antonio. She wishes that nobody would talk to her, that Enrique would not inform her of his admiration of Mia, that Isabella would not try to hug her, that teachers would stop praising Mia's skills in the classroom. She sits perfectly still, not drinking the wine, as well-meaning communicants come and go, acknowledging them with a nod of her head or slow blink of her eyes.

Antonio comes to sit beside her and explains that many of those present, talking in little groups, are former pupils of Mia's, or people on the periphery of her life – the groundskeeper and the secretary from the school, the woman from the laundrette, the man who kept a vegetable stall that Mia had passed on the way to work.

'The tall man,' Evie says, her voice soft and hollow. 'In church. Silver hair. Did you notice him?'

Antonio shakes his head. He has no idea who she is referring to, and Evie cannot see him in the room, cannot point him out, so she sinks back into semi-oblivion.

SEVEN

LUCY

1999

Taylor arrived with all the ingredients for lunch, laying them out on the counter one by one. Avocado, courgettes, aubergines, chickpeas, tomatoes, almonds, flat-leaf parsley and couscous – 'a feast,' she said, to build me up because I was always too weak and pale. She set about making us a warm salad, to be followed by rhubarb poached with honey and ginger.

I felt truly cared for and it was heaven. Taylor was right about cooking being *her thing* and I was in awe of her cooking skills. While she worked, she told stories about her employers Orlando and Persephone. Apparently, they glided around their house like ghosts, barely speaking. 'You should see them at dinner,' she said, widening her eyes. 'Matching purple silk pyjamas, both staring at spreadsheets on their laptops.'

I found myself laughing more when Taylor was around. The constant knot in my stomach eased and, at times, I actually felt light and funny, hardly aware of the chaos in my head.

'They sound really weird,' I said.

'Everyone's weird, once you scratch the surface,' she replied, concentrating on slicing a courgette.

I laughed and told her all about Sam and his media world where the women are upper class and cool and flirt with him the whole time. 'They have the biggest opinions on everything, and are always a hundred per cent certain of themselves,' I said. 'They're all called Rachel or Annabel or Isabel and had ponies and Labradors when they were children, and their parents have houses in France or Tuscany. Oh, and they walk like they own the world...'

'Show me!' She looked up expectantly as she swept the courgette into a bowl. I did an impression of Sam's closest friend, Rachel Tang, who strode about with her chin up, doing narrow sexy eyes at Sam, while she said something outrageous like, 'Of course Britain is so *finished*. Not a hope.' Or, 'Who gives a toss about the green belt? I mean, there's always Wales if you want countryside.' I was looking down my nose and pulling faces, making it up as I went along. Taylor roared with laughter and demanded more impressions. I felt a little guilty. I was being unfair to Rachel, to all of them really. It wasn't their fault that I flinched at the mention of ski lodges in Verbier and second homes in Tuscany. Not their fault I felt like an imposter in their world.

That evening Sam was late home – long hours in the edit suite – and in a tetchy mood. I pushed my food around my plate, searching for the right words to reach him. 'I'm doing better, you know. Really better. Taylor's been such a help with everything—'

'That's great,' he said flatly, barely looking up. 'Really good.' His tone said it all: *About bloody time you found a London friend.*

. . .

Orlando and Persephone didn't give Taylor much work, leaving her free most afternoons. She'd appear at Russell Drive soon after lunch. 'Treat time!' she'd announce when Evie went down for her nap, producing her morning's baking – muffins, scones, banana bread. Sometimes, she'd whip up smoothies, packed with apples and avocados, even beetroot.

Then there was the massage. She'd knelt over me on the bed, her soft hands kneading the tension knots in my back and shoulders. The tension melted down my arms, draining from my fingertips. A few days later, she brought me a present – a diffuser and essential oils – bergamot, geranium and jasmine; presenting the kit with a 'ta-dah!' and a theatrical flick of her hand. 'We'll get this going and I'll give you another massage,' she said.

I thanked her but suddenly felt embarrassed. 'It's too much! Why?'

'Well, the simple answer is, I like you, Lucy. We're friends. I was pretty alone in London until I met you.'

'And the complicated answer?'

She paused, looking thoughtful. Then a gentle, 'I feel for you. There's something wrong, isn't there? You don't talk about it, but I can tell.'

I tried to laugh it off. 'I know I'm a little shaky sometimes. And I worry too much about Evie…'

In that moment, I wondered whether I could tell her my secrets; but what if I drove her away? Instead, we did our usual things – settled on the sofa, put our feet up and watched daytime TV together, back and forthing a running commentary on properties for sale in Andalucia, ornate water-features in small gardens, sheepdog trials in the Peak District. I was soothed by the dogs, and the farmers whistling in the rain and calling out 'Jess!' or 'Dot!' or 'Fly!' Sometimes, I thought that if my life were very simple, I'd be able to cope with it.

Taylor's birthday was coming up. She was turning twenty-six. I wanted to show her my appreciation and the day before her birthday I made a Victoria sponge. I followed a handwritten recipe that my mother gave me years ago and, to my relief, the thing didn't turn out too badly – a tad biscuity at the edges and crest-fallen in the middle, but it was presentable. I slipped a voucher inside her birthday card: *Spa Day for two, including champagne lunch.* At the Whittingdon Club in Chelsea. A facial for each of us and a whole load of lounging around. It had been Sam's idea. 'I can take Evie to work,' he'd said. 'I'll book her into the BBC crèche and go down to check up on her. It will be good for you to have a day off... Use the joint account.' He sounded relieved. Our friendship took the pressure off him.

The birthday was a success. When Taylor hugged me at the end of the day, she held on so long, I could practically feel her heart beating. Perfect, I thought. The spa day – that's when I'd finally tell her everything.

A strange thing happened when we entered the Whittingdon Club – Taylor grabbed me and pulled me behind a marble pillar.

'What?'

'It's Seph. Persephone. I don't want her to see me.'

I peeked out and saw a tall woman with white-blonde hair chatting to a receptionist. She had a straight back, perfectly even shoulders and a long neck, giving her the look of a high-fashion model; she was wearing smart blue sports gear and carried a gym bag over her shoulder. I watched her pop a complimentary mint into her mouth, looking like she belonged there.

'Blonde ponytail?'

'That's her.'

We huddled together like schoolgirls hiding from a teacher.

I peeked out again. Persephone was on the move, heading

elegantly towards the front door, a strip of morning sunlight her catwalk. 'Okay, let's go,' I said, and we started out towards the reception desk. But Persephone stopped to hold the door for someone, looked around and saw us. At least, she looked right at Taylor with a shocked expression – one arched eyebrow and a note of confusion – before she turned and hurried away.

Taylor giggled. 'Did you see that face? Do you think we caught her doing something illicit? I mean, she's supposed to be at work.'

'Why did you want to hide?'

'No real reason. I mean – this is *our* day. I didn't want her interrupting it.'

'You're strange,' I said, trying to keep my voice light. We checked in and loaded ourselves up with fat white towels, still warm from the dryer.

Facials, steam room, sauna and showers later, and we were in robes, lying on poolside recliners, our salads and glasses of champagne on a low table between us. I shifted about on the recliner, no appetite for the salad, and swigged some champagne, summoning courage for my planned revelation. 'Taylor...' I said with trepidation. 'It's sensitive of you to realise that something's wrong with me. You're very kind about it.'

'The thing you don't talk about,' she replied sweetly, forking coleslaw into her mouth. 'No pressure, Lucy – but I'm always here—'

A young woman in a white uniform appeared. 'More champagne ladies?'

'Yes, please.' I offered my empty glass and Taylor did the same. The woman left and we were alone again apart from a bald man wearing goggles splashing effortful lengths of the pool.

'Can I tell you something in confidence?'

'Of course,' she said absently, still shovelling up her salad. Her easy-come easy-go manner disarmed me. I wanted to tell her everything – about my father's death and the mess it left inside me; about my constant terror of being left alone. But the words wouldn't come. Not here. Not with all these people around. It was too much. I swallowed hard and focused on the present instead. 'It's about my marriage...' I said. 'You've probably worked out that things are... difficult.'

'No. Not at all.' She looked up now. 'Oh. I'm sorry, Lucy.'

'What I mean is that *I'm* having difficulties and it's because I'm kind of screwed up. I don't seem to be able to pull myself together and I'm sure I irritate Sam. I mean he's always distracted when we're together and—'

'Hey. Back up. What do you mean *you're screwed up?* Nobody's perfect – you do know that?'

'I don't fit in with his world, Taylor. That media-artsy-literary world where everyone went to the same universities and know the same people – and they speak in a special language that's full of codes.' I gulped some champagne. 'I mean, they're always making little jokes that I don't really get, or sounding off on politics and international affairs and stuff – like I told you when I made fun of Rachel Tang. And it's all in this flirty, flirty, clever, clever, sharp way... I feel so completely different from them. Sort of isolated and substandard – I have these mental problems you see...'

She brushed that aside. 'Lucy, you're just lacking in confidence...'

I felt a stab of hurt. But Taylor couldn't see inside my head. She couldn't know what was going on. 'It makes me think – why did he marry *me* when he has so much more in common with *them*? It's getting to me. I'm doing bad stuff.'

'What bad stuff?' She put down her plate and sat up to face me, moving her legs from the recliner, putting her bare feet on the floor.

I glanced around to see if anyone could overhear us, but we were still alone apart from the splashy guy doing lengths.

'I'm becoming paranoid – off the scale paranoid – and I'm

drinking way too much. White wine – I drink it down like Coke – all the time, every night. It's like I'm always on the point of losing control... and...'

I stopped and lay there looking blankly at the pool. She said nothing, waiting for me to go on, but I couldn't do it after all, I couldn't tell her just how low I'd sunk. I changed tack. 'Sometimes, they come to dinner, the Rachels and Annabels – and I hate every minute of it. Watching the rapport that Sam has with them, and the little looks sparking across the table – and I know that's how it is at work as well. Banter and flirting for half the day – and sometimes half the night. They have all these massive certainties and opinions that overwhelm me, and I just sit there like a lump, getting everything wrong.'

'Like what, Lucy?' Her hand reached across the fruit bowl, out to mine. 'What do you get wrong?'

'Small things mainly – but they feel huge.' I searched my mind for an example. 'Like the first time that Sam invited some work friends back for dinner. I was terrified about the cooking, and I made something easy that my mother used to make. Can't-go-wrong fishcakes. Basically, tinned pilchards mashed up with potato and salt and pepper and fried. But Rachel Tang was part of the group, all touchy-feely with Sam...'

'How touchy-feely? On a scale of one to ten?'

'I don't know. Sometimes, I think a three, sometimes I imagine it's an eight... When I wake up in a cold sweat at 3 a.m., it's an eleven.' I was trying to sound light-hearted and jokey but could hear a tremor in my voice. 'So, Rachel said – in this sultry voice – *hmmm – what's in the fishcakes, Lucy?* While she kind of prodded a fishcake like this...' I poked a radish on my salad plate with a fork, moving it half a centimetre to the left, half a centimetre to the right. 'I told her it was just pilchards with potato, and she made this totally gobsmacked face at Sam as if she'd just learned something extraordinary like, I don't know, a family of giraffes had moved in next door, and she said, "*Praise the Lord! I always wondered what pilchards were. I thought they were for making glue."* Glue!' I took a sip of champagne and could feel my lips quivering on the glass.

Taylor sat still for a second, then she doubled up, her towelled shoulders rising and falling – she sounded like she was trying to suppress a small explosion. Looking at me, her eyes starting to water, she said, 'That's so funny! Glue.'

'It's not funny! Honestly, it's not. You know, in the next breath she said the fishcakes were delicious – but I had to scrape them all into the bin, barely nibbled at. I was mortified.'

'I'm sorry.' She was smiling coyly, making pretty eyes. 'But you are a very sensitive flower.'

'I know. I know. I'm the problem. Sometimes, I think I'm going mad. But I can't bear that people like Rachel look down on me and don't care if they humiliate me in front of Sam... and that maybe Sam looks down on me too.'

She was struggling to take me seriously. I could see it in her face. 'Have you talked about it with Sam?'

'It's hard. I tried to talk to him after the pilchard incident – stop it. Don't laugh.' She was working hard to look serious and made an exaggerated concerned face. 'I've tried – but Sam thinks I'm imagining it.'

Taylor swivelled back into her reclining position and took up her champagne glass, contemplating the room. The turquoise tiles on the walls, the marble pillars, the bubbling jacuzzi beyond the pool, and the swimming man. 'He's right,' she said. 'You're being idiotic. Look at this wonderful life you have – be grateful. It's like we're handmaidens at the court of Cleopatra.' She took a small bunch of green grapes from the table, dangled them daintily above her pouting lips and deftly bit one off.

'Yeah. I feel so guilty...'

'Oh gosh. I'm sorry... I've been making light of a serious situation,' Taylor said, her eyes suddenly intense, her voice compassionate. 'It upsets me that you're feeling bad. I really want to support you. What can I do?'

She looked at me with such kindness in her face – I think more kindness than I've ever seen from anyone. 'Just listening means a lot,' I said.

'We need to build you up – psychologically speaking. Have you ever thought about going back to work? You could go part-time at first. It's just that you've been so isolated at home – that can make people turn inwards and doubt themselves, you know. Maybe it would help to be out and about, mixing with people?'

'But what about Evie? I couldn't leave her in a nursery, or with a nanny.'

'I could look after her if you like. She and I adore each other – you know we do; I could take her to the park and the swings. And I'd love to cook for her, I'd make such fantastic little meals. Truth is, I'm totally fed up with Orlando and Persephone and their purple pyjamas. It's like a living death over there.'

Sometimes, I'd watch them from my window, the evening commuters trudging up from Warwick Avenue tube. Exhausted but purposeful. Connected. I'd catch myself envying their rushed goodbyes, their 'quick question' phone calls, their lives full of meetings and deadlines and adult conversation. But then Sam's voice would sound in my head: *You're my anchor, remember? That was the deal.* He'd said it like a compliment, back then. Now it felt more like a cage.

'I'm going to think about it,' I said.

That night I woke at 3 a.m., my head aching with thoughts about my failure to fit in with Sam's friends. Their talk of sailing in the Mediterranean or skiing in Whistler. The constant name-dropping of politicians and artists and intellectuals. Their invisible rulebook – the right clothes, the right books, the right opinions. Everything that I got wrong. Other women sailed through their world effortlessly. But not me. I was falling into an abyss, and I thought of Taylor's voice telling me I was idiotic. She was right.

Would work save me or destroy me completely?

I glanced at Sam, making sure his breathing was deep and steady. Then I crept downstairs to my laptop and visited a familiar website. I needed more little blue pills. *When your head hurts, you take paracetamol. When your heart aches, you take a Valium. It relieves mental suffering.* A few clicks and, once more, I was spending my husband's money on numbing my broken brain.

EIGHT

SEPTEMBER 1999

TL – By the time I arrived on the scene, Lucy and Sam already hated each other. She was a total fireball of resentment, and I realised later that Sam couldn't stand it – he was staying at work later and later and doing everything he could to spend less time with her. But Lucy, jeez, every time she talked about him, it was to complain that she didn't *fit in* with his world, didn't like it at all. But she'd *chosen* this life – and anyway, Sam's world was fantastic. Loads of money; luxury flat in Little Venice; entertaining, clever friends; expensive restaurants; amazing holidays; and an easy child who was a breeze to take care of. All that, and Lucy was always whinge, moan, bellyache, self-pity.

But I felt sorry for her all the same. There was something very fragile about her, physically I mean. Her hand would shake a lot. And she was pale and had a quiet never-say-boo-to-a-goose voice… You felt that she could break at any minute, like a twig, if you stepped on it. I guess that made me want to look after her and protect her. And I thought it was good for Evie that I was around. Then something happened.

AR – Go on...

TL – Lucy gave me a birthday present – it was totally over the top. A luxury day out – with her – at a spa resort, the Whittingdon, do you know it? It's super expensive – the pool has underwater music. And ozone. Anyway, while we were there, she cracked up and told me she was an alcoholic. I thought, fuck me, what do I do? Should I tell Sam? Call the social services? I mean Lucy was in charge of Evie all day. When there's a child involved, you can't just walk away... Then I had this brilliant idea of encouraging Lucy to go back to work, to get her away from Evie. I figured that she might pull herself together if she was in an office, mixing with people...

AR – So Lucy went back to work and that's when you started looking after Evie, is that right?

TL – Correct... but there's something I've left out.

AR – Which is?

TL – The truth is that I'd already tracked down Sam. That is, before I went to the fancy-pants spa with Lucy. It wasn't difficult – given that he was on the TV the whole time and I knew where he worked. I'd phoned him up because I was having doubts about Lucy being a danger to Evie. I thought maybe Sam would think I was the crazy one and would hang up on me. But it wasn't like that at all – it was almost as if he was expecting my call. So I arranged to have coffee with him at his work.

AR – Why are you slumped over like that, Taylor? Are you okay? Do you need a tissue?

TL – I'm fine – but this is hard... So I took the tube to the BBC – out in White City – and we went to the staff canteen. I told him my worries about Lucy and concerns about Evie. When you first meet Sam, he seems like this really nice guy. He looks you straight in the eye and seems to care about you. Know what I mean? I'm not surprised he's a journalist – he could get anyone to open up to him. Being good-looking helps. Always does, doesn't it? It's not fair when you think about it. So, yeah, I trod really carefully talking about Lucy – not saying anything extreme – but he encouraged me to go on and agreed with me and told me to stay close to her and to see her often. He told me to persuade Lucy to go back to work, so that we could be sure that Evie was safe during the day when Sam wasn't there. I was starting to get a sense that he was keen to control her actions, if you know what I mean? Looking back, it was sinister, even then.

AR – Lucy knew nothing about this? Your meeting with her husband?

TL – Nothing…

AR – If I'm understanding this correctly, you are alluding to a building sense that Sam was abusive to Lucy, which is how we ended up here, with Lucy's death. At that time, did you get a sense of Sam's behaviour towards her?

TL – From Lucy?

AR – Yes.

TL – She was obviously afraid that he'd leave her… But back then, I didn't know she was afraid of him for any other reason. That came later.

AR – Did you have further contact with Sam at that time?

TL – Yeah, he phoned me loads. He'd do it in the evenings – from work, before he went home. He'd ask about Lucy, whether she'd done anything unhinged.

AR – He used that word?

TL – He always used insulting words about her – unhinged, unbalanced, insane – that sort of thing. He said he was really worried about Evie – the poor kid. That incident with the knife under Evie's cot made him mad – I'd told him about it of course.

AR – Taylor?

TL – Oh God...

AR – Are you okay? Sinead, could you fetch some tissues for Taylor? Thanks. For the record, Taylor is slumped on the table again, head hidden. Sinead Somerville is leaving the room.

While Sinead is absent, Adra sits back and observes her witness once more. She can't see Taylor's face for the mass of hair that has fallen out of its messy updo and is cascading onto the desk. The brazen self-confidence is no longer on show. Instead, Taylor's body is tense and angular, her shoulders raised. Perhaps she *is* genuinely distressed. Adra has interviewed hundreds of people over the years. Is Taylor real? Or is she disseminating? Acting? The truth is, Adra can't call it yet.

Sinead Somerville returns. As soon as Adra restarts the tape, Taylor sits up and speaks:

TL – I'm sorry. I'm trying to be tough, so that I can do the right thing. But it's really hard. Maybe everything's my fault. I mean, I totally encouraged Sam. If I hadn't – if I'd kept my distance – maybe Lucy would still be alive... Can you tell me? Have you found her body yet?

NINE

LUCY

1999

I caught myself watching Taylor – so tiny and feminine in her grungy clothes. All quick movements, her face animated, her eyes bright and intelligent and knowing. I felt a thrill when she touched me, when her hand brushed mine, or she gave me a massage. I loved the way she filled the house with stories and would grant me occasional glimpses of her background: a memory of playing barefoot outdoors in the South American sun, another of a polar bear sauntering through the coastal town of Churchill, Manitoba. 'I don't belong anywhere,' she said. 'But I like it that way. I'm a free spirit and I make my own rules... Nobody imposes their stupid, hypocritical moralities on me.'

She became the warp and weft of my everyday life, joining Evie and me on trips to see the ducks in Regent's Park and to sample the pastries at the Polish café in Primrose Hill. One time we went to the London Aquarium and watched the sharks slide by the glass, shrieking and shivering at their dead eyes and flicking tails. On the way home, we sat at the front upstairs on the bus with Evie on my lap, then her lap, the three of us just enjoying the ride.

'I feel like I'm coming back to life,' I whispered when we were in a traffic jam at Piccadilly Circus. She leaned into me, and I took in her citrussy scent.

'The miracle of Lucy Bliss,' she said. 'Raised from the dead.'

'Mummy not dead,' Evie said in a matter-of-fact voice.

Taylor and I froze, exchanging a startled glance. How did she know the concept of 'dead'?

'No, darling.' I squeezed her tight. 'Of course not.'

We kept returning to the subject of my going back to work. Taylor said it would build my confidence about everything – being a part of Sam's world, being Evie's mother. We were in the kitchen eating smoked salmon salad. 'What does Sam think about it?' she asked as she took another forkful of rocket.

'I haven't mentioned it to him,' I told her. 'I don't want to alarm him – not until I've properly made up my mind.'

'Alarm him?'

'Well, you know – our deal. The idea was always that I'd be at home.'

'The anchor.'

I smiled. 'Yes – the anchor. The more I think about that image, the less I like it. I mean, who wants to be a deadweight?'

'Haha! Anchors aweigh! The good ship Lucy is sailing out of harbour...'

She put her fork down on her plate. 'Show me your hands.'

I held them out across the kitchen island, and she gently touched my fingers and inspected them from different angles. 'Hardly any eczema,' she said.

Her home-made remedy had been working. Taylor was good for me in more ways than one – I was taking fewer blue pills.

'I know. Isn't it wonderful?'

. . .

It was such a beautiful day – one of those late spring days that feel like summer. I was wearing a loose cotton dress; Evie was in a T-shirt and shorts. Taylor wasn't around, and I was at home, just putting Evie down for her afternoon nap when I heard the front door shut, and voices in the hallway. I went back into the kitchen and heard a woman say, 'Amazing, Samsy, I've always wanted to go down those tunnels. Legendary.' Samsy? I'd never heard Sam called that.

They clattered down the stairs and I followed them into the kitchen. Despite the warm day, Rachel was in tight low-rise jeans and heels, although she wore a sleeveless distressed T-shirt rather than her usual leather jacket. Her chin up and her smoky eyes peering between the curtains of her straight black hair, she belonged in the Kit Kat Club, the main attraction stealing the light from Sally Bowles. Sam was hot in the face, and he wiped his hand across his forehead. 'We've bunked off school!' He pecked me on the cheek. 'Going to work in the garden – the weather's too good to miss.'

'Oh. Great! Do you want anything? Shall I bring cold drinks? Sparkling water?'

'Don't suppose you've a beer in the fridge?' Rachel said, pulling her hair up away from her hot neck.

'Beer for me too, darling,' Sam said. 'And, I don't know – do we have crisps?'

'You two go out – I'll bring refreshments,' I said breezily. *Samsy?* Who the hell was *Samsy?*

Evie was fast asleep in her cot, and I went into the garden carrying the plastic bowl from the sink, filled with ice and cans of beer under one arm, in my other hand a family pack of salt and vinegar crisps. I was barefoot, so I negotiated the width of the gravel path carefully. Sam and Rachel were leaning up against a tree, legs out on the grass, laptops on their laps. I had the baby monitor in a pocket in my dress, thinking I'd sit with them a little while and have a beer of my own.

Their thank yous were enthusiastic but short, and they were back to their conversation analysing the latest developments in the war in Kosovo, then wondering about China-Vietnam relations and whether they'd be able to film there freely, without a government minder following them everywhere.

'Are you going to Vietnam?'

'Possibly,' Sam said, and started talking to Rachel about the vast network of tunnels that the Vietcong had built during the Vietnam war.

Ah – the 'legendary' tunnels that Rachel wanted to see with 'Samsy.'

I listened a little more, then returned to the house. My heart was beating a little fast – but I knew I had it under control. I wouldn't go upstairs for a blue pill. I took some deep breaths, and reminded myself that I should trust Sam and I did myself no favours by beating myself up about my ignorance about the war in Kosovo or Vietnamese politics.

Rachel stayed for supper. I made a simple pasta with pesto and salad, and she didn't make any snide comments, though most of the conversation was still set on work subjects – foreign affairs, and then British politics: how Tony Blair was doing, and the ups and downs of the feuding between Gordon Brown and Peter Mandelson. Then they were on to the Euro and how good it would be for the British economy when we joined. I zoned out, of course. But I didn't suffer. I just enjoyed several glasses of Australian Sauvignon Blanc and listened politely.

After she left, my head was hazy from the wine. I looked at Sam, his brown eyes soft in the lamplight. 'You and Rachel,' I started, then wished I hadn't. 'When you talk about work and stuff... you sound so sophisticated, like you're on the telly or something.' I tried to laugh. 'I feel stupid. Like they all think I'm...'

'Like you're what?' He made a tense face.

'I don't know. Not knowledgeable about politics and

economics and all that... Not able to join in the conversations and when I do, I get things wrong.'

'What are you talking about? Of course they don't look down on you. You're imagining things, Lucy. You're being neurotic.' He shook his head, stood up and started loading the dishwasher. The clatter of crockery, the jangling of glass felt like little stabs of mockery.

Sleep wouldn't come. Each time I closed my eyes, I saw them together – Sam and Rachel, trading jokes about current affairs, finishing each other's sentences. Then Sam's voice in my head: *You're being neurotic. Of course they don't look down on you.*

But they did. All my mistakes proved I didn't belong. Asking for a serviette instead of a napkin. Not knowing what 'urbane' meant. Saying Magdalen College wrong – apparently, it's 'Mawdlin'. Who knew?

While Sam slept soundly, his back to me, gently snoring, I imagined my life falling apart. Divorce. Sam getting custody of Evie. He'd use his money to get the best lawyers. I would disintegrate mentally, of course. He'd say I was unstable. A bad mother. I couldn't help myself. I quietly got out of bed and found my key and my locked jewellery box. A birthday present from Melody for fourteen-year-old me; a pretty wooden thing painted white and adorned with a blue rose. I took two pills. I really wanted to sleep.

TEN

EVIE

NOW

Evie has woken early, and she's lying in bed, admiring Antonio's sleeping face and his dark curls, splayed across the white pillow-case. She's reminded of the day they met. Of being in a crowded university bar, standing behind a stranger, gazing at his raven-black hair and thinking that it was the Renaissance hair that she'd seen in a dozen ancient portraits.

The crowd had shuffled forward; the guy with the hair had asked for a Corona and, turning as if he knew she was there, right behind him, he'd said, 'It's such a crush in here, let me order for you.' She'd thought, *he also has a Renaissance face.* It was a moment of pure joy as she said thank you, she'd have a Coke. Nothing more. She was going to work late.

He refused to take her money and carried the two drinks back through the throng. When two students vacated a low sofa, she'd grabbed it without thinking and patted the space beside her. He'd smiled and introduced himself – 'Antonio'.

'Evie,' she'd replied.

If Evie hadn't been right behind him in the crowd, if

Antonio hadn't turned around at that moment, (it was an instinct, he said), if the two students hadn't chosen that instant to leave their places on the sofa – Antonio's and Evie's lives would have taken entirely different paths. Him being in science, she in art and not having friends in common, it was unlikely that they would have met. They were both in wonder of their luck.

In the following weeks, Evie had discovered that Antonio, like her, was a quiet, reflective person. In the lab he worked alone on his project, happy in a near-silent atmosphere of diligence. He was well-liked for his occasional wry and perceptive remarks and was the person people confided in, telling him of their personal worries – doubts about a new romance, a new haircut, a sick cat – almost anything.

Within three months, they'd moved in together, sharing a double room in a student house. Antonio proved to be a good cook, a reader of serious books, a connoisseur of art-house movies and a craftsman – he repaired a broken chair, hemmed an old curtain and made a decent job of cutting Evie's hair and styling it into a short, choppy bob.

Evie had never been happier. She had loved their domestic life, their long hikes in the forests of Los Dinamos National Park, their deep companionship. Most keenly, she loved that extraordinary black hair, hanging in loose curls, his dark hooded eyes, his bony shoulders, the smoothness of his skin. She found him unspeakably sexy and was sometimes frightened by the depth of her physical and emotional response to his mere presence.

So, it had been strange that, in the months before Mia's death, she'd become restless. Sometimes, she wanted to come home to an empty flat, to be alone with her art, totally involved with it, totally disengaged from the day-to-day elements of being in a couple. She'd sensed a rising desire to escape, to start over as an artist, even if it meant a period of extreme uncertainty and no income. That chat with Mia had been so deeply needed; but Mia is dead, and Mia wasn't even her real mother. The pain, at times, is unbearable.

Evie slips out of bed. In the kitchen, she makes coffee and thinks of the past weeks. How could Mia have withheld the truth of Evie's existence? How could she have guarded that horrendous secret so completely?

She hears Antonio coming down the stairs and into the kitchen and, instead of saying good morning, greets him with the words: 'My entire life is based on a falsehood.'

'Love is the most important thing,' he replies. 'And Mia loved you without reservation.'

'I slept really badly... I'm obsessing about it all.'

'It will get better with time,' Antonio says. 'You have to give it time.'

'No,' she replies sharply. 'It's too big. Too fundamental. You're not understanding me.'

Later, at the coffee shop, Evie's busy, taking orders, working the coffee machine, navigating the hissing steamer, piling blueberry muffins and almond croissants onto plates. But her mind is returning repeatedly to the same questions. Mia and Melody – two names for the same person. But who was she really? A friend who rescued a child from a horrendous fate, or someone else entirely? As for the dead woman, Lucy Bliss – had she known her life was in danger?

The image of the silver-haired man from the funeral appears in her brain. Something about him sparks a memory – a figure from her childhood, a visitor who had brought brightly wrapped presents, had swung her round and round in the garden, under the oleander tree. And he'd spoken in English. Did this man have answers to her questions? Was it possible that he was her father? Was Sam Preston? No... it was too much...

'Excuse me?' A woman's sharp voice cuts through her thoughts. 'My coffee?'

A young mother, toddler on her hip, is staring at her, eyes narrowing.

Evie tries to focus, reaches for the woman's cup, but her fingers fumble and hot coffee spills down the sides.

'I'm so sorry!' She grabs a cloth. 'I'll make a fresh one.'

The woman rolls her eyes and purses her lips, and Evie realises that she can't live like this, with constant overwhelm, her mind manically flipping from one question to the next while her life unravels. She needs answers. Real ones, not these wild theories she can't share with anyone, not even Antonio.

She's home before Antonio that evening and she opens her laptop to search for information about the case – as she has done before on countless fruitless quests. It has become more of a ritual than a serious expectation of discovery, but this time, as she clicks on places and names and dates, she does come across something new: a chatroom on a website headlined *True crime – the unsolved cases.* The name of the thread is *The murders of Lucy Bliss and Jackson Wu.* She opens it up and starts to read, noting that nothing new has been added in the past eight years.

Some of the entries are bizarre conspiracy theories. The young man who was murdered had been, according to someone calling herself MagnificentMarple, connected to a Chinese triad. Lucy must have witnessed the murder and been killed because of it. The disappearances of Sam and Evie, along with the nanny Taylor Love, could all be explained by fear – they were supposedly in hiding from the same Chinese gang. But such fanciful accounts are the minority. Most of the comments assume that Jackson Wu had witnessed Sam Preston taking Lucy's body across the garden to the gate. That Sam had killed his wife in a fit of rage before leaving the country with Taylor and Evie, or in despair had murdered Taylor and Evie too, before killing himself. A few were 'Sammites' who believed him innocent, suggesting that the nanny was somehow responsible for the entire mystery.

Didn't these opinionated commentators have anything better to do with their lives? She's about to shut her laptop, but something makes her stop. A name.

Melody King.

More people need to look at Lucy's friend Melody, wrote TruestCrimeFan, *she lived near me in Gloucestershire, and I know she was really close to Lucy. After the murders, she disappeared too. She went to Mexico. Maybe Melody knew that Sam had gone to central America with Evie.* Evie scrolled down to see if anyone else had known Melody personally, but few seemed to be interested in her; the comments were cursory acknowledgements of the post, a mere *Good theory!* and a couple of people saying that if Sam was in Mexico twenty-two years ago, that didn't mean he was there now.

Evie now slams the laptop shut. Her mother had indeed come from Gloucestershire. She had once described the countryside there, the hills, the gardens, the woodland and the farms. Evie had asked – *did you grow up on a farm? What were your parents like?* But Mia, as always, had closed down the conversation.

Later, at supper, Evie looks despondently at her lasagne; she has no appetite at all. Antonio, meanwhile, is wolfing his food down as Evie explains that she's living in a constant state of anxiety. She can't even make art; each time she takes out her paints and brushes she feels a wave of panic spread through her body, her entire being seeming to be shaking inside. 'Actually,' she says with a bitter laugh, 'I'm in no fit state to make coffee... I'm not coping at work.' Antonio suggests that she ask her boss for a few weeks' compassionate leave, or sick leave.

He's right. Her boss, Daniel, would understand, and it wouldn't be difficult to find someone to cover for a short time.

'Maybe you should see someone?' Antonio holds her gaze, looking a little trepidatious. 'The doctor, or a counsellor...'

'I don't think so. I don't want to drug myself into suppressing this... this desire, this thing inside me that needs answers. That's what the doctor would do – he'd write a prescription and call that the solution. That would be awful!'

'Evie...' Antonio looks pained. 'Mia wanted to protect you.' He looks down for a second, and even at this distressing moment, Evie notices the beauty of his closing eyelids and black lashes. Antonio stands up and she thinks he's about to embrace her, hold her in his arms, but instead he goes down on one knee and says: 'Evie Segura, I love you. I will always love you. Will you marry me?'

She looks at him, bewildered. *Now! You ask me this now? When I don't know which way is up!* Love and sadness rise inside her with equal measure and her eyes fill with tears. 'Stand up,' she says. She stands too, and they hold each other close. 'You know I love you too. But I can't answer that question... It's impossible while all this is going on.' Her heart is burning, and she keeps the words tucked inside: *I was thinking of leaving you. I'd gone to Mia's that night to talk about it.*

Antonio kisses her neck, then holds her head with both hands and looks into her eyes, his own softening, his lips forming a half-smile. 'I'm an idiot,' he says. 'It was the only thing I could think of saying... to be of help or something.'

Evie mumbles, 'You meant it, though?'

'Of course.'

That night, as they lie in bed, Evie tells him that she has decided to go to Britain, to London, to see what she can find out about Melody's life and her relationship with Evie's birth parents. 'Before I make any decisions, I want to get to know these people,' she says. 'I need to know what happened in that house. The one in Little Venice.'

Antonio offers to come with her, but they both know that he can't; he isn't able to take the time off work and that the expense would be too great. 'Thank you,' she says. 'But this is *my* story. I have to go alone.'

ELEVEN

LUCY

1999

I sat with Evie in the upstairs sitting room, looking out of the window, waiting to see Melody striding along the pavement in her confident Melody way. She'd phoned earlier to say she was in London, at last, and had an hour to spare. I was thrilled.

Within minutes, she turned the corner into Russell Drive walking at twice the speed of the average Londoner. Her rucksack was slung over one arm, and she was kitted out in work clothes – green gardener's trousers and a zip-up green fleece with a large yellow logo on it. She spotted us and waved, smiling broadly. Evie and I dashed to the front door.

She got down to Evie's level and gave her a quick hug, then unfurled herself and wrapped big arms around me. She always smelled of outdoors and trees. 'Tea outside? Or something stronger?'

'A glass of white, I think. It's been a long day. I can't wait to see the garden!' She's a massive fan of Charles Fairbrother, our trendy designer.

'I wish you could have done it – but Sam was paying, so...'

'Hey, don't be silly, Lu. Charlie is the business. Proper talented.'

So we sat in our intimate private garden, the communal garden and distant mansions providing the backdrop, the evening sun on our faces, and she told me about her day. At one point, a dog slipped under the gate and was suddenly in our garden, sniffing about amongst the plants. I recognised it immediately as the golden labradoodle I sometimes saw, and looked up to see his owner peering over our fence. 'Oh, I'm so sorry! Rupert! Come here,' he said without conviction.

I stood up and grabbed Rupert by his collar. 'No worries,' I said. 'He's a gorgeous dog.'

'Gorgeous but wayward. He gets me into trouble.'

I laughed.

'I'm Jackson,' he added.

'Lucy.' I handed over the dog, which he took up in his arms and carried away.

Melody said she adored dogs and imagined herself one day living in a country cottage with two golden retrievers. She'd been visiting the top London nurseries to look at their stock and the current trends. 'You'd be gobsmacked at how it works. One year London decides to go mad for digitalis lutea and verbena bonariensis, and the following year they are lapping it up in Gloucestershire – you can't move for digitalis lutea and verbena bonariensis.'

'Like straight jeans or flares – or maxi skirts or mini skirts? I had no idea they did that in gardens.'

She laughed. 'Yeah well. I don't bother with clothes fashions, as you know. I like them to be functional and comfortable and that's it. You know, Charlie's done a great job with your garden. It's not faddish. The irises are gorgeous – you can't beat a generous splash of purple iris. Purple's the colour of wisdom and bravery. I love it in the mornings.'

Melody took a sip of her wine, casting her eye over the

bigger shrubs and our silver birch. Even after all these years, something about her remained unknowable – like she held part of herself in reserve, separate from the world. That quality made her the perfect keeper of secrets. I felt a rush of fondness.

'Do you remember that first day at St Mary's?' I asked. 'When you rescued me, the lonely new girl?'

She nodded, her eyes softening. 'The human chain in the playground? God, we ran so fast, we almost took flight...'

'You spotted me cowering away in a corner, and just grabbed my hand and pulled me in...'

'Two redheads with freckles... I spotted my twin soul.'

She didn't mention that, although we looked alike, we were different inside. She was happy and I was sad. She came from a good family. Mine was poisonous.

We sat in silence for a while, watching Evie digging a hole in a patch of earth with her miniature spade. Then, looking thoughtful, Melody told me that I had the most romantic marriage she'd ever come across. 'God, Lu, before Evie was born, I remember you telling me about your idyllic evenings together. Sam asking you to play the cello – then, when you ate, he'd read aloud to you from Graham Greene or Joseph Conrad or Louis MacNeice or Robert Graves...'

'You remember that! You've got all the names right – those are actually Sam's favourites. How do you remember?'

She made a 'duh' face. 'It's not hard. I mean, it's such an image – like from *Brideshead Revisited* or something. So culturally lah-di-dah. Like you two should be played by Gwyneth Paltrow and Leonardo Di Caprio.'

'That's the most atrocious casting. Good job you went into gardening. I was so happy at the beginning...' I said.

'I'm sensing a *and then things changed*,' said Melody cautiously.

'Well, things were bound to change... After a while, we had nothing to talk about. I mean he was spending his days talking about war zones and corrupt politicians. I'd given up work and was clearing out the cupboards or chatting to the man who came to fix the radiators. And he was spending more and more time away...'

I broke off, finding that I didn't want to go further into the deterioration of our relationship. Didn't want to tell her about my efforts to get Sam's attention. How a simple question about his workday would cause him to accuse me of prying, or being needy... How an interest in an overseas trip would cause him to snap back that I had to stop being jealous, or suspicious of him. He'd tell me that I made him feel trapped and that I should stop it. Should become more self-sufficient. He'd fall into a mood, and I'd find myself right back in childhood, scared of upsetting my overbearing father.

I did stand up to Sam, once, when Evie was a baby. She'd been screeching with colic all day and I was at my wit's end, rocking and calming her. Just as she fell asleep, Sam came home from work, announcing that he'd dropped by for his forgotten debit card. He was off for drinks with Rachel and the lads.

'Do you have to?' My voice cracked with exhaustion. 'It's been a hell of a day.'

Well, apparently, my tone irritated the hell out of him, and he launched into a lecture about the pressures of his job, and the awfulness of coming home to *this*. It made me, he said, about as attractive as an old dishrag.

'What do you mean *this!*' I shot back. '*This,* as you call it so disdainfully, is motherhood. *This* is the reality of looking after a sick baby!'

He froze. I'd never talked back before. Then he erupted. 'If you weren't going to embrace *motherhood*, Lucy, you should never have become a mother.'

He shoved past me so hard I fell back and landed on the floor. Later, he came home with apologies for his words and behaviour, and the next day he brought flowers, huge white lilies. But I saw it in his eyes – he'd marked me down as trouble. I knew that the punishment would come, slowly, in cold silences and dark moods.

I changed the subject, and told Melody all about Evie, and how happy motherhood made me. In return, she shared her news. She was going on a walking holiday in South Africa to clear her head. 'I'm thinking of shaking my life up. I'm ready for a big change.' When she dashed off to catch her train, I promised not to leave it too long before I came to Gloucestershire. Somehow, in all the time that I'd been chatting with Melody, I didn't mention Taylor.

One early evening, I had Bach playing in the kitchen, and was feeling good as I shooshed onions and spices in a pan. I'd managed three weeks with no blue pills, for which I credited Melody. Her visit had lifted me.

I heard Sam come in the front door. His step was light as he came down the stairs to the kitchen.

'You're early,' I said, happily, thinking that things might, just possibly, be improving between us.

He picked up Evie and reached out to me with his free arm. 'Group hug?'

I couldn't remember the last time he'd done that; it must have been months earlier or even a year. I joined the hug and said, 'Claudia Roden for supper. Tunisian meatballs. How about that?' (Taylor had managed to find an ingredient called rosebud powder).

'Yeah. Good.'

My ingredients, chopped and prepped with Taylor's help, were set out on plates, ready to go. She'd talked me through the recipe and rehearsed it with me. Sam took Evie and sat on the sofa, holding her, while I peered at the instructions.

'There's something different about you today,' Sam said, eying me up and down.

'You noticed!'

'Yeah. I'm doing man-noticing. I know it's there but not what it is.'

I stepped out from behind the kitchen island and did an impression of a model, swishing my hair about and puffing it up.

'Okay. It's the hair. Very nice.'

'Not just the hair.'

'Don't tell me. New dress?'

'Yup. And?'

'Ooooo. Now I see. Mmmm. Not sure about the boots. They're not you.'

I was wearing biker boots with bare legs. My new dress was a floaty wrap affair in cornflower blue from DKNY. I'd spent the day with Evie and Taylor – Taylor acting as my personal stylist – schlepping down Bond Street and back, winding up at the John Frieda hair salon in Marylebone. Taylor had brought along pictures from a magazine of a long-layered cut which she thought would suit my face and she'd read *The Hungry Caterpillar* to Evie, while I watched myself in the mirror, being transformed.

I'd loved the makeover and loved the boots, but now anxiety hit like a jab to the gut. I told myself not to ruin the moment.

'Mmm. Maybe you're right about the boots. I'll think about them,' I said as brightly as I could muster, slipping them off my feet. I turned off the music.

'Can they go back?'

'Not really – I've worn them outside.'

'Were they expensive?'

'Six hundred.' They were Jimmy Choos. Actually, they were £650.

'Christ almighty, Luce!' His voice was ice cold. Evie watched the exchange from Sam's lap, her big brown eyes focusing on Dad, me, Dad, me. Her mouth was a little rose-coloured o.

'Yeah,' I said. 'I'll resell them. No problem.'

I worked in my bare feet, trying to give the recipe my full attention while Sam got down onto his hands and knees and played with Evie on the kitchen floor, lining up toy cars and sending them down a little slide.

An hour later, Evie was sleeping. Sam and I had cracked open a bottle of red wine to have with our meatballs. I took a sip and trepidatiously asked Sam about his work. He was planning the trip to Vietnam, he said matter-of-factly, the one that he'd discussed in the garden with Rachel Tang.

'Oh, nice – tell me about it.' I was trying to sound soft.

'Two days in Ho Chi Minh City, then upcountry to Danang and Hanoi.'

'With Rachel?'

'Yeah, Rachel, she's producing. She's a pro. You know that, Lucy. Don't get paranoid.'

I tried to ignore the hostility in his voice and pushed away thoughts of Sam and Rachel together. Of her sharpness and her beauty. 'Great,' I said. 'You'll have a great time.'

I took a breath. 'I've been thinking about making some changes.'

'Yeah?'

'I sent off an email to Philpott and Sterne.'

He swung in, to eyeball me. 'What?'

'Yup. I've asked Ed about the possibility of coming back to work. Part-time. Not full-time obviously.'

'Really?' He was absorbed, processing the information. 'They'll want you, of course they will.'

'I know I said I wanted to stay at home. And that you want me to be at home with Evie, and I honestly thought that was best. But I'm not so sure anymore. I think I need adult company – and Taylor could look after Evie. They adore each other...'

He studied his glass, the silence stretching between us. I waited patiently, understanding that my proposal was a big deal. We'd always planned on giving Evie a sibling, but I'd grown increasingly resistant. Each time Sam brought it up, I'd deflect. Not now. Not yet. And the more Valium I took, the more certain I became – another child would risk my fragile brain breaking down completely.

He looked up, pulled me towards him and kissed the top of my head.

'Yeah – it's a good idea. I get it. Tell me more about Taylor. Does she have experience with small children? We'll need references and all that.'

'Sure,' I said. 'But first things first. You need to meet her.'

TWELVE

SEPTEMBER 1999

Adra Roy contemplates the interviewee. The way she leans back in her seat, one arm over the side, the other hand playing with her hair. She keeps gazing at the ceiling and constantly switches from a bored look on her face to an intense, engaged one, and back again. The confidence in the young woman's body language suggests that she thinks she's casting a spell over the policewomen, has them under her control. Adra is not impressed.

AR – We're still looking for Lucy, Taylor… Can you return to your account please?

TL – Sure… So, Sam and Lucy interviewed me for the job – which was a total charade, of course. Sam and I pretended we'd never met before and part of me wanted to laugh through the whole thing. We both performed magnificently – we deserved Oscars, we really did. I brought along scones – spelt flour and oatmeal with apricot and ginger, one of my specialties – to show off my cooking skills. And I was pleased that he really liked them. Back then, I saw Sam as a special guy – one of those people who fill a room and make the world seem more exciting, you know what I mean?

AR – Not really, Taylor. What *do* you mean? That he impressed you? That you were attracted to him?

TL – What are you implying?

AR – Nothing. Carry on. Tell us how things developed between you and Sam.

TL – Well, there was no *developing* as such at that point. But I felt that I knew him pretty well. From the meeting at the BBC and all the phone calls about how insane Lucy was. Anyhow, the meeting went well. I talked about the things I'd do with Evie, like reading to her, making her meals, going on outings… Sam asked me about my experience, so I talked a bit about working in kids' clubs, and working as a nanny in Brazil. Lucy just sat there like a potato and watched; but she was pleased with how it went, and they offered me the job, right there.

AR – Did you start straight away?

TL – No, it was a couple of weeks later. There was a hitch with my references and that took a while to sort out. I don't think Sam had realised that I'd have to be full-time because I needed the salary. I had to move out of Sanderson Road obviously, and I needed to find somewhere else to live – you can't rent a room in London on a part-time salary. I was on a two-week notice period with Orlando and Persephone; it must have been later in June when I started. And Lucy started work, three days a week.

AR – But *you* worked five days a week.

TL – Yup. When Lucy was home, we both looked after Evie.

AR – And the job went well at first?

TL – I thought so.

AR – In July, you took Evie to St Mary's Hospital. Could you tell us about that?

TL – Yeah. Lucy was at home, and we'd not done much because it rained all day. Evie was sulky and out of sorts and kept coming to me for comfort, and that infuriated Lucy. She'd developed this new neurosis, that being away at work would damage her bond with Evie. So, it was after lunch and the three of us were on the sofa in the kitchen and we were watching *Toy Story*. Anyhow, Evie wanted to come to me and Lucy said, 'No, I'll take her,' and took her onto her lap, but Evie cried and held her arms out to me. I had to think what to do and I said something like, 'Why don't I take her for a bit, and then she can go to you?' I'm such a diplomat sometimes… And Lucy screeched, 'Oh take her then, for fuck's sake!' and she stormed off, up to her bedroom.

AR – Are we talking about the day you went to hospital here?

TL – Sure. I'm giving you the background.

AR – Okay. Carry on.

TL – So, after a couple of hours I said to Evie, 'Shall we go find mummy?' I carried her up the stairs and knocked on Lucy's bedroom door. There was no answer, so I said, 'Can Evie and I come in?' I heard some sort of murmuring and took it as an invitation. Lucy was sprawled on her bed, face down, with her arms spread right out. She glanced our way and she looked a total horror show. Swollen eyes, mascara all over her face, like that old rock star, what's his name, Alice Cooper? Snot hanging out of her nose, drool seeping out of her mouth. I wasn't sure what to do. I didn't want Evie seeing her mother looking like that. But I didn't think Sam would want me to walk out and ignore Lucy, like pretend not to have seen her.

So I put Evie on the floor. She just curled up on her side and stuck her thumb in her mouth. I went to Lucy and said, as gently as I could manage, 'Lucy, what's the matter? What is it?' And she said, 'Fuck off Taylor,' in a crazy, slurry voice.

AR – Did you think she might have taken something?

TL – It did occur to me. I thought, *fucking hell, has she overdosed?* I asked her, but she said, 'No. I really haven't' in quite an irritated way. Then she hauled herself up and said 'What's wrong with Evie?' And I said, 'Nothing's wrong with Evie. I mean she might have picked up a bug or something. That's normal.' We were both looking at Evie on the floor and she *was* pale. Then she puked up this green vomit on the bedroom carpet. A white carpet by the way. Or probably *taupe.* Anyway, it was like Lucy was jolted out of a stupor, like someone had punched her. She said, 'That's it. We're going to A&E.' I tried to reason with her. Toddlers throw up all the time. They get bugs all the time. It's just one of those things.

AR – Lucy was Evie's mother, Taylor. Didn't she have the right to be the judge of her daughter's condition?

TL – Oh yeah of *course* she did! I wasn't going to deny her her mother's rights or anything like that. I just thought that if we went to A&E, it was going to be bad for Lucy. They'd make her out to be crazily overprotective. And, even worse, Sam wasn't going to like it. It would be really bad – *really* bad – for their relationship.

AR – What made you an expert on their relationship?

TL – I'm not calling myself an expert. I mean, only the two of them could know what was going on in that shitstorm of a marriage. But I knew Sam well enough by now, and that he thought Lucy was a basket case. I mean, at that stage, I had no reason to believe that there was more to it.

AR – Tell us about the hospital.

TL – They did a quick assessment straight away, then we sat for two hours waiting to see another doctor. I called Sam and he spoke to Lucy for a bit. I went outside with Evie to give Lucy some privacy, so I don't know how that conversation went, but I can imagine. Anyway, when we eventually saw a doctor, he said, she probably had a mild bug. Told us to keep an eye on her. Bring her back if anything changes. It was all so obvious. That trip wasn't about Evie. It was about Lucy wanting attention for herself – to get Sam's sympathy I guess – but it had the opposite effect. All the drama made him hate her more.

THIRTEEN

LUCY

1999

Taylor was shining her eyes at Sam, head on one side, big wholesome smile – and he responded with a warm voice and eager grin, the two of them sparking off each other right through the interview.

'Where do you see yourself in five years?' Sam asked, only half seriously.

She did a little, *hmm* – high and pretty like a bird. 'Maybe somewhere like this but with a view of the sea and a helipad.'

Sam laughed. 'Yeah, I hate that question too. It assumes either fierce ambition or that you're good at making stuff up. I don't know why I asked it.'

'It's a weird one, isn't it?' she said. 'I mean, life takes so many twists and turns. We can't know what they're going to be. All I know, is that I adore Evie and would love looking after her.'

We offered her the job right there and then. Sam and I agreed that we should get references even though she's a friend and it's totally clear that she's a good and responsible person.

'Not from Orlando and Persephone, though,' I said to Sam. 'They're going to be highly pissed off that we're stealing their housekeeper. She's only been there a few months.'

Taylor agreed to provide something from a kids' clubs company, and said she'd track down Daniela and Paolo, the couple who'd employed her as a nanny in Brazil.

I was suddenly impatient with the process; excited by the idea of going back to work; relishing the beginning of a new phase in my life.

Two weeks later, and no references had materialised.

'God, I'm so sorry, Lucy,' Taylor said. 'Nobody at the kids' club knew who I was... all the people who knew me have left. It's one of those businesses with a massive turnover of staff, you know how it is?'

'Oh gosh – don't worry,' I reassured her. 'What about the people you worked for in Brazil?'

'Daniela and Paolo... I phoned them and it was a dead line, no longer active. They must have moved, I guess.'

I discussed the situation with Sam.

'I know her really well,' I said. 'I trust her completely... and you've seen her with Evie – they love each other to bits.'

Sam didn't put up a fight. Not at all.

'I love her zest for life. It's exceptional. We shouldn't let her slip through our fingers...'

I delivered the good news when Taylor arrived at number 37 one morning, knocking on the kitchen door as she always did, coming in with a little prancing dance.

She picked Evie up, saying, 'You and I are going to have such a wonderful time together, little cabbage.'

'I've never heard you call her that before.'

'Oh, haven't you? I'm sure I've said it before. It's like the French say, petit chou. I knew a French mother who called her little boy "mon petit chou-chou" all the time and I picked it up from her.'

'When was that?'

'Oh, a while back. I lived in Kensington once, lots of French people live around there.'

'You've had so many lives. I lose track.'

'You're right,' she said. 'It's nice to be settling down at last.' She twirled Evie around, and the two of them collapsed together onto the sofa.

After three years in leggings and shapeless tops, wearing tailored clothes felt like putting on armour. I bought myself sharp little jackets, fitted trousers, spent time on make-up and hair. Looking the part made me feel strong.

The first few weeks in the office went well. I was as excited and pleasantly nervous as a child starting school. Ed Dawson, the owner of our little firm, welcomed me back warmly. I thought of him as my work-father – and he was everything my real father wasn't. Where Dad had ruled our house with cold precision, Ed ran the law firm with cheerful disorder, constantly losing pens and forgetting appointments, but never missing a legal detail. I loved having a father figure who didn't terrify me.

I started prepping on new clients. I had Megan Curtis, a stay-at-home mum with four-year-old twins whose husband had left her for a Hungarian ballet dancer, and Nduka Obi, married for thirty-five years, grown-up children, whose wife Chioma couldn't cope with his retirement, telling him, to his surprise, that she simply couldn't face seeing him shuffling about gloomily all day every day for the rest of her life. I'd seen how quickly marriages could implode when one side had a sudden panic about their mortality. But helping others through their crises gave me purpose. Perhaps their chaos helped me forget my own.

At the end of the working day, I'd rush home and would usually find Taylor and Evie in the kitchen. No more mounds of beans on toast for tea, or eggs with soldiers for my little girl. Instead, Taylor made bean and vegetable stews with mashed sweet potato, miniature fish-pies, apple crumbles, veggie snacks and sugar-free treats. As I'd come down the stairs, discarding my jacket on a chair, dropping my bag to the floor, she'd minister to me too – putting the kettle on, making tea as she gave an account of Evie's day. They would go to Science Museum or take the train out to Kew Gardens or meet with other children at a local café. Through Taylor, Evie was hanging out with the children of the Little Venice women that I'd always found too intimidating.

As Sam got home late most nights, Taylor took to phoning him during the day to give reports on Evie's activities and well-being. I'd never done that – I'd assumed he was busy and wouldn't like the interruption. But Sam seemed to like it. Twice, he'd asked Taylor to bring Evie to his work and the three of them had gone out to lunch at the Brackenbury restaurant, a favourite restaurant of Sam's and mine when I was pregnant. I'd thought it was special to *us*, but I made a conscious decision not to be upset or make a fuss.

Mainly I felt fine. But I snapped a couple of times when, in the evening, Sam would mention Evie's activities, things I hadn't known about. 'What? Evie went down the slide by herself? With no help?' Like I was interrogating a prisoner. But Sam was kind – making a joke of it and saying, 'Hey, have you taken your meds today, darling?' or 'Do we need to up the dosage?' I forced a laugh and said, 'Yup – I do need *bigger* pills!' But it was painful to miss those little moments when Evie did something for the first time and I wasn't there to see it.

·   ·   ·

I was at home with Evie and Taylor today. It was raining, so we stayed indoors. Evie was crawling around the floor, playing with a garish baby doll called Bunty which Taylor had bought for her. When Evie bashed its tummy, it squeaked 'hello' 'mama' 'dada' or made irritating cooing and purring sounds. In truth, I loathed Bunty, so I went into Evie's playroom and came back with a fifteen-piece jigsaw of baby animals in a bus, but I couldn't interest her in it. So I said, 'How about *Toy Story?*' We started the DVD, but Evie stayed on the floor, bashing Bunty again – two sounds going on at the same time, the TV and Bunty. Then Taylor and Evie were laughing together as Taylor started making up irritating sentences around Bunty's inane responses. *Mama mama, is looking so grumpy on the sofa. Dada dada, when will he come home to make her happy again?*

It was too much, my head couldn't take it – but Evie protested when I suggested putting the doll away and cried when I wanted to stop the film. I tried to be calm, but out of the corner of my eye I saw an expression on Taylor's face – a hint of a smirk, lopsided and suggestive, loving the fact that her teasing was getting to me, and that Evie chose her toy over mine. Then Evie started mewling and turned to Taylor for comfort. I put out my arms and said, 'Come to Mummy, darling,' but she shook her head, and grabbed Taylor's legs. It killed me to see that, and I found that I was shaking and losing control as Taylor watched me disdainfully. 'Excuse me,' I muttered as I ran away, up the stairs and to my room where I threw myself on my bed and sobbed until I fell asleep.

Later – I'm not sure how much later – Taylor brought Evie up to the bedroom, and I could tell immediately that there was something wrong. Her irises were unfocused and drifting, her colour was deathly – then she threw up a strange watery green liquid. That brought me to my senses. I leaped out of bed and showered while Taylor stayed with Evie. I called out, 'Hold her! Make sure she's safe!' I was ready in no time, and we drove to the hospital. To St Mary's. Thank God, they said Evie was fine, that it was a bug or something. Sam called and I assured him that Evie was okay. Coming out of my madness, I apologised to Taylor. 'I don't know what's wrong with me. I've been on edge lately.'

She squeezed my hand sweetly and said, 'Don't worry. We all have our moments. It's natural.'

In the following weeks, things improved between Taylor and me and at times it was almost like the old days. She baked little treats for when I got home – her cherry and almond brownies were particularly good – and I'd tell her about the Megan Curtis case, relaying stories about Megan's self-obsessed husband and his beautiful Hungarian ballet dancer. I shouldn't have been sharing the personal lives of my clients' cases, but I was desperate to reconnect with Taylor and knew she loved the juicy details. Then everything changed.

One afternoon, a work meeting was cancelled, and I was delighted to leave early. I called Taylor, to tell her I was on my way, but there was no answer. I hailed a black cab and headed home, where I dashed down to the kitchen, expecting to take Evie into my arms, but the room was empty. I called out and looked in the garden. No reply. I thought, *oh well, they're probably at the park* or something, and put the kettle on to make a cup of tea. I texted Taylor. No answer. I didn't panic. Instead, I took my tea upstairs and ran a bath, listening to some soothing Tibetan chanting that Taylor had introduced me to. I closed my eyes, dipping my head under from time to time.

I must have drifted off into a semi-sleep and after about an hour, all pink and wrinkly, I scrambled out of the bath, wrapped myself in a towel, fixed another around my head and tiptoed down the wooden stairs, being careful not to slip. Sam and Taylor were in the kitchen. They'd opened a bottle of wine and were about to take their first sip. I checked the clock. It was five-thirty. They looked at me in surprise, their faces colourful from the fresh weather outside. That was the obvious inference, anyway. But my stupid mind saw it as the high colour of intimacy, and I couldn't think what to say. My towel was coming loose, and I tried to pull it tight again.

'Lucy!' Taylor said perkily. 'Glass of wine?'

'Are we celebrating something?'

'Just relief,' Sam said.

'Oh?'

'Evie was unwell again,' Taylor said cautiously. 'Like before. So, knowing you wanted to go to A&E last time, I thought it best to go to St Mary's. But she's fine. False alarm.' She stood up and put her hand on my arm, looking at me pleadingly, like I was an imbecile. I brushed her arm away, feeling sick.

'Where is she?' I was already backing out of the kitchen.

'In her cot. Napping,' Taylor said softly.

'Why didn't you call me? Why didn't you call me?' My voice shrill. My wet face burning.

Her hand went to her eye. Was she wiping away a tear?

'I'm sorry,' she said in a tiny voice. 'My phone ran out of charge. I forgot to charge it last night. It was silly of me.'

Sam was still sitting at the kitchen table leaning back on the chair legs, and I looked to and fro between him and Taylor. I could tell they were shutting me out, were in collusion about mad Lucy.

'Is it a coincidence that you all came in at the same time?' I continued, clutching at my towel. 'Or did Taylor somehow get a message to you, Sam? Did *you* go to the hospital?'

'Darling... I feel that I'm walking on eggshells.' He, too, was talking gently, like I was an idiot. 'Everything's fine. Evie's fine. They checked her out and sent us home – that's good, isn't it?' I could see the irritation and annoyance that he was trying to hide, plain as anything.

Taylor tried to put her arm on mine, but I took several steps backwards, retreating towards the stairs.

'Lucy. Lucy... I was on the bus with Evie, and she was all weak and floppy like before, then she threw up on the bus seat. I didn't know what to do, and the bus was going to Hammersmith, so I thought – the quickest thing is to get her to Sam. I'll just stay on the bus for ten minutes longer.'

'And *you* went to the hospital with them?' I stared at him.

'Of course. Why on earth shouldn't I?'

'Sam! Why didn't *you* call me?'

'I sent an email.'

'You sent a fucking email? I haven't looked at my emails since lunchtime! Why didn't you call? Why?'

Sam stood up now and came towards me. 'Luce... There's nothing sinister.' He reached for me, took me in his arms, held me tight and stroked my hair, but none of it was genuine; it felt like damage control. 'When Taylor and Evie arrived, I happened to be on email, and I was so focused on getting to the hospital that I just dashed off something to you before we left. It didn't occur to me that you wouldn't see it. It was just a mistake. Just a mistake.'

I was humiliated; my every pain and weakness was exposed, my abandonment issues were on full display. I gave way, and descended into pitiable wretchedness. 'I'm sorry,' I murmured into Sam's chest. 'I'm behaving like a mad woman. I'm sorry.' I turned to Taylor. 'I'm sorry,' I repeated. 'Enjoy your wine, you two. I'm going to get dressed and check on Evie.'

I stepped into Evie's nap room and leaned into the cot, smelling the soothing scent of the top of her head. 'Sorry, darling,' I whispered. 'Mummy's bonkers again today.'

Later, just before bed, I checked my emails, but there was nothing from Sam.

FOURTEEN

SEPTEMBER 1999

AR – Okay, Taylor, perhaps you could talk us through these illnesses of Evie's.

TL – The mystery illnesses?

AR – For now, we will just call them illnesses if you don't mind.

TL – Sure. That's fine. Well, after that first visit to A&E, there was this second… second *event.* It was a month or so after Lucy had started back at work, at Philpott and Sterne. I don't think her job was that demanding. It wasn't some big city law firm. It was just this little high street solicitor's office that did family law, but she didn't handle those cases you read about in the papers, where the wives get mega-millions and all that. It was ordinary. You know, how she was obsessed with getting back to *normal?* Well, it was that. But still – she kind of overdid it. She let work get to her, like it was a whole new drama.

AR – And this is related to Evie's illnesses?

TL – Yup. That's the way I saw it. Lucy was always hypersensitive about stuff. And she became like that about her clients. She'd talk endlessly about someone called Megan Curtis whose husband had left her for a woman in the Royal Ballet. It was unprofessional of her to talk about such personal stuff at home I suppose. But still, she did it. She just felt too much for this Megan. Like Megan was pulling at her heartstrings. It was always 'Megan's so lovely, such a kind person. Her bloody husband, leaving her for Zsofia just because Zsofia is young and sexy and astonishingly bendy. It's all about the status, isn't it? Nothing about real human connection? Blah blah blah…' And 'At least he's not interested in taking the children. I think that would kill Megan. Poor Megan…'

AR – Could you come to the point?

TL – It was like this: Lucy was using Megan to feed her own neuroses – her fear that Sam would leave her for someone more glamorous – and the more she did that, the more she became obsessive about Evie. It was like – *my world may fall apart, but I'll always have Evie. Evie is mine.* And she was all over Evie, clinging on to her like her life depended on it. And I think that's why she started becoming, well, fixated on proving that if Evie becomes unwell, then it was Lucy that she needed. So, on the second occasion that we took Evie to St Mary's, Sam and I, well, Lucy practically had a breakdown because she hadn't been *the one true rescuer* of Evie. She was screaming and ranting because she, Lucy, wasn't the queen bee. We knew she'd be like that about Evie's illness, Sam and I. That's why I persuaded him to come to the hospital with me, and we'd tell Lucy afterwards.

AR – And Evie's symptoms?

TL – The same as before. She was floppy and listless and throwing up. I mean, later, I knew it was Lucy making Evie ill out of some crazy need of hers. But that day, it happened hours after Lucy had gone to work and she seemed totally surprised. So I guess that day was different.

AR – Let's break for five minutes.

TL – You don't want to know about the third time? When it was Sam's birthday? That was a real Grade A catastrophe.

AR – After the break, Taylor. After the break.

FIFTEEN

LUCY

1999

I was up most of the night. Why did Sam say he'd emailed me, when clearly he hadn't? Why would he lie? I should have confronted him before he came to bed. Instead, I'd watched him fall asleep, had stared at him for hours, trying to work it out. In sleep, that big handsome face seemed gentle. His dark lashes fluttered, and his pink lips trembled with all the innocence of a child. But my thoughts about him didn't soften. They were hostile.

Twice, my hand reached out to wake him and twice, I lost my nerve. It was about six in the morning when I fell into a fitful sleep. I woke up again around ten and staggered down to the kitchen to find Sam having a relaxed late breakfast, taking big bites of toast and marmalade, reading *The Guardian*. 'There's no bloody email. It's not there,' I said.

'For fuck's sake.' He dropped the toast onto his plate and reached for his laptop while I leaned on the table with both hands, staring at him with burning, tired eyes. He was scrawling, hunched over like a troll. 'Of course I sent it... Why wouldn't I?' But there it was, the supposedly sent email, still sitting in his drafts file. 'Oh fuck.' He leaned back and scratched the back of his head, made a shocked face at me. 'God, Luce. I don't know how that happened.'

'How can you possibly write an email and not press send?' I folded my arms high across my chest. 'That's not something anyone does by mistake. It doesn't happen.'

There were other questions on my mind. *What else are you lying about, Sam? Are you sleeping with Taylor?*

'Well, obviously it does, and it did.' He was sneering.

'I don't believe you.'

'Oh for God's sake.'

He turned his back, then picked up his laptop and marched across to the cupboard to retrieve his messenger bag and jacket. 'Have a nice day,' he shouted sarcastically as he left.

'Have a nice day,' I snapped back.

I waited for the front door to slam, then picked up his discarded toast and ate it. Suddenly hungry, I made more toast. Poured coffee, but didn't finish it, my cravings overtaken by exhaustion. I curled up on the sofa and dozed off.

Taylor woke me. She had Evie in her arms.

'Lucy, are you okay?' she said softly.

I tried my best to tame my rampant thoughts, to think like a sane person would.

'Yes, yes... Just having a little nap.'

I focused on Evie who, fresh from her cot, had her thumb in her mouth while she played with Taylor's hair. Her total innocence struck me. Her vulnerability.

For her sake, I needed to get a grip. I knew I should put the confrontation with Sam behind me and try to give him the benefit of the doubt, like a mature person would. Be a good wife who wants to rescue her failing marriage. And I should shut down my neurotic ideas about Sam and Taylor. Assume the best! A thought came into my head.

'It's Sam's birthday next week,' I said. 'I'd love to host a dinner for him... Not my forte, as you know. Would you help me?'

'I'd love that! You know how I love to cook!'

'Great, that's a plan! Can you look after Evie while I take a shower?'

I'm good at thinking in the shower, and while the water poured down on me, I became increasingly convinced that the dinner was a good idea. It was so hard to buy actual gifts for Sam. He didn't wear a watch or fancy clothes. There were no shirt or cufflink opportunities, and he didn't care about toiletries. Other men might have wanted to see their family on their birthday, but Sam wasn't close to his father, who lived in Italy with a new family, or his mother Clemency who was a stern and critical woman. The less said about Clemency the better.

Most importantly, the dinner idea seemed like a peace offering. It seemed loving and generous.

Later, when I suggested it, Sam was thrilled. Possibly by my gift, possibly by our return to normal, cordial communication. 'I couldn't wish for anything more,' he said, a sense of relief in his voice. 'And no presents. Really no presents. I'm done with *things*.'

SIXTEEN

LUCY

1999

Tapping into my better self, I made Taylor a coffee and gave her a profound apology for the scene I'd caused in the kitchen after she and Sam had taken Evie to hospital. 'I think I was pre-menstrual.' A terrible excuse, but it just slipped out of my mouth. 'I was just so on edge. I'm worried about these episodes Evie's having. Truly, I'm grateful you took her to hospital and I'm so sorry I reacted like that.'

'No worries, Lucy. Honestly.'

'Thanks. In case you don't realise it, I love having you around, I really do. You know how I get stressed and over-whelmed, you understand that – it's mainly work at the minute; this Megan Curtis case matters a lot to me. Her life is in total freefall, and I want to help her get back on her feet. God, poor Megan.'

'Hey, she's lucky to have you.'

'She's terrified of having a breakdown and becoming inca-pable of looking after her children. Can you imagine how awful that would be?'

'I don't really understand it.' She was fixing her mass of hair, which had been precariously held up in a messy bun by a red pencil. I wasn't sure she was concentrating on what she was saying.

'Oh?' I said. 'How come?'

'Wouldn't you have to be weak inside in the first place if you became like that? I mean, if your children are so important to you, you'd hold it together for them. I honestly can't bring myself to care about the richest people on the planet having no greater problem in life than getting through a perfectly ordinary middle-class divorce...'

Her words irritated me. 'Gosh. No, I totally get it!' I said too eagerly. 'If all your emotional infrastructure collapses around you – if the husband you love with all your heart runs off with a ballet dancer and you're humiliated in front of the world and then you fear that you can't take care of your children. It would be like falling into an abyss! Unliveable.' I was speaking too loudly.

'Oh!' She let go of the pencil in her hair, leaving it sticking out like an aerial. 'I'm such a clodhopper.'

I turned away and went upstairs, where I lay on my bed and looked at the ceiling. Why did I have to overreact again? Just minutes after apologising for my previous overreaction, so keenly aware that she knew everything about my paranoia and insecurity. I found myself sinking into a moment of self-loathing, hating the way that everyone had to walk on eggshells around me (Sam was right about that). I tried to tell myself that things couldn't go on like this, that I should make a bigger effort to stay on an even keel. I desperately wanted to be the calm and rational person that I knew was inside me, somewhere deep down. That person wouldn't drive everyone away.

The little jewellery box at the back of my underwear drawer was calling to me. Just one, I thought, to help me transition to sane Lucy, to help numb my crazy sensitivity, to help me go downstairs and re-establish normality with Taylor. As I found the key, buried in the 'special underwear' that I rarely wore, I convinced myself that I was making a rational decision not an emotional one, I opened the box, and downed a single Valium with a glass of water. I'd cracked. But I told myself that the drug was the lesser of two evils – that I'd stay in control.

A few days later, I arrived home from work and went down to the kitchen, where I picked up Evie, twirled her around and kissed her happy face while Taylor said, 'Let's think about the food for Sam's birthday. It will be fun.' She was flipping through the pages of a cookbook written by Jessica Willoughby. Taylor's purchase – she'd said that all the Little Venice mums were raving about it.

I settled Evie with her toys, and Taylor and I examined the recipes together. Taylor suggested a vegetarian curry with coconut and lime. 'Suitably sophisticated,' she said. 'Sam will love it.'

'Fantastic.' I trusted her judgement.

The guest list was short. Rachel Tang, of course, a couple of Sam's friends from Oxford – Daniel Speck, a barrister and Zak Weston a film producer who hadn't yet made a film. Daniel was bringing a boyfriend and Zak a girlfriend. Also on the list was Rosie Jones – Rosie was Sam's first girlfriend at Oxford. She'd studied English and was sweet and shy and from a comprehensive school in Bolton. She'd found Oxford intimidating at first and Sam had helped her acclimatise. Since university, she'd switched to psychology and was training as a counsellor. I liked Rosie. She was down-to-earth.

I'd half decided to wear the dress that I wore on the day that Sam and I met – a perfect-for-playing-the-cello wrap dress in rose-coloured jersey, with the necessary long, full skirt. I hadn't worn it in years – not because I didn't love it, but because it barely went round me after Evie was born and I spent ages getting rid of pregnancy fat. 'I've slimmed down a bit recently,' I told Taylor. 'Shall I try it?' She was keen, so we went up to the bedroom and fished it out of a bag at the back of the wardrobe. I tied it around me and looked in the mirror.

'No! It looks dreadful. It's not supposed to cling to all my lumps and bumps like that. I look like a failed macaroon.'

'You look amazing! You actually have curves. Curves are sexy!'

I turned around, twisting to keep my eyes on the mirror, inspecting myself from all angles.

'Curves aren't supposed to have sub-curves. I mean, I have curves all piling up on top of each other. And there aren't supposed to be curves rippling down your thighs.'

She sat on the bed, eyeing me up and down. 'Stop it. There are *no* curves rippling down your thighs. There are just thighs, like everyone has and then knees. You're being ludicrously self-critical. Honestly, Lucy, you're an intelligent professional woman, you mustn't let those confidence issues get the better of you. The past is not the present.'

I sat beside her. 'It's true. I do need to develop a bit of... What?'

'Sass. You need a bit of sassy in your life. What about shoes? Do you have some heels?'

'You know me. I don't generally do heels. I like your approach. The biker boots.' I allowed myself a moment of bereavement for the Jimmy Choos.

'I'm a twenty-six-year-old nanny who dresses like she's off to Ibiza,' Taylor said. 'You're a thirty-something professional solicitor with a shit-hot reporter husband. Get a grip lady!'

I opened the wardrobe again and rummaged around in a big raffia basket at the back. 'I do have these!' I held up my sky-high Louboutin heels. "Bought in St John's Wood nearly three years ago and never worn. I got them when I was eight months pregnant. Not to wear *then* obviously. But to remind me that I wouldn't be a mountain of blob forever.'

'There you go!'

They were wonderful – bubblegum-pink patent leather, pointed pumps, with silver three-and-a-half-inch heels. Thin as pins. I put them on and shimmied around the bedroom.

'You're channelling Marilyn Monroe in *Gentlemen Prefer Blondes*,' Taylor said.

'I am, aren't I – in a Gentlemen Prefer Redheads kind of way?'

'Sam won't know what's hit him! Will you let me do your hair and make-up?'

'Oh thank you. I'd like that.'

I was happy – cautiously happy – that we were being girlie together again. Love and Bliss.

Sam's birthday was on a Saturday, so he was around all day. In the late afternoon, Taylor and I sent him to Regent's Park with Evie while we got ready and prepared the food. I wore the dress and shoes, and Taylor came up to the bedroom to give me scarlet lips and smoky party eyes. She styled my hair into big, floppy waves and stood behind me shooshing it up and letting it drop, like a hairdresser would do. I looked fabulous, but my heart was fluttering and my mouth was dry. When Taylor went downstairs, I found myself getting nervous about the evening, overly concerned that it should be a success. I looked again at myself in the mirror, then took two Valium – reasoning that I'd been good, taken none for several days. This was topical medicine self-prescribed to prevent a crisis of nerves; a sensible precaution. I joined Taylor in the kitchen and poured myself a glass of Chablis.

Taylor was using all the strength in her skinny arms to saw a butternut squash into slices. 'I feel like a lumberjack!' she said.

'But it's going to be sensational. I can cook while you're chatting and you'll get all the amazing smells. You'll feel you're by the river in Bangkok – at the Oriental Hotel.' We'd bought flat breads and dips to keep people going and had already set out olives and nuts on the table.

'Wine?' I brandished the bottle.

'I need a clear head for cooking.' I stepped back and admired her brightness, her peculiar charm. 'You're some kind of woodland sprite,' I said.

'What?'

'You're of the air and the earth...'

'Not like you to sound new-age.'

'I know. I'm just feeling strangely, creatively... me.'

She looked bemused as she arranged ingredients neatly in little saucers and dishes. Onion, garlic, peanut oil, ginger, chilli, coriander, spinach, fennel seeds, tomatoes, coconut milk, mango powder, coconut paste, pomegranate seeds, maple syrup and limes. 'You're a work of art,' I went on. 'Your ingredients are a glorious installation...'

'Is that your first glass?'

'Yes, Taylor. It is.' I kissed the back of her head. 'May I say that you're looking especially beautiful today?' I meant it. She was wearing a simple shift dress of loose grey linen, black espadrilles, no make-up other than a smear of terracotta red on her lips. Her hair was tied back with a roughly torn strip of black linen. 'Stripped down to your essential loveliness,' I said, feeling in that instant that all was well with the world.

'I did give Sam a little present this morning.' I was leaning on the counter, watching her work. 'Even though he said not to.'

'Oh?'

'Just a couple of decent notebooks. Moleskines. I thought – who doesn't love good stationery?'

'That was nice.'

'I hope the others don't bring gifts. He'll hate it if they do.' I glanced at the clock and saw that it was ten past seven. The guests were due at seven-thirty, and I felt another shot of nervousness. I poured a second glass of wine and went upstairs to check myself once more in the full-length bedroom mirror, spinning round, so that the skirt of my dress billowed prettily. 'You sexpot,' I said to the mirror, just as the front door clicked shut – Sam and Evie returning from the park. I tottered on my heels to greet them, stopping halfway down the stairs to pose like a film star.

'Wow! Really. Wow!' Sam's eyes were shining too bright. His hand was gripping Evie's.

'You like?'

He nodded his head, a nod too far.

'Honestly?' I said. 'I know it's a bit... different.'

'You look gorgeous. Is that a new dress?'

I went down. 'Don't you recognise it?' I twirled.

'Hmmm. No. I don't think so. It's not Taylor's?'

'No! It's not bloody Taylor's!' I tried to inject humour into my shriek. 'Sam! It's the dress I wore the night we met.'

He threw his head back and roared with laughter. Evie started laughing too, caught up in his mirth, and I joined in.

'Family hug,' Sam said, picking Evie up. The three of us squeezed together. I looked sideways and saw Taylor watching the scene from the hallway, a kitchen knife in her hand. 'Come on, Taylor! Hug!' Sam and I said it together.

Zak and his girlfriend Okki arrived first. A warm evening; no coats to take, but a bottle of Veuve Clicquot to accept and admire, yellow tulips to put into vases. I was kind of fizzy. 'Zokki!' I said brightly, 'it's so good you can *never* split up.' They smiled indulgently and we went downstairs to the dining table in the kitchen; people sat down, happy birthdays were said. The door buzzed again and I trotted back up the stairs. Daniel and Victor. I've met Daniel a few times already and think him *a stuffed shirt* – a phrase of my father's. Victor was new, though.

Handsome, tall and sculpted. Dark, smooth skin, long straight nose, prominent cheekbones and, evidently, he worked out. I searched my brain for a joke. Dictor? Vaniel? No – impossible. There was a dick in there and almost an anal. I took Victor's bottle of Barolo, said a dignified thank you and ushered them downstairs.

Rosie had called to say she couldn't come – a family emergency – and Rachel texted Sam to say she was running late; so Taylor opened the champagne. She handled it like a professional, holding the bottle with a tea towel. A small pop, no explosion, and she poured it into flutes, cleanly and swiftly, no fizzing froth all over the place. The shapes made by her bare arms and thin hands as she poured the drinks and handed them out were mesmerising – at least to my vague but joyful mind. We sat around the table drinking, while she worked next to us at the kitchen counter, the spicy aromas drifting across. Evie was on my lap, playing with strands of my hair, staying up late. I turned to Victor and said: 'What do you do?' I sounded like the Queen. 'Young man,' I added.

He was in business, he said. He had his own kitchen design company and had offices in five cities. 'What?' I downed my champagne and, with the hand that wasn't holding Evie, refilled my glass. 'You're not old enough.'

'Well, I obviously am.'

'You're not *obviously* anything, Victor,' I said, feeling like my nonsense meant something, that I was being impossibly witty. 'You are a very *unobvious* person.'

'Is that a compliment?'

'Totally! Isn't there just too much *obvious* in the world? Obvious this.' I gestured with my glass, indicating our kitchen. 'Obvious that.' I gestured towards Evie.

He looked quite shocked.

'Oh no! I only meant thirty-something woman thrilled to produce perfect child with perfect man.' I thought I was totally hilarious – but he turned to talk to Okki. They were sort of neighbours in Islington or Highgate or somewhere and they both knew someone called Henrietta Crow, who was an artist – they both couldn't stand her and found her work overly-sentimental.

'You know she's self-taught?' Okki said, making a face.

'Nooo.' Victor touched his lips and made a face. 'I'm sure I've heard her mention the Slade.'

'Well, she might have shagged someone who worked there.'

'Or been a life model.' Victor did wide eyes and pursed lips.

'Eeewww. The mind boggles.'

'Doesn't it just! Don't you just know that she'd leave *stains...*'

'And there'd definitely be indefinable *fumes...*' They laughed uproariously.

I looked across to Sam at the other end of the table and attempted to blow him a kiss, but he was too deep in conversation with stuffed-shirt Daniel and when he did look away, it was to check on Taylor in the kitchen. Fair enough, I thought. She was working hard on our behalf.

I turned to my left. An empty space for Rachel, and then Zak the filmmaker. He was staring grimly at the table. I became the Queen again, 'So Zak,' I said, 'what do you do? In your spare time?' I sensed that I was adrift, losing touch with my surroundings. Zak started talking about a project he was working on, but I couldn't follow it. He was somehow saving the world by filming travelling circuses in Eastern Europe. I blinked at him, wondering if I should make him repeat it all. 'Excuse me, could you hold her for a minute?' I said, passing Evie across, while I nipped upstairs for another Valium. I was pretty sure it was the third, but there might have been one that I'd forgotten about.

As I came down again, the doorbell rang and I let Rachel in. Or, rather, I waited while she finished texting. She handed me a bottle of champagne still in its plastic bag – from The Winery at the end of the road and not chilled. 'Party's started,' I said distantly.

'Oh, Lucy, look at you. A vision in pink.' She breezed past, trailing a wisp of fragrance – Jo Malone and Marlboro Lights. As usual, she was wearing tight black jeans, a black vest top, sneakers, and a leather jacket with dangly bits – *not so much distressed as chewed* I thought. She was wearing biker boots too. Remarkably similar to the ones that I had bought! I wanted to loathe her, but I couldn't; even when she said bitchy things, I couldn't find any malice. I was still drifting around in my head and gripped the handrail as I negotiated the stairs and sat down again by Victor, leaning towards him. 'What's it like being gay?' I thought I was being funny – but he excused himself and went to the bathroom.

I took Evie from Zak who was trying to talk to Rachel over her bobbing head and sang our lullaby quietly into her left ear. 'I left my baby lying here, a-lying here, a-lying here...' I noticed Sam standing up and joining Taylor. He was admiring the food. I carried Evie into the kitchen area.

'Happy?' I said.

'Of course.' He put his hand on my back. 'And Taylor making this was inspired. I only mentioned it once, didn't I?'

'That's right,' Taylor said with a sideways glance. 'That day when we were talking about things with lime in.'

'Things with lime in?' I hadn't been part of this conversation. I felt a sweat breaking across my forehead.

'Yeah,' Taylor said. 'I'd put lime in a sneaky gin and tonic one evening, when we ran out of lemons. And Sam and I started talking about how we liked things with lime in.'

'Where was I?'

'Oh, late home from work I guess.' My underarms felt sweaty now, and my thighs. She was so casual about it – was it normal for the nanny to be having sneaky gin and tonics with my husband? And she'd chosen a recipe with lime in like it was *their thing.*

'Right,' I said, taking Evie back to the table where Rachel was holding forth about Zak's travelling circus project. Her voice was kind of penetrating and words kept shooting at me – primitive, discipline, misfit, underclass. I was suddenly extraordinarily tired and closed my eyes, tipping sideways to rest my head on Victor's shoulder. He straightened up jerkily and I apologised. 'How did you and Daniel meet?' I said stupidly.

I never got an answer because Taylor announced 'grub's up' and was bringing dishes to the table. Her curry in a large yellow bowl, followed by pink and green bowls of salads. Everyone's eyes turned to the food. Pronouncements of wonder were made, and Rachel chipped in with, 'Is it Jessica Willoughby? Fuck, she's a genius. Makes you wonder what we ate before.' Taylor nodded vigorously, while Evie became wriggly and irritable on my lap.

I stood up, holding her tight, loud-whispering to Taylor as I passed, 'I'm taking her to bed? Do you mind keeping mine warm?' She gave a smile that said, *don't worry. I've got this,* which made me feel worse. Evie cried a little into my hair; she didn't want to leave the party, but I rocked her in my arms as we went up to her room and laid her gently in her bed.

When I returned, the party chat had turned raucous. I retrieved my curry and sat down. At the other end of the table, Sam shot me a friendly glance. Raised a glass.

I took a long drink from my water glass. The coconut and lime curry was, as predicted, delicious. Zak and Victor were talking across me about politics, something about Tony Blair and the Millennium Dome. I zoned out and looked blearily at Taylor who got up from her seat and disappeared into the hall, returning with a wrapped present which she presented to Sam. I couldn't hear what was said, but I watched Sam kiss her cheek and touch her bare arm. He untied a ribbon. The paper was plain silver and the ribbon the same black linen that was tying up her hair.

A book. Like an exercise book but with a hard cover. Sam flipped through the pages, smiling and looking up at Taylor, his eyes shining with delight.

But he'd said – very firmly – no presents! She knew that he'd said no presents! She hadn't told me about a present. Why the fuck not? I felt the chasm inside me opening up and in slow motion I scraped back my chair and tottered round to his side of the table, my face burning and bloated.

'Hey. What's this?'

'Just a little gift,' Taylor said sweetly. But her eyes weren't sweet – they were knowing.

'Oh – but it's no presents. Definitely no presents.' I must have been too loud, because everyone looked at me.

'It's very special,' Sam said nervously. 'And it's for both of us really.'

'And Evie,' Taylor added. 'For when she's older. She'll have it to keep.'

Sam handed me the book. A photo album. It was full. Every page featuring pictures of Evie, Evie and Sam, Evie and Taylor, a few of Evie and me. Just one with Sam, Evie and me – which was stilted and formal. The rest were delightfully intimate and fun. *Now I get it.*

Recently, Taylor had brought a little camera to work and had taken to saying 'Oh do take a picture, Lucy, it would be so nice,' as she posed with Evie, pushing her on a swing, feeding her at the table, playing games on the kitchen floor. It was for this – *the perfect present*. The present that *I* would have given Sam if I'd had the wit. The present that should have featured me and Evie on every page, not every fourth or fifth page. Taylor had written little comments under the photos in her curly, backwards-sloping script. *Evie the mud princess* – the day Evie sat in a puddle. *Taylor and Evie go shopping* – Evie sitting in the trolley at Waitrose while Taylor reached for a can of beans. Who took that? A passing customer? A member of staff?

'Well, gosh,' I said. 'That's lovely. Very thoughtful.'

Sam looked relieved. 'Isn't it?' He touched Taylor's hip and she twinkled her eyes at him.

'Very thoughtful,' I repeated stiffly, and placed myself between Sam and Taylor as I inspected the photos, manically flipping the pages of the book. Everyone was looking at me. Rachel's face said it all – she was leaning to one side, her head resting on her pretty crooked fingers. *Lucy acting jealous and neurotic. Sam's impossible wife. Lucy, who thinks it's okay to ask 'what's it like being gay?'* 'What the fuck are you all staring at?' I said in someone else's high-pitched voice. 'Taylor is an extremely, pathologically thoughtful person.' Dead silence.

'Excuse me.' I thought I might faint and turned to leave the room, but I twisted my right ankle on its silver pin. An image flashed in my head. *Who's Afraid of Lucy Bliss?* I removed the shoes and stumbled towards the stairs, the humiliating, deafening hush following me all the way up. I went to Evie's room, picked her up and took her into my bed, snuggling the two of us under the covers. At last, I was where I was meant to be. She wriggled and I cried into her hair.

Sam came into the bedroom and then Taylor. He turned to her. 'Can we have some privacy?'

Sam lunged forward, ripping Evie from my arms. 'For God's sake,' he hissed. 'You're suffocating her!' It was true. She was panting, trying to get her breath. I pulled myself up, engulfed by shame.

'I'm sorry, I'm so sorry.'

I watched helplessly as he rocked her, and saw her turning green, about to be sick. 'Please, Sam,' I said in despair, 'we have to take her back to the hospital. Something's wrong – this isn't normal.'

SEVENTEEN

SEPTEMBER 1999

During the break in the interview, Adra Roy and Sinead Somerville stand by the water cooler. Adra tries to collect her thoughts about Taylor. 'What do you make of her? A credible witness?'

Sinead laughs. 'Well, a voluble witness, that's for sure... Strange manner she has, don't you think? Too casual, then too sincere, then too upset. It's hard to know whether that's her personality, or if she's hamming it up and spinning a tale...'

'Yes.' Adra places a paper cup onto the cooler tray and pours herself water. 'But we'll find out soon enough – if she carries on talking like this, and if she's involved in the death of Lucy. She's over-confident and she'll talk herself into trouble...'

'Do you reckon she's actually unhinged?'

Adra raises her eyebrows. 'We're about to find out...'

An officer passes by. 'Any news, Dougie? Any trace of a body?' Adra says. 'Any news of Sam Preston and the little girl?'

'Not yet,' replies Dougie. 'How's it going in there?' He nods towards the interview room.

'It's the weirdest domestic situation I've ever come across,' says Adra, throwing her paper cup into the bin. 'And that's saying something... We're going in softly, it's the best way. But we need a breakthrough soon. We need to find Lucy, and Sam and Evie, the clock is ticking...'

Adra opens the door to the interview room and the two policewomen take their seats.

TL – Thank you for the break, Inspector Roy. I needed it.

AR – Okay, Taylor. Now, back to business. To that final visit to St Mary's.

TL – Same old, same old. We took Evie in. Lucy wanted them to keep her in overnight, but they wouldn't, and Lucy came across as seriously unhinged. She was drunk and slurring her words and the staff had to check that Sam and I would take care of Evie. It was totally obvious that Lucy was incapable.

AR – It was from here on in that you became close with Sam, is that correct? Taylor? Can you look at me?

TL – Sure, sorry I thought I saw something outside the window. An interesting bird… So, that night, back at number 37, Lucy was sleeping in Evie's room, on a futon on the floor, while Sam and I cleared up the kitchen. It was a total mess from the party. Sam was really shaken by Lucy's behaviour, and I just blurted it out: 'Is Evie safe upstairs? With Lucy in there?'

You know what Sam did? He picked up a dirty wine glass and threw it at the wall. Like this!

She stands up and throws her arms furiously at the policewomen.

AR – Please sit down, Taylor.

Taylor sits back down and leans forward.

TL – But he did it again! Another glass and another glass. I went to calm him down and I ended up wrapping my arms around him. That's when I said what had been in the air: 'Do you think it's Munchausen's by proxy? Do you think she's hurting Evie on purpose?'

Sam sort of melted. Like he'd been bottling up his knowledge for so long, and now it wasn't his secret anymore; it was in the open. We moved over to the sofa and talked until the sun came up. He told me all about Lucy's fucked-up, dysfunctional family. Her mother was this overprotective, fussing parent, but kind of emotionally mean. And her father was a classic fuckwit. You know the type: controlling. Manipulative. Alcoholic. The full package. He used to hit the mother – Geraldine.

One night, when everyone was asleep, Lucy's dad fell down the stairs, drunk. The next morning Geraldine found him there in his pyjamas, unable to move. Crying and begging for help. You know what they did? Lucy and her lovely mum. They left him there – for days. Lying in his own piss, I mean, what the actual fuck? Lucy played her cello in the sitting room, knowing her dad was outside in the hallway whimpering and begging, and her mother was saying crazy shit like, 'Don't worry darling, Dad will be better soon – play him some nice music.' People are dark, aren't they, Inspector Roy? I guess you get a lot of that here.

AR – Okay, Taylor. What else?

TL – So much *else.* Lucy's father died in an ambulance after her mother eventually dialled 999. And, you know what? Lucy's life was one hundred per cent improved. Geraldine got the pension and shedloads of sympathy. You know how everyone's so fucking lovely when you're grieving?

AR – This is interesting, Taylor, but is it relevant?

TL – It's hugely relevant, Inspector Roy! That's where it all began for Lucy. Associating misfortune and neediness with receiving attention. And that was at the root of Sam's anger and his violence... knowing that Lucy wasn't the innocent angel he'd taken her for.

It was that night that Sam told me about his intrusive thoughts and wanting to knock the living daylights out of Lucy when she was clingy and pathetic. I told him that thoughts were harmless if you didn't act on them. God, I've messed up in so many ways...

Do you know about Sam's friend Rachel Tang? She knew Sam was going mad...

AR – We're about to interview Miss Tang. What can you tell us about her?

TL – Force of nature! When Rachel came into that house, it was like an electric shock. Everything jolted into action. She was so fucking cool and beautiful. Of course, she was the opposite of Lucy – wouldn't take any shit, or be pushed around... Lucy was terrified of Rachel.

Just after the party Sam and Rachel had this work trip to Vietnam. He'll have told her all sorts of stuff then, I'm sure of it. She might even know about the drugs that Lucy was taking.

And I'm sure he's since confessed to Rachel, about the murder, I mean. He was texting someone. It must have been her.

AR – Hang on. Drugs? What drugs?

TL – Just before Vietnam, Sam found a whole load of drugs in Lucy's underwear drawer – hidden away inside a box. There was no turning back after that.

EIGHTEEN

EVIE

NOW

Evie stands at the foot of the steps up to a flat-faced, white mansion in west London and tries to make sense of it. Weird that it looks so bland, given its history. Like it's been anaesthetised by layers of new paint, or neutered. The street is empty and still, lined with identical white mansions. Not quite real. She doesn't know what she expected – maybe it was this. Maybe not. Did she think that Little Venice might somehow resemble the real Venice? Not really.

She's cold and dizzy with jet lag and stamps her feet as she checks her phone. The policewoman, Adra Roy, is to meet her here. Evie's been waiting five minutes, but it feels longer. At last, a car draws up, the front left tyre wedging into the pavement and a slight, serious woman gets out, flips the door shut and offers Evie her hand: 'Adra Roy. Chief inspector. Are you ready to go in?' Adra says.

'Yes.' Evie's hands are trembling and she buries them in the pockets of the black woollen coat that she bought for the trip.

'The owners said they'd rather not be here.' Adra unlocks the front door and Evie stares at it.

'Was it always this colour?'

'Black? No. I don't think so. I think it was blue. Or maybe green. We'll have photos on file. Would you like me to check for you? Afterwards?'

Yes. She wants to know everything, right down to the colour of the front door. While waiting, she'd counted the stone steps from the street – eight; registered the ironwork fence at the kerbside – neck height; the dejected row of half-dead miniature daffodils; the vastness of the window to her right. 'May I see the case files?' Evie asks.

'No, I'm afraid not. We will have to reopen the case – now that you're here.'

Adra Roy unlocks a second door, the door to the flat, which is light green in colour. An internal hallway is revealed and Evie's surprised by her reaction; she instantly imagines herself as a toddler running up and down; can hear steps on the wooden floor; and is beguiled by a cold silvery light creeping in from a far window. Maybe it's her imagination, but it seems familiar, although only in sensation; she can't remember anything distinct – she'd only recently turned three when the murders happened, when she was last here in this hallway. 'What's that smell?'

'Floor polish.'

'Oh yes.'

'Where would you like to start?'

'The kitchen.' Evie has travelled all this way to discover her history; she may as well get straight to the heart of it. She'd read online that her birth mother's blood had been found in the kitchen. That Lucy Bliss died there. Adra Roy leads the way down a smart, angular staircase which seems out of place in such a grand old house. 'Were these modern stairs here back then?' Evie asks.

'Sorry. I can't remember.' Adra Roy's voice is clipped. She's keeping a professional distance from Evie, who has appeared from nowhere after all these years.

The kitchen is huge and shiny, occupying the full length of the lower-ground floor. The blinds are down at the front but light floods in from bifold doors at the back, that same silvery light. Adra returns to the pale wood stairs, and is crouching, stroking a pointed edge. 'I take that back,' she says. 'I do remember the stairs.'

'The flat runs over three floors, right?'

'Yes. Upper ground has the living room and a formal dining room. Top floor the bedrooms.'

In this part of London, with a magnificent communal garden – a private expanse of greenery in the congested city – the property is worth three or four million pounds. At the time of the murders, her family was wealthy and that seems extraordinary. Wealth – a foreign concept. A word that won't fix in her bewildered brain, so different from her modest little life with Mia, an ocean and a continent away. There are prosperous people living here in the flat now – and a small child. A wooden high-chair is perched at the table; children's garish paintings are taped onto the fridge door; a soft-toy polar bear slumps on the floor.

Evie finds that many of her questions are mundane – were the kitchen and table at the front, like now? With a seating area at the back? Are these glossy kitchen units new? She supposes that small details will make this early life of hers seem more real. She has to make an effort to ask the important questions about the killing of Lucy Bliss that happened right here – she's still struggling to think of this woman as her birth mother. 'Tell me about the evidence,' she says. 'About the blood and the knife and the forensics.'

'You're sure?'

'Of course. It's why I've come to London.'

'Okay, Evie. Well, Lucy's blood... Sorry, I mean *your mother's* blood, it was here, near the back door – although it was a different back door, narrower. So, about here.' Adra trails her finger along the tiled floor. 'It was localised. No splatter... And it was smeared across the floor, here, towards the garden. Tiny smears, barely visible, but still relevant. Are you okay? Shall I go on?'

Evie pulls out a dining chair and sits at the table. 'Yes, please.'

'We had evidence that your mother struggled – a fragment of Lucy's fingernail right here, with Sam's DNA on it.' Adra is examining the base of the bifold doors. 'Maybe she was still struggling right here, as she was dragged outside. Or maybe the fingernail had come loose earlier and was knocked off by the door. We had DNA evidence for all of you – you, Lucy, your father...'

'And Taylor Love?'

'There was substantial DNA evidence of a fourth person in the kitchen and we assumed it was Taylor.' Adra sighs and moves away from the door. Evie thinks of the lurid phrases in the newspaper cuttings that she's read over and over, and discussed endlessly with Antonio. *Little Venice Love Triangle Murders: Where is Sam Preston? Where is little Evie? The impossible disappearances...* On and on, each one of them tying knots in her brain.

'We found threads of a sweater that your mother owned – here on the floor,' Adra continues softly. 'Some blood and some of your mother's hair.'

'And the knife?'

'In a bush in the communal garden. We found Lucy's blood on it. Would you like to see where it was? I have the key for the back door.'

'In a second. Give me a second.' Evie leans forward, holding her head in her hands, pushing her blonde hair away from her face – her sensitivity now so heightened that a wayward hair on her skin feels electrically charged.

'The body of the young man, that was in the garden too, yes?'

'Jackson Wu. Yes. Near the knife. Most of the blood was his.'

Adra stands calmly by the door. Waiting.

'I'd like to see the garden.'

'Okay.' Adra turns the key that is sitting in the lock and Evie goes outside, walking through a pretty patch of private garden that leads to an area that seems large enough to be a park – enormous centuries-old trees line its edges, along with dozens of houses, as splendid and old as the Preston-Bliss house.

She sits down on a bench, unsure of whether she's made the right decision in coming, not knowing how much she should tell the policewoman of her own side of the story, of her life with Mia in Mexico, or when she should tell it.

Evie gets up and strolls around the garden, the only person out there in an unpleasant, cold wind, and the image comes into her mind of the young man, Jackson Wu, who'd lain dead for hours, under a bush, before his body was discovered.

She pushes her hands back into the pockets of the black coat and walks slowly around the path that runs next to the houses, wishing that she knew more about the young man, offering up a little prayer for him to a God she doesn't believe in. Then she thinks about the questions that she plans to ask Adra Roy – about her birth parents Sam and Lucy, about the witnesses to Lucy's murder, the details of the evidence and the mysterious disappearance of Taylor Love. And about dear, beloved Mia in her *Melody days*.

NINETEEN

LUCY

1999

I was pretending to read a book while Sam packed for Vietnam, moody and stiff, chucking his clothes miserably onto the duvet, coming to life when he couldn't find matching socks. 'Sweet Jesus!' Hissed at an old sock, but meant for me. It took some effort, but I ignored him.

Sam threw his rucksack onto the bed next to the pile of clothes. 'I wish I could cancel this trip,' he said sternly.

'Me too, I wish you didn't have to go.' It was true. After the disastrous dinner party, we'd been told that Evie was fine. Just keep her hydrated. Check her temperature. But I was still convinced something was terribly wrong. That her father should be at home – and not on an Asian adventure with Rachel Tang bonding over *the problem of Lucy*. The idea filled me with horror. I glanced unthinkingly at the drawer where I kept the Valium and saw Sam flinch.

He stuffed a T-shirt into his rucksack and came to sit beside me. 'What are you reading?'

'Oh nothing. Just recipes.' I showed him the cover. *How to*

Eat by Nigella Lawson. 'It's the latest craze.' He cupped his hand over mine.

'Lucy.'

'Yes, Sam.'

'You know I love you?'

'Sure...' I sensed impending disaster and pulled my hand away.

'We need to talk.' His delivery was portentous, like talking was a grave and difficult endeavour.

Nervously, I set the book aside and folded my arms across my chest. 'That old cliché?'

'Lucy...' He stopped talking and ran his fingers through my hair to get it away from my face. A gentle touch, but patronising, and I felt stupid in my pyjamas.

'Lucy... This is hard to say, but—'

'I'm not an idiot.' I interrupted. 'I know you're worried about me. I know I've been weird...' I reached pathetically for a justification. 'It's hormones, Sam. They're all over the place right now. You know. It happens.'

'You're not pregnant?' There was fear in his brown eyes. Definite fear.

'No. That's not what I meant.'

'Good.' He sighed and slumped against the headboard, reaching for my hand again. 'Lucy, I think you should go away. Go to your mother's or something. Just until I'm back from Asia.'

'What are you talking about? I can't go away. I have work.' He looked down at our hands dejectedly. I softened. 'I suppose it's fairly quiet this week... It's not impossible for me to take a couple of days' holiday, and Mum would love to see Evie.'

'Without Evie. That's the point.'

'What?'

'Without Evie.' He got off the bed and stood over at me, readying for a fight.

An icy silence. Then, from nowhere, my head was thumping to a deafening drumbeat, and I heard myself shriek: 'Never! Never! How dare you!'

'I don't feel comfortable leaving her with you,' he said calmly. 'I don't think she's safe. I mean, look at you.'

I got up off the bed and paced up and down trying to control myself. It was hard to slow my breathing, and I struggled to get the words out in a reasoned voice: 'Sam. This is me. Lucy. Who loves you and loves Evie more than life itself. Why the fuck would Evie be unsafe?'

'You're not well.' There was despair in his voice.

'I'm just as worried about Evie as you are! These strange episodes, these sicknesses are not normal, Sam. Do you think I'd leave her? You want me to leave her with Taylor?'

We were eyeballing each other across the bed.

'You know what I'm talking about,' he said, his voice cracking. 'I suspect... I strongly suspect... that you have been harming Evie in order to take her to hospital. It's your background. Your history. It's always there like a poison.'

'No, Sam, no.' My voice collapsed to a whisper. My legs weakened, and I fell to the ground. All my worst fears about Sam and Taylor were happening, now, in real life. They wanted to destroy me utterly, and to take Evie too! I could barely breathe.

'I hate to say this, Lucy, but you need time away from Evie and you need treatment.'

'What are you talking about! Treatment?'

Slowly, he turned away and opened my underwear drawer, removed my jewellery box, shook the key out of its hiding place inside a pair of tights and started opening the lock. I crumpled into a ball, my eyes level with the bed, watching him, this handsome husband with disdainful eyes, his long slim fingers holding my little white box in the air.

As he threw the drugs on the bed, packet by packet, he

called out the names, like a roll-call at school: 'Rivotril, Diazepam, Tramadol, Lorazepam, Xanax.'

So many pills. Where had they come from? I curled up tighter, rocking like a baby, the beat in my head now becoming distant, as though it was in some far-off, unreachable room.

'If you don't get out of the house, tonight,' he said, 'I'm going to social services. You'll lose me. You'll lose Evie. You'll lose everything.'

TWENTY
LUCY

1999

It was raining when I arrived in Gloucestershire and the fuchsia bush by the gate was heavy with water and weeping. I dashed up the front path, dragging my suitcase on wheels, rainwater dripping down the back of my neck. A pathetic, desolate figure.

Mum lifted the net curtain in the front room, and I waited in the porch for her to answer the door. I hadn't seen my mother in months, and she greeted me with a look of pity in her watery eyes. I dragged the bag indoors, registering immediately the old blue pile carpet in the hallway scrubbed pale at the bottom of the stairs. Why did she never replace it? On the wall, the painting that Dad had lain under. A field of poppies. Scudding clouds. A mother and a child. Together. As a mother and child should be.

'You should visit more often, Lucy,' Mum said sharply as she led us into the sitting room. 'Living alone isn't easy when you're old. Don't get old.'

'I'm sorry.' I sat on our sofa, which smelt of toast. She sat at the other end, brushing invisible crumbs from her brown trousers, wiggling her feet inside her fleece slippers, altogether uneasy.

'I wanted to see Evie,' she said in a self-pitying voice.

'I know, Mum. I'm sorry. I couldn't bring her this time.'

'So you say.'

'She's going to a party,' I lied. 'She was so looking forward to it.' At the best of times, my barriers were up around my mother. Now, in my horrendous state, I was constructing a fortress.

It didn't help matters that every time I went home to Gloucestershire, I was back in my childhood nightmare – back at the death of my father. I closed my eyes and became that little girl again – the messed-up twelve-year-old pleading with my mother: 'Daddy's not okay, Mum...'

'You're right, Lucy, he's not okay. He's a bloody drunkard and that's why he's sprawled across the corridor.'

'What should we do? Should we call an ambulance?'

'Don't be stupid, Lucy. He just needs to sleep it off. That's the way it is with drunkards.'

'Can't we do *something*?'

'Go into the sitting room and play your cello, why don't you? He likes that – it will help him pass the time.'

And that's what I did. I played the cello for hours, while my father was dying, convincing myself that it was the right thing to do, that I was doing my bit to help.

'Well, party or not, at least *you're* here,' my mother said, bringing me back to the present. She flicked her tongue back and forth across her upper gum like she was trying to remove flecks of food. 'Would you like a cup of tea?' she asked stiffly. 'Have you eaten? I have some beef casserole from yesterday. With mashed potatoes? You like that, don't you?'

'Yes. I do. Thanks.' The tears were welling up.

'What's the matter, Lucy? Whatever it is, it can't be that bad.' Her voice softened: 'Come into the kitchen and help me cook.'

The way she said it, with concern, surprised me. It was warmer than anything I remember from childhood. Her little daughter coming home with a freshly scraped knee or tales of the bullying big girls had always been greeted with a frosty voice: 'I'll put a plaster on it. Now stop whimpering and go and do your homework.' Or 'You need to toughen up, Lucy.'

Suddenly, I wanted arms around me. Not hers. That would be too alien, too jarring. But somehow our little kitchen embraced me. The familiar pots and pans hanging from hooks, the wooden clothes' airer ornamented with damp tea towels, the multicoloured tiles, some of them bearing raised ceramic fruits. A plum, an apple, a peach. The cat-flap and the red-fleece cat bed. 'Where's Cupcake?'

My mother sniffed. 'When did I ever know where Cupcake is? You know what she's like.'

'You don't have any wine do you, Mum? I think I'd rather have that than a cup of tea, if you don't mind.'

'Look in the back of the larder.' She was peeling potatoes, getting them ready for boiling, happier now she had something to focus on.

I opened the larder door. Weetabix, blackcurrant jam, Nutella, Bourbon biscuits. Tins of tuna, tins of pilchards and on a top shelf, behind the orange cordial, two bottles of Shiraz. I reached up and extracted one, noticing a dust-covered half-bottle of Johnnie Walker Red Label whisky. Dad's favourite. I wondered why she kept it.

'Would you like one?'

'Oo no. Not at this time. I'm fine with tea.'

I drank slowly, watching her as I cut crosses into Brussel sprouts. Her rounded back. Her right shoulder always a little higher than her left.

'I can tell that you've had a to-do with Sam,' she said. 'But I won't force you to go into it. I've made a blackberry and apple crumble for sweet.'

'Thank you.'

'I'd have made it anyhow.' She dropped a potato into a saucepan.

Later, I told her that Sam and I had argued. But I made it sound bland, almost like a tiff. She didn't press me for details, and we turned our attention to the TV and *Masterchef*. Before bed, she told me about goings-on in the church choir where she sang and how they were closing down the Spar and the difficulties she was having getting her lawnmower fixed.

At eleven, I went up to my old bedroom in the eaves – same rust-red sheets and autumnal patterned pillowcases on the bed; same yellowing lace at the dormer window. I lay heavily in the dip in the mattress made by my body over the years and I could hear voices from long ago. My father yelling at my mother, complaining about the small things that were never right. Her sewing materials out on the table when they should be away in a cupboard. Her failure to polish his shoes to the required shine. Her habit of talking too long to people after church. Then the punishments – the endless days of his dark moods and belittling criticisms. I could practically hear my mother scurrying up to bed early, for a little peace. To her credit, she didn't complain about him to me. She kept everything to herself. Coldly so. Maybe she thought it was safer to shut me out entirely. No kisses, no hugs. But nonetheless a buffer between me and Dad. The time he spent criticising her was time off from criticising me.

I turned towards the wall like I used to as a child, curled up in my bespoke cradle – but this time, as an adult, I had my phone in my hand and I texted Melody, desperate to see her again.

We'd agreed on The Plough at Recton, – a twenty-minute walk from my mother's house. I arrived first, bought a lime soda and sat in the corner watching the locals: middle-aged men who came in for a lunchtime pint, chatting loudly at the bar.

Through the window, I saw a dark green van pull up and park at an angle and knew immediately that this was Melody. She'd always driven old vans filled with tools, or garden waste, or plants. She strode into the pub like she was bringing the outside in with her, like a breeze rustling up fallen leaves, and the men at the bar looked over with interest while she stood widely, scanning the room. Then, 'Lucy-Lu!' Big arms, a toss of her fabulous red hair, and a swift embrace. She smelled of the garden centre where she worked, of top-soil and geraniums.

I bought her a half of cider and she told me she'd handed in her notice at work; it was her last week. She loved Greendales, but it had been five years and she wanted a change. And, guess what, she'd got herself a six-month contract at the super-posh Tredenham Nurseries in London; half an hour on the tube from Little Venice. She was bracing herself for flat-hunting, or rather room-hunting, in noisy, dirty London. 'Stupid rents! I won't stay forever of course. But I gotta live in London at some point in my life and it's a good moment.'

'Oh my God!'

'You know me and adventure,' she said.

'How was South Africa?'

'Just the biz. It's a beaut of a country, Lu. The walking around Cape Town – it was *up there...* In all senses.'

'Who did you go with?'

She took a slug of cider. 'Myself. You know I like travelling that way. Just me and God's good earth. It was good thinking time – about the job change and new experiences generally.'

'How about your love life?' I asked.

'Zilch.' She was beaming. 'That's one reason it's easy to pick up sticks and do a stint in the big City.'

I'd only known her have one boyfriend. A guy on her gardening course called Lennie. I never met him, but she'd shown me pictures of a big, ruddy lad wearing a Nordic jumper – he was like a male version of her, a big honest smile, practical, happy outdoors. The relationship fell apart after a year when Lennie moved on to someone else, but all I got out of Melody was, 'Totally gutted. Like you gut a fish gutted.' Shortly afterwards, she took herself off to Asia and went trekking in Nepal. I wondered whether this latest move was prompted by another ending – romantic or otherwise. But I didn't pry.

'You in London!'

'Yep. Well, I have a friend there, you know!' I smiled.

But she said, 'Lu? What's up?'

'Gosh. Is it that obvious? Oh Mel. Things aren't good.'

'Oh?'

I took in a breath and began the story, telling her that things were even worse than I'd let on last time we met. I told her everything about Taylor and Sam and Evie's illnesses and how I'd grown paranoid – like I'd been in the old days after my dad died. I didn't tell her about the Valium. 'Sometimes,' I mumbled, 'when I'm at my worst, I'm afraid that I'm incapable of looking after Evie. I wonder whether I'm a danger to her.'

'Lu, that's paranoia speaking... You're being too tough on yourself. I know it.'

'Sam's lost faith in me.'

'Don't you lose faith in Sam! He knows about your background. He understands.'

'I suppose.' We shared a sad grin and sighed at the same time. It's a relief that Melody knows all about Sam, how his childhood was nearly as damaged as mine. Ages ago I'd told her about his parents' vicious divorce and how sixteen-year-old Sam went off the rails – skipping school and heading into the city for weed, and sometimes cocaine.

'Remember Willow Kelly?' I said.

'The girl Sam fell for when he was young?'

I'd shared the story with Mel years ago. Sam's first love and his first obsession.

'Yeah, he was infatuated with her, and stalked her when she dumped him for another boy... She was ruthless – humiliated him in front of his friends, mocked his family, brought up his parents' horrific divorce...'

'God, poor Sam...'

'Here's the thing – the worse Willow was to him, the more infatuated he became with her. Instead of turning him off her, she was turning him on...'

'Oh dear... That's sick.'

'Yeah... He said damaged kids do that. They can't accept the truth and try to fix everything emotionally... Whatever it takes.'

'You think he might behave like that with Taylor?'

'Maybe, at some point. She's beautiful and she's cruel and she has Sam under her spell.'

'I'm here,' Melody said. 'If ever you need to talk about it. And I'll be in London soon to look after you. I can't wait to see Evie – you know how much I love that little girl.'

Her warmth broke me and I fought back tears. 'Oh God, Mel! Thank you so much. You've no idea how scared I am of losing her!'

'Hey, Lucy... We've got this! We've got this...' Her words were strong, but the look on her face was anxious. About me, about Evie.

'We'll sort it out when I'm in London,' she said, still troubled. 'Now I have to run – get back to my gardener's world. Can I give you a lift home?'

She dropped me off at Mum's. I opened the front door with a borrowed key and peeked into the sitting room where my mother was slumbering on the sofa, covered by a crocheted patchwork blanket. She was snoring softly, her glasses trembling halfway down her face. I crept out, and went upstairs to check my emails. There was just one new message:

Dearest Lucy,

I want you to get professional help. You know you need it, and we can get you the best in London. You've never dealt with what happened with your father. That's part of it. I think that, for a while, you and I should not talk. It's clear that I'm part of the problem. I make you worse. The world I'm in makes you worse. I'm worried about you, and leaving Evie with you. I've rented a flat in Queen's Park. Only ten minutes from Russell Drive. Make yourself cozy there. Come and see Evie, under supervision, while we sort this mess out. If you want to go to the flat, rather than stay with your mother, while I'm in Vietnam, contact Taylor. She has the key and can help you move in.

Sam.

TWENTY-ONE

SEPTEMBER 1999

TL – Yes, the drugs discovery – that was really shocking. Sam found a whole smorgasbord of sedatives and tranquilisers in her underwear drawer – it was like the stuff that guy Damien Hirst calls art – all the different pills and their pretty colours. The truth was Sam had put them there – he was gaslighting Lucy, messing with her head – but I had no idea at that point. I just thought he was amazing and that the two of us had so much in common. I mean we're both sharp and funny and all that. And a bit flirty.

AR – What do you mean *Sam had put them there*?

TL – Just that. The guy turned out to be as cruel as fuck – I guess he wanted all her breakdowns so he could be in control, or something like that.

AR – But that's extreme, isn't it? Planting drugs in her drawer?

TL – Yeah, well, Sam *was* extreme, as we now know. I guess when you've been in warzones, face to face with the depths of humanity, planting a few drugs is the least of it.

AR – It was around this time that Lucy left the family home?

TL – Yes. I mean, she didn't leave voluntarily. Sam expelled her and, like an idiot, I went along with it. I absolutely believed that Lucy was totally off the rails and a danger to Evie. I stupidly thought Sam was doing the right thing – that it was noble of him to be decisive and to put his child first. I had him on a pedestal at that point. Like a skyscraper of a pedestal and I didn't see through him. I mean, he was so charming and engaging and I liked the flirty stuff – it made my day.

AR – He expelled her from her own home? Tell me more about that.

TL – God, he was such a manipulator. He'd told me how desperate he was about Lucy; then he went off on a work trip to Vietnam, leaving me to do the actual expelling. He outsourced the actual dirty work.

TWENTY-TWO

LUCY

1999

The email was so calculated. So uncompromising. *I make you worse... I'm really worried about you, and scared of leaving Evie with you... I've rented a little flat... Make yourself cozy... See Evie, under supervision...* My own daughter – under supervision! That's why he sent me to Gloucestershire – to take control and get me away from Evie for good. I didn't sleep, not for a minute.

At 3 a.m., I switched on the bedside light, sat up and stared at the familiar objects from childhood. Sylvanian families, music awards, CDs from the time I tried to teach myself Spanish. I felt completely alone. Abandoned by my husband, ripped away from my child. I dialled Sam's number, over and over, and listened. *You've reached Sam Preston. Leave a message. Cheers.*

I left only one: 'God, Sam, what have you done? Call me.' Then, in the dim light, I stared at the opposite wall and listened to a dozen imaginary conversations. I'd say: *How could you? You've made a terrible mistake? I would never ever harm Evie. How dare you keep me from my darling girl.* And he'd say: *It's all over, Lucy. You've gone too far. Evie isn't safe. I'm divorcing you. I'll take custody of Evie.* At eight, I dialled Taylor's number – rage in my heart, but knowing that I must feign calm.

She picked up straight away. 'Lucy.' She sounded blunt and firm.

'Hello, Taylor.' I controlled my voice as best I could. 'I don't want to discuss what's going on with me and Sam. I just want to speak to Evie. To hear her voice.'

'Sure.'

I heard a sweet, affectionate voice: *Come on, darling. Mummy's on the phone. She wants to say hello.*

'Evie's here – I'll pass you over.'

Mummy. It broke my heart.

'Hello, sweetheart. Are you having a nice time?' I kept my voice light and soft, trying to be brave. Evie didn't answer, but I imagined her nodding her head and smiling.

'I'm at Granny's house. She says hello. I'm going to see you very soon. Listen...' In a shaky voice, I sang the lullaby about the lost and found baby and imagined her softly nestling her head into Taylor's neck, her thumb in her mouth.

Taylor interrupted, 'That was lovely, Lucy... Evie looks so sweet and tired. I'm sorry about everything that's happening – really. I'm sure things will be okay soon.'

'Okay, Taylor... Just look after her.'

'I will. You know I will.'

I took a shower, got dressed in old jeans and a sweater and called Melody. 'Mel, I'm really sorry – but could you bear to see me again today? Something's happened and...'

'Of course. But you sound awful. What's up?'

'It's Sam... He sent me an email last night and...' I couldn't think what to say next. How to explain it.

'Hey Lulu – absolutely I can see you. I could nip out in half an hour – we could have a coffee at the pub. I'll pick you up on the way – how would that be?'

'Amazing. Thank you.'

Downstairs, Mum said she'd had breakfast already, but there were eggs and bacon in the fridge if that's what I wanted, or bread for toast and marmalade. But I couldn't face anything and sat frozen, unnaturally upright, while she took out her crochet and worked her way around a yellow square, dozens of others piled up on the kitchen table.

'Is it a blanket?' I said, remembering one that she'd made for Dad when he moved into the spare room.

'For the church. They'll send it someplace where it's needed.'

Two beeps from a car horn and I picked up my bag and coat.

'You off?'

'Melody. Just to say goodbye.'

We were soon settled next to an open fire at The Plough and I came clean about the drugs – and the gaslighting.

'Sam was packing for the Vietnam trip – the one he's on now – and he was really tense and hostile. Then he stopped packing and went to my underwear drawer and found the jewellery box I keep there and the key, and right in front of me, he opened it up and threw all these little packets of pills on the bed, full of disgust, chanting their names at me.'

'I don't follow. Pills? Your pills?'

'A few were mine. I bought Valium online. Illegally. Which is dreadful, I know it is. But there were all these others too, which I *hadn't* bought. Rivotril and Tramadol and Lorazepam and Xanax. I knew all the names, because I'd researched them. But they weren't mine, Melody. They weren't mine. I told him, but he didn't believe me... I think he hates me...' My words felt remote, like this was someone else's story. Not mine at all.

She looked up. 'This is crazy.'

'I'm so unsure of myself, Mel. What if I did buy them, and I've sort of blocked it out of my memory? You know what it was like after Dad died. How I imagined all sorts of impossible things. I had hallucinations, do you remember? One night, I saw Dad lying at the bottom of the stairs spread out like a starfish, as clear as I see you now. But he'd been dead and buried for two weeks.'

'God, minds are powerful, aren't they?'

'Yes. They're bloody untrustworthy. Mine's unbearable at the minute. It's been torturing me... I haven't slept.'

She coughed a big throaty cough. 'Dunno. It made a kinda sense when you hallucinated your dad. This doesn't. Not really. It's too... factual. Too detailed. There was so much emotion around the death of your dad. Buying drugs? It's not in the same league. Have you ever had blackouts before, where you didn't remember something?'

'Well no. I guess not.'

'So someone put them there. Taylor or Sam—'

'Taylor,' I chipped in. 'Sam wouldn't do that.'

'And she's in charge of Evie while Sam's away?'

'She adores Evie, she's always kind with her. It's *me* she's messing with – for whatever reason.' I glanced out of the window as though the oak tree outside was reassurance that I was right.

Melody lowered her voice. 'I know you're suspicious. But is there really something going on between Sam and Taylor? Might you be imagining it?'

'I'm pretty certain,' I said quietly. 'They really like each other – that's for sure. And she's very pretty. And much younger than me.'

'Hey!'

I told her the story of the disastrous dinner party and my embarrassing behaviour and the humiliation of the moment I tried to leave but wobbled on my silver heel. 'The problem's *me,* Mel. It always is,' I said.

'Come on. You've had your troubles. But every year you get better and better. Don't go backwards, Lu. Promise me?' She held her mug to her lips, waiting for my response.

I smiled weakly. 'How can I stop it?'

She took a mouthful of coffee and wiped her mouth with the back of her hand. 'Let me help you, Lucy. I reckon you need a cool head and a good friend. I'll help you plan...'

It was just what I needed to hear – and I loved her so hard for it.

'But what?' I asked. 'Plan what?'

'You need to toughen up, Lu, and do something positive. Do research. Find out who this Taylor person really is. If your suspicions are right and she's gone this far to steal Sam from you, she'll have previous.'

I looked at Mel's wide freckled face with love and gratitude. 'It's odd how I thought I knew Taylor so well. But I don't know her at all,' I said. 'Like, she doesn't seem to have friends. Or much work experience. In this country anyway... I didn't push her for references... Oh Mel, I've let her get so far on – what? A sort of charisma, I suppose. She's overflowing with bloody charisma.'

'All the more reason to do a little digging,' she said. 'There's always something.'

I took a taxi straight from Paddington to number 37. My wobbly fingers struggled with the key to the internal door, the one to the flat, until I realised that the lock had been changed. I dropped my bags to the floor, overtaken by uncontrollable anger, rising inside me like puke.

I pounded the door with my fists and shrieked, 'Taylor! Let me in!'

She opened it a notch. It was on a chain latch. A new one.

'For God's... sake... Let me in.' I was wheezing out the words.

'You need to calm down, Lucy.'

'Don't... you... dare to tell me...' Exhausted, I bent right over, hands on my knees, trying to return to myself.

'Don't be angry with *me,*' she said gently. 'I'm really sorry about this. It's awful. But Sam insisted.' She made kind eyes at me through the slit of space, while I heaved and concentrated on trying to control my hysterics.

My breath back, my anger channelled, I spat out, 'Where's my daughter? I want to see her.'

'She's napping.'

'Fetch her.'

'Are you sure? It might be upsetting for her to see you out there, upset and with the door on the chain like this?'

'Fucking take it off the chain then.'

'I can't. I promised Sam. It's his way of making sure social services don't get involved.'

'Taylor? Really? Social services?' But even though it was insane, there were the drugs in the drawer. Me apparently smothering Evie with my body on the night of Sam's birthday. The knife Taylor had found on the floor under Evie's cot.

'I'll go outside and I'll sit on the front step,' I said desperately. 'You can bring her out.'

It was her turn to think.

'If you try to snatch her, Sam will go to the police,' she said. 'He told me to say that.' Her voice was still sympathetic, but for a second, she played with her hair, like you might if you were flirting, and it seemed that she was enjoying her power.

'I won't snatch her. I just want to hold her.' I struggled not to yell again. *This is my house for God's sake. Evie is my child.*

'Okay,' she said eventually. 'But control yourself, Lucy. Stay calm.'

I collapsed on one of the stone steps and waited.

The front door clicked open and there she was, my little girl, all sleepy in Taylor's arms. Her hands shot towards me, fast and I took her, happy in that instant.

We sat on the step together in the sunshine, she on my knee, my nose in her hair or my cheek against hers. Taylor stood by the door, monitoring us like a prison guard. I pretended she wasn't there and whispered to Evie quietly, told her the story of Goldilocks and the three bears, which she loved and she joined in with *who's eaten all my porridge!*, I explained that I wasn't coming into the house today, but I was very close by and would see her in the morning. She accepted this like it was perfectly normal. She didn't cry or ask to come with me and when I handed her back to Taylor, she was happy to go.

'You heard? I'll see her again in the morning,' I said boldly, determined not to cry in front of her.

'Okay,' Taylor said in her kind voice. 'Don't forget this.'

She reached into a pocket and handed me the key to the flat in Queen's Park, with a label showing the address. I wheeled my suitcase to the tube, off to my temporary home, telling myself that this nightmare arrangement would soon be over – that I'd be back in Little Venice, back with Evie, by the end of the week.

The Queen's Park flat was on the first floor, over a pharmacy. As I entered, I realised that this was the first night I'd ever spent alone in a property. The place was light and bright, white walls, white bed linen, minimally furnished. A kind of sanitorium. The small kitchen possessed a large fridge, which I opened to find that it was stocked with milk, butter, cheese, yogurt, broccoli, bagged salad, olives, Parma ham and two bottles of Chablis.

In an overhead cupboard, I found pasta, passata, sundried tomatoes, eggs, sourdough bread, olive oil, Comté cheese, balsamic vinegar, sea salt and black pepper. On a counter, was a bowl of fruit. Apples, oranges, black grapes and bananas – a thoughtful welcome pack for the mad woman! I supposed this was Taylor's work and I resisted throwing everything in the bin.

Instead, I opened one of the bottles of Chablis she'd left and shuffled into the sitting room with my wine and some bread and cheese. Not that I could eat. The food felt like cardboard in my mouth and I struggled to swallow. But I drank a glass of wine and then another until I'd finished the bottle. If I'd had my Valium, I'd have reached for it. But my drugs were at Russell Drive.

At midnight, I called Melody. She answered immediately. I knew she would – she's a night owl.

'You should definitely see a family lawyer.'

'I *am* a family lawyer, Mel! That's how I know how horrific this is. If I go the legal route, Sam will make allegations against me, social services will get involved. God knows how often I'll be able to see Evie and under what conditions. Also, there's the small issue of the drugs in my jewellery box. I could be charged with a crime – and struck off. There has to be a better way.'

'But you only bought the Valium, right?'

'Yes. I told you. Unless I've blocked the memory of the rest. And that can't be right.'

We sighed together in harmony.

'Being away from Evie,' I muttered, 'it's intolerable.'

'Be strong, Lu. You're in this wretched flat for now – but make the most of it. Use it as your war room for your fight back. I'm here, and we'll find a way.'

'Thank you.'

'What for?'

'You know. Being close. Your friendship is everything...'

'Stop it!' She laughed. 'We're going to dig for dirt on the she-devil, remember? Starting in the morning.'

'Melody... This flat's not bad. It's quite big, has a terrace and stuff – and two decent bedrooms. Would you come and stay when you arrive in London? If I'm still here, which I hope I'm not.'

'And I hope you're not. But thanks, Lu. I'd love to.'

Before bed, I tried Sam's phone again. I had left dozens of messages. He hadn't answered any of them. I wondered where he was right now. In a bar in Hanoi getting cosy with Rachel? I closed my mind to that, got into bed, switched off the light and almost immediately flicked it on again. In the living room, my phone was ringing. I stumbled through and saw the name on the screen.

'Sam.'

'Hi. How are you?' The line was poor; he sounded faint.

'Awful.'

A pause. Then, 'I'm sorry about all this, Luce.'

I wanted to say: *Well, you should be sorry! You have committed a monstrous act – throwing me out of my own home, separating me from my daughter!* Instead, I replied as softly as I could manage, 'Sam, let me go home. Evie needs me and honestly, honestly, I would, could never harm her. You know that deep down... Let me back, then we can talk it through properly when you're back in London?'

There was a painfully long pause. Then, in a haughty voice, he said, 'I *am* sure this is the right thing, Lucy.'

'So you're not sorry then? About *all this*.'

'I know it happened quickly,' he said. 'But it had been coming for a long time... I need separation from you, to work things out. And I'm worried – more than worried... I'm – I don't know what the word is – but you can't be alone with Evie. Not until we've got to the bottom of this—'

'No! No! I would never ever hurt Evie! How can you think that? How! It's unbelievable! You're being ridiculous. And cruel. Sam, please. Please.'

'I can't talk to you while you're like this, Lucy. You need to *listen* for once. You've forced my hand... Do you understand? And don't call me again. I'll call you.'

The line went dead. I stupidly dialled his phone again and again – punching numbers into the void, overwhelmed with shame and humiliation. Dazed, I walked to the bathroom and, hardly noticing what I was doing, I stripped, tossing my night-clothes on the floor and stepped into the shower while turning the tap all the way to cold. Instantly, I was engulfed in a torrent of freezing water. The coldest cold that I'd ever felt, an assault on my body, an extreme sensation to match my despair.

TWENTY-THREE

EVIE

NOW

As Evie crosses the communal garden and returns to the house, her mind turns to her father Sam Preston. He must have loved her once, just as her birth mother had. What if he's alive? Maybe he's here in the UK or close by in Europe, in France or Denmark or Spain. Maybe he's innocent of Lucy's murder and there's some other explanation for his disappearance. For all she knows, Sam Preston has spent the past twenty years trying to find her. But he was a journalist, wasn't he? A good one too. Surely, he'd have succeeded by now. Her mind returns to Mexico City and the hazy memory of a handsome man with white hair, who'd swung her round and round, who brought her a present and spoke to her in English.

Inside the kitchen, Adra Roy is sitting at the table, typing on her phone. She lays it down, and Evie joins her, pulling up a chair and reaching down for her handbag which is on the floor.

'I have these,' she says, laying out her collection of press cuttings so that they face Adra. 'But I don't know much else about what happened. What can you tell me? Did my father ever reappear?'

Adra studies the news stories forlornly, moving them around the kitchen table with her forefinger, saying nothing.

'Well?' Evie says.

'I'm sorry, but no, your father never reappeared. We have no idea what happened to him.' There's sympathy in her eyes; a vague, heavy sympathy borne of decades of delivering bad news. 'Shall we see the rest of the flat,' she says gently, 'then go and have lunch somewhere?'

Evie takes one last look around the kitchen. Maybe there were family dinners here – friendly chat and jokes. Her father probably hugged her in this room and played games with her. Perhaps he swung her in circles or lifted her on to his shoulders. Her birth mother would have hugged her here, made her meals, played little games. Mia would have come by, not as her mother but a mere visitor, her mother's friend. It seems impossible.

She follows Adra back up the stairs and they quickly tour the rest of the flat, but Evie can revive no memories, not even in the bedroom that she had once slept in, or in the enormous luxury bathroom that should belong to a celebrity or an oligarch – over the top, more suited to some glamorous diva than a little girl. As they leave, she takes one last look at the whitewashed façade and finds that, although she demands answers about the people and events of her early life, she has no desire ever to visit this house again.

Adra drives them to Queen's Park where they queue up in the bakery, order salads and find a table in a corner by a window. The place is buzzing with young mothers and babies – buggies everywhere – and it's noisy; nobody will overhear them.

'Your mother lived in Queen's Park for a while, in the weeks before she died,' Adra says.

'Really? Why?'

'Well, as you know from the press cuttings, she and your father were estranged – and this is where she came.'

A female member of staff squeezes between the buggies and sets out the salads in front of them with a hearty: 'Enjoy!'

As soon as she's gone, Adra Roy continues: 'The key to the case was the nanny.'

'Taylor Love.'

'Yes. But that wasn't her real name. At least we don't think so.'

'Oh?'

'She said she was born in Brazil – but we couldn't find any documents in that name, certainly no passport – not in Brazil and not here. I suppose there was a possibility of a bureaucratic mix-up or that she was using some variant of her real name. But we never found out.'

'You interviewed her, though? Before she disappeared along with the others?'

'Yes. She was a vital witness. She presented us with a lurid account of what happened...'

Adra prods her salad with her fork. Beetroot, lentil and goat's cheese. She doesn't seem hungry and repeatedly glances out of the window, trying to collect her thoughts.

She continues: 'It was an extraordinary case. The parents of a small child had disappeared, along with the child – the mother's blood at the scene, on the knife and clothes, a witness to the murder and the removal of the body, and the body of a neighbour in the garden. The tabloids were all over it, of course, because it happened in such a wealthy part of London and your father was a TV reporter and well-off and rather good-looking. The press thought it was just a matter of time – we'd find him.'

'But you failed.' Evie leans her elbow on the table, her fork dangling from her fingers.

'We did everything we could, Evie. There was an almighty manhunt, the whole nation was desperate to find you alive. We put out appeals on TV and thousands of people called in with sightings and leads – but we were overwhelmed, even when we scaled up the manpower and it came to nothing...'

A shriek of laughter and general merriment from the nearby mothers forces Adra to lean earnestly across her salad, towards Evie. 'I'm sorry. I suppose we concluded that Sam had started a new life somewhere with you and Taylor. Or had killed Lucy, and then you and himself. It's a familiar enough story. But here you are. A young woman and very much alive. Of course, we will reopen the case.'

Evie doesn't want probing questions from Adra right now and changes the subject. 'Are my grandparents still alive, do you know?'

'Your mother's father died when she was young– and her mother, Geraldine, I remember, died soon after the investigation... It's all so long ago.'

'More than twenty years.'

'On your father's side, his parents were divorced. The father, I think, went to live in Italy with a new family – I don't know what became of him after that. His second wife was Italian, so I suppose he stayed there. As for Clemency...'

'Clemency?'

'Your paternal grandmother. A striking name, isn't it? We went to see her down in Sussex – she was living alone in a Georgian country house somewhere near Chichester.'

'What was she like?' Evie asks. 'I mean – what sort of person?'

'Old-school, a stoic – perfectly in command of herself. You know how they are, English ladies of a certain background and era? Or maybe you don't. Anyway, she was quite someone – beautiful posture I recall and what they call *exquisite taste*. Tailored clothes, perfect make-up – and the house! Very organised and traditional – antique furniture, Persian rugs on the floor and portraits on the walls – Georgian and Victorian. Maybe they were family portraits, Evie.'

But Evie's not interested in her history in that sense. She finds it dry and remote. 'What else?'

'Her reaction to Sam's disappearance, and yours, was strange. She seemed determined not to show emotion, at least not while we were there. I think it was a matter of pride. It made her seem haughty – like we were an imposition, not there to help.'

Evie almost replies, *She was right. You didn't help.*

Adra looks pensive. 'I sometimes wonder if Sam sought refuge with her for a while. She was his mother after all... Clemency may still be alive. She probably is, statistically speaking. You might find her.'

'Is it possible that you have her address or a phone number?'

'I'll see what I can find.' Adra pops a lump of beetroot into her mouth. 'It's the least I can do...'

'What was the nanny like? The press cuttings don't say much about her.'

Adra shakes her head. 'Sharp as nails. Incredible confidence. Sassy... She had a self-possession that you rarely see in someone so young.'

'I don't remember her at all.'

'Maybe that's best. She was engaging – fascinating even – but not a good person. Not at all. She'd been a close friend of Lucy's, then she set her sights on Sam – and in no time they were having an affair. He was infatuated with her.'

'How do you know that? I mean – how could you know my father's emotions?'

'It's a fair question. Taylor described it that way, and she was a supremely manipulative young woman... She was certainly skilled in crafting stories for her own advantage...'

'But you took her word for it?'

'No, it wasn't like that – I didn't trust her at all. In fact, I was highly suspicious of her. But others said the same thing. Sam's closest friend was a woman called Rachel Tang – she confirmed that Sam was infatuated with Taylor and having an affair – and Melody King, too, your mother's oldest friend. She was adamant about it.'

Evie feels a stab to her heart. 'Tell me about Melody King?'

'We only interviewed her once. She told us about the events leading to the murders, and she confirmed that Sam was infatuated with Taylor – totally enthralled. I think she used the word enslaved.'

'Oh.' Evie feels distressed on Mia's behalf, imagines the suffering she'd endured as she'd talked to the police about her murdered friend. 'Anything else about Melody? What was she like?'

'She made a good impression on me, I can say that. She was upset, of course – but she had a quiet dignity. Oh, I remember that she worked at an upmarket garden centre. Tredenham Nurseries.' Adra smiles. 'During the investigation, I went there to talk to her, to arrange the formal interview, and on my way out I bought a plant. A white hydrangea. It's still in my garden and I love it...' Evie thinks of Mia, always tending her garden so carefully.

Adra interrupts her thoughts: 'Would you like a coffee?'

'Yes, please. Black, no sugar.' Evie's grateful for an emotional break as the policewoman goes to the counter to order. Evie reaches into her bag for her notebook and looks at the questions she'd prepared. Who else had the police interviewed? How long did they spend on the investigation? She needs more information.

Adra brings the coffees over, sits down, and before she can take a sip, Evie asks, 'Why did you make it a murder investigation where my mother was concerned? Without a body?'

Adra sighs. 'There was so much more than the press knew about. Taylor told us she took part in the removal of Lucy's body from the house. And there was overwhelming forensic evidence – Lucy's blood on the knife, her clothes, her hair. And, I'm afraid to say, that in the days leading up to Lucy's death, Sam had been openly fantasising about it... and had been violent. He'd assaulted someone at work. And he confessed to Rachel Tang. I'm sorry, Evie – Lucy was terrified that he would kill her, and he did. It seemed beyond question.'

'It must have been awful for her friend, for Melody King?'

'Yes. Melody was staying with Lucy at the time. She knew what Lucy was going through... As for the young man who'd been killed in the garden – Jackson Wu – we understood from Taylor that Sam killed him because he stumbled on Sam dragging Lucy's body across the garden to his car. It was dreadfully sad. We couldn't find any direct connection between him and your family, other than that of being a neighbour...

'I'm afraid this case was rather a low point in my career. It fizzled out – we got no resolution...' She takes a sip of water and as she puts the glass back on the table, she holds Evie's gaze. 'But Evie, now you have appeared, I want to know your story. Has your father... has Sam been in touch?'

Evie pulls her woollen cardigan close around her, leaving the question hanging between them. She looks past Adra, focusing on an abstract painting on the wall, blocks and stripes of muted yellows. She's had these moments since Mia died, when grief and confusion engulf her like a wave. She takes a sip of her coffee and says, 'May I leave it a day or two? I have jet lag and my head's a mess.'

'Okay. But it can't be delayed too long.'

Evie tries to focus. 'I definitely want to track Clemency and Rachel down,' she says.

'I've heard Rachel's name on the radio – I'm pretty sure she's still at the BBC.'

Evie is puzzled by this woman. Her neat little features, her precision bob, her tidy clothes. Everything about her so serious and precise and workmanlike – and yet she's failed to solve those long-ago murders. As they leave the café, Adra looks up at the shops across the street and points one out: 'See the apartments above,' she says, 'that's where your mother lived in the weeks before she died.'

Evie stops and stares at the windows, a sudden breeze chilling her face. It seems impossible that in those rooms, her mother had planned Evie's escape with Melody. Had trusted her closest friend with her child's life. The love between the two women, she reflects, must have been absolute.

Evie says goodbye and heads for the tube, making her way back to Paddington.

TWENTY-FOUR

LUCY

1999

Melody drove to London in her green van, which was packed with gardening tools. I gave her a bunch of parking permits. We ordered in pizzas. There was so much to say – so much to plan. At one point I told her about Orlando and Persephone who lived on the other side of the garden and who'd employed Taylor for a while and we agreed that talking to them would be a good place to start the fight back against her, the fight for the recovery of my life and my daughter.

'Mad names!' Melody said. We laughed and tried to imagine what Orlando and Persephone would be like in person.

That night Melody went to bed at midnight, and I went to my room, opened a drawer and took out a little notebook that I'd named *My Fortitude Book*. I wrote:

Week one: Recovery, exercise, plan, cold showers. Week two: visit Orlando and Persephone.

On the first morning of *Week two*, Melody and I made

ourselves a substantial breakfast of oats, berries and yogurt and I joked that I was now a warrior queen.

'Great,' she said. 'And when you feel like the warrior queen needs to scream or lash out, do it here. Never to Taylor or Sam. Punch a cushion or something.'

'I don't think punching a cushion will do it. I need to stab a small animal to death. A squirrel or, I don't know, a stoat.'

'Lucy!'

'I don't mean it! I'm just trying to sound tough.' I smiled but, in truth, I was shocked that those words had come out of my mouth.

Melody had a few days before she started her new job at Tredenham Nurseries and she explored the city while I was at work, visiting the sights – the Tower of London, Buckingham Palace, Big Ben – places that Londoners forget about. Afterwards, we cooked together in our tiny kitchen, using ingredients from the 'welcome pack'.

'They're probably poisoned,' I said.

With Melody there, I began to breathe again. Queen's Park felt like sanctuary – anonymous crowds, everyday life continuing around me. I channelled my fear into action – cold showers, running laps of the park until my muscles burned. Anything to make myself stronger.

On workdays, I saw Evie twice a day. Taylor met me in a Little Venice café before I went to the office, and again in the evening, I'd drop by the café on my way home. I said nothing to my boss, Ed, about what was going on. Instead, I focused on my work, especially on the Megan Curtis case.

Her husband, Peter, had rewritten the story of her marriage by claiming that she was 'incapable of showing genuine affection' to him and Megan was adjusting to a new world. I hoped that, while Peter was in the grip of his new love affair, on an emotional high, we could persuade him to sign a good settlement for Megan and the children. I knew the score – if negotiations dragged on for months, he would convince himself that Megan was a monster. Before long, it would be *her* fault that he had fallen into the elegant arms of Zsofia the ballet dancer. It would be *she made me do it.*

On non-workdays, I spent longer with Evie. We met up in Regent's Park or Queen's Park and fed the ducks or visited the giant rabbits in the children's zoo while Taylor trailed a few paces behind, her mind on other things. She often looked bored. Occasionally, I'd ask about Sam, keeping my voice as neutral as I could manage. How is he? Does he have any more travel plans? But Taylor was always short and sharp: '*Sam's fine.*' or '*No idea.*'

I was watching her, though. Watching intensely. Her behaviour, her mannerisms, any little clues she let slip in her speech. Hints about her past, or her duplicity. I checked her clothes and her jewellery too – for signs that she was being manipulative, dressing for Sam, dressing for seduction.

One evening, I came home to Queen's Park after an outing with Evie. It was still light, the weather was glorious, and Melody was on the terrace, tending to plants. She'd bought terracotta pots and planted them up with a mixture of herbs and flowers – mint and chives and trailing thyme, white geraniums, a few tall wispy verbenas. It looked so pretty. 'Beautiful. Thank you so much,' I said.

'Agh! You made me jump! I was miles away.'

I went to fetch Sauvignon Blanc from the fridge, and root vegetable crisps and we sat together, sharing our day's news. I wondered why it had been difficult for me to find such a sense of companionship and security with Sam. I had never relaxed fully with him like I did with Melody or Evie.

'It's my last *recovery day,*' I said. 'I think I'm ready.'

Mel leaned forward, her elbow on one knee of her green gardening trousers, her chin resting on her hand, her red hair tumbling forward. 'Ready for action?'

I raised my glass. 'Yes. Exposing Taylor!'

'Exposing Taylor.'

'It's weird how she has no friends. At her age. You'd think she would go to bars or night clubs or something. But nothing.'

'It's not natural.' She took a handful of crisps.

'Definitely not natural. I'm going to find Orlando and Persephone,' I said. 'I bet they have a Taylor story... and they'll have references from her – that would be a lead... It could be very revealing...'

'I like your attitude,' Melody said. 'Are you just going to ring the doorbell and introduce yourself?'

'Yes. I'm a private detective now. Isn't that what a private detective would do?'

I didn't have to ring the doorbell. I was coming out of Warwick Avenue tube, en route to see Evie, and I spotted Persephone. I recognised her immediately from the day at the spa. Her pale blonde hair was in a loose bun, and she was in business clothes, wearing a bottle-green jacket with the arms slightly pushed up to leave her wrists bare. She had a fast, swingy walk – back straight like before – I scurried to follow her. A hundred metres down Sanderson Road, she stopped at number 22, fishing for her key and unlocking the door. I called out. 'Persephone?'

She looked at me suspiciously. 'Y... es?'

'I'm Lucy – I live on the other side of the garden. On Russell Drive.'

She still looked suspicious.

'Sorry to accost you in the street,' I said. 'I wondered if I might ask you about something. We employ a nanny, Taylor Love, and I think she worked for you before us?'

'That's right.'

'I hope you don't mind. I was wondering if I might ask about her time working for you. From a references point of view.'

She looked slightly alarmed. 'Oh... okay,' she said. 'But not now. Do you mind coming back tomorrow? Around eleven?'

'Sure. Thank you.' As she went inside, I called out again. 'Thank you. Much appreciated.'

When she answered the door the following morning, Persephone was different. Dressed down for the weekend in loose shorts, a white T-shirt and Birkenstocks, a welcoming smile on her face. She ushered me in. 'L-L-Lucy.' She had a stammer.

My first thought as I followed her into her kitchen was that the house wasn't as I'd expected it to be. It was bright and homely. Flowers in vases, big abstract paintings on the walls. Positive colours, lemons and apple-greens. Taylor, I remembered, had described the place unfavourably; I'd thought it would be stuffy and soulless.

'Can I offer you a c-c-coffee?'

'Yes, please. How it comes. No sugar.'

I looked around for signs of Orlando – but didn't see any.

We sat at her kitchen table which, like ours, had a view of the garden. Except here we were on an upper floor not the lower ground. I could just about see number 37 and the window of our bedroom, Sam's and mine.

'So, Taylor,' I said tentatively. 'She's been working for us for a couple of months.'

'A little late for a r-r-r... reference then?' She raised an eyebrow, but not unkindly.

'I know.' I smiled, to imply *silly old me.* 'We got other references at the beginning, but then I saw you in the street, by chance, and it struck me that I'd forgotten to talk to you about her.'

'Right.' She seemed bemused. 'And you recognised me how?'

'Taylor once pointed you out... From a distance. And I remembered. That's all.'

'So, Taylor. How is she getting on with you?'

I felt uncomfortable acting a part; Persephone was so welcoming. But I continued, 'Yes. Yes, okay. She really loves Evie, my little girl. And she's great with her...'

'Am I sensing a but?'

'I'm not sure. She's been great – a fantastic cook, always on time... but I thought I should check that you were happy with her too, just in case...'

Persephone looked pensive. She sighed and stirred her coffee. 'Between us?'

'Yes. Strictly between us.'

'Taylor seemed great. She did the work. She was reliable and was always coming up with little extras. You know what I mean? Essential oils she thought I might like. A green smoothie that she said was good for stress...'

'Oh, that's so her!'

'We loved her at first.'

'You mean, you and your husband? Orlando?'

'Not husband. Partner. As was.'

'Oh? I'm sorry...'

She shook her head dismissively. 'The point is, after a while, I began to feel there was something not quite right. But it was really hard to pinpoint what exactly. Until, it gradually dawned on me, that she was just a l-l-l... a little... t-t-too close to Orlando.'

I put my hand over my heart. 'No.'

Persephone shrugged sadly. 'I don't know what happened. He said they slept together just once and that was it. I didn't know whether to believe him and to be honest, I blame him more than I blame her. We've split up now. Luckily, the house is mine.'

'I'm sorry. I had no idea. I mean, Taylor's never said

anything. But she wouldn't, would she?' I was shocked – I'd expected some small notes of concern about Taylor – some clues to her past, but not this. Her behaviour seemed like an enveloping violation, at odds with her positivity when she arrived at number 37, at odds with these surroundings, which were citrussy and light, a betrayal of a woman who seemed sweet and sincere. 'How long were you and Orlando together?'

'Two years. Not that long, I suppose, and I'm not sure that I trusted him completely, even before Taylor came along.'

I thought about Sam's Brackenbury lunches with Taylor, the sneaky gin and tonics, their obvious rapport. But, somehow, deep inside and despite everything... I still believed him to be faithful to me, to our wedding vows. 'When did all this happen?' I asked tentatively.

'In the spring. Taylor told me on the day she moved out.'

'What?'

'Her parting gift. I hate her.'

'God.' It was hard to know how to go about asking the rest of my questions. 'Actually, this is quite a blow... I should have been more careful, you know, trusting her in my house with my family.'

She touched my arm. 'Don't look so down. I'm fine. I'm seeing someone else and I'm happy. Good came out of bad. I'm sure it was a one-off – it won't happen to you.'

I remembered my quest: 'Did you get references when you employed her?'

'She gave me a note from someone who'd employed her as a nanny...'

'Did you check it out? Speak to the person?'

'I'm afraid I didn't... I regret that now... At least, I phoned once, and the number was wrong. Taylor apologised and said she'd made a mistake and would get the correct number, but somehow that never happened. She was part of the household so quickly, and references didn't seem to matter.'

She had been as fooled as me, I realised. Trusting in Taylor's personality and allowing that trust to make her less-than-professional where references were concerned. 'Do you still have the note?' I asked, hopeful that it would contain something useful.

'I don't, I'm afraid.'

'Are you sure?'

'I hate clutter. I don't keep stuff.'

I tried not to let my frustration show. 'Do you remember the name of this employer?' I asked.

'All I can tell you was that she was a French woman – lived in Kensington – near the Lycée – husband English. He worked in TV, at the BBC. Taylor may have f-f... forged it all, of course. She may have been called Françine or Claudine... I know it seemed very French... Anyway, I should get on with my day.' She looked at her watch. 'S-s... sorry. I have tennis.'

'Thank you. That's been helpful.'

We walked together towards the front door. Persephone stopped. 'Hang on. One thing. She left behind a few belongings that I'd like to get out of the house. Can I give them to you to pass on?'

'Sure.'

She ran up the stairs and returned with a thick paper carrier bag from Harvey Nichols. In her pristine tennis whites, she looked preppy and American. 'Here you go.'

I took the bag and left.

TWENTY-FIVE

LUCY

1999

I was on my way back from Persephone's house and about to go down the steps into Warwick Avenue tube when I saw Sam, Taylor and Evie in the street. Taylor was pushing Evie in her buggy, Sam at her side. Taylor and Sam were laughing about something. I stopped and watched a confected little family that looked so much happier than the real thing, so perky and light. Sam touched Taylor's back – the small of her back – for a fraction of a second as they crossed the road, then held her arm as they pushed the buggy onto the opposite pavement. I gripped the iron handrail at the top of the steps, winded by their intimacy, feeling it like a physical blow. I ran down the street and down the stairs into the tube, desperate to be out of public view.

At Queen's Park, I ignored Melody and ran to my room on weak legs, burying myself under the covers. I pulled the duvet down to my chin and stared at the ceiling. Taylor was living my life with my husband and my daughter, as though I did not exist. It was unbearable, and I wanted to curl up into a ball, tighter and tighter until I disappeared. But I told myself, that I was the mother of a little girl, of my darling Evie. I closed my eyes and remembered the day she was born. Lying in the hospital bed with her, taking in the scent of her soft, downy head, placing my little finger in her tiny palm. I'd made a promise in that moment – that I'd not pass my childhood trauma down to my daughter. I would always be warm and tender to this child. I'd devote my life to her. I would always be her protector. I had to be strong.

I dragged my body out of the bed and to the bathroom, where I ran an ice-cold shower. I stepped in, ordering my brain to resist my weakness, to overcome my pain. As I stepped out again, my skin was fizzing and my mind was clear. I was almost human again.

Returning to the sitting room, I found that Melody had made leek and potato soup. We sat at either end of the sofa, sipping from bowls. I'd started to shiver and needed the warming liquid inside me. Between sips, I told Melody what I'd seen.

'I know it hurt you,' she said. 'And it seemed like the end of the world. But Lu, it's not the end of the world.'

'I do know that... I mean intellectually. But my emotions went wild. You know how they do?'

'Yes. I know.' She'd seen it all before, after my father died.

I spotted the Harvey Nichols bag on the carpet where I'd dropped it. 'Persephone gave me some of Taylor's things,' I said. 'Nothing exciting – just T-shirts and a couple of dresses.' I tightened my bath towel around me, put my soup bowl on the floor, picked up the bag and riffled through it again. 'Oh, hang on...' Buried inside the clothes was a scrap of yellow paper. I read the words written there in blue pen, in Taylor's handwriting. 'Look at this?' I passed the paper across to Melody and sat down again at my end of the sofa.

She read out loud in a puzzled voice. 'Alaska 15 – Edinburgh 17 – Mining – Kids Clubs Portugal… What does it mean?'

'God – she was making notes about things that she told me when we first met! That's weird. She told me she'd lived in those places – and "mining"… I'm guessing has something to do with her dad. She said he was a mining engineer.'

'Kids' clubs?'

'At holiday resorts – like crèches with entertainment for toddlers and little kids.'

'So what? So she writes it down?'

'But why would anyone do that? And what about the numbers – the 15 and the 17? They're the ages she was when she lived in those places.'

'So? It's a doodle. I do that sometimes, if I'm on the phone, I'll start writing down bits of the conversation and names of people who come up. It's a habit.'

We made eyes at each other. She was just being devil's advocate.

'That's just to keep your hand busy while you're talking,' I said. 'She wrote this *after* our meeting. Or maybe before it. Don't you see? She's written the words down because she was telling me stuff that she was making up. These are reminders – to stop her slipping up another time.'

I waited for Mel's counterpoint. She stretched out her legs along the sofa and warmed her feet under a cushion. 'It's possible, I suppose. But why would she bother to make things up? It doesn't serve any purpose. It's just random bits of her past.'

'Maybe.' I turned the paper over and read more seemingly random words: *Shopping. Oatmeal. Baby steps. Limes.*

'Look! She's written down limes!'

'So?'

'Sam's birthday. She made a dish with limes in, like she and him both liking limes was a massive deal. It was all done to suck up to him and exclude me.' I was talking more quickly now.

'Or it was to remind herself to buy limes, if she was making food with limes?' Melody shrugged.

'Oh, I don't know. But... It makes the most sense.'

We took our bowls to the sink. Melody washed and I dried. I told her about Persephone. 'God knows how she has that house. She's too young to have earned the money. Inherited, I guess. It was nice. Taylor had made me think it was kinda dark and dreary. But it wasn't like that at all...'

'It's hard to know,' Melody said, 'if she's just a bad person... or if she's, you know, some kind of evil.'

'She planted drugs in my bedroom,' I reminded Melody. 'That's evil.'

'If she did, if it wasn't Sam, then that's the smoking gun.'

I picked up the bag again and pulled out Taylor's old clothes in order to put them in the bin. Something else fell out, another strip of paper. I was about to throw it away with everything else, but realised it was a strip of photos – passport photos from a booth. I studied them. She was wearing no make-up, her hair was pulled back from her face, and she looked straight ahead with dead eyes and a blank expression. It was totally different from her normal look. 'I'll hang on to these,' I said. 'Evidence, I guess.'

We returned to the sitting room with two Magnum ice-creams, and I told her about the couple in Kensington who'd employed Taylor, and how the woman was French, maybe Françine or Claudine and how Taylor had once called Evie her little chou, or chou chou, and mentioned Kensington. 'The French woman's husband works at the BBC apparently. Sam might know him. Do you think that's weird?'

'Hmm. It might be weird, I guess. Or a coincidence.'

At work the following today, Megan Curtis came in and signed a separation agreement with her husband Peter. He was going to pay £80,000 a year for alimony and maintenance money for her two boys, and give her the family house. A lot of money, but she was still devastated. Nothing could make up for Peter's betrayal and the sickness Megan felt when her two boys went to stay with him and his Hungarian ballet dancer two days a week. 'It will get better with time,' I told her. 'It always does.'

'I don't want it to get better. I want my old life back,' she said quietly.

'I know... I really do.'

When she left, I phoned Melody who was at her first day of work at Tredenham Nurseries.

'How's it going?'

'Good. Nice people. Nice plants. What more can I ask for?'

'Listen, I'm going to contact Rachel Tang. Remember, I told you about her? She works with Sam. She'll know what's going on with Sam and Taylor and might know who the guy with the French wife is. What do you think?'

'Maybe.' She sounded distracted. 'Sorry – I have to go. Customers.'

'Bye.'

I didn't have Rachel's number, so I went online hoping to find her contact details on the BBC website. No luck. Then I remembered that I knew the way BBC email addresses worked. I composed a short message, hoping I'd got the tone right.

Hi Rachel, I wondered if we could meet for coffee or a glass of wine. You probably know that I'm not living with Sam, temporarily. Things are strange and I'd love to discuss with you. I hope you don't mind, and I understand totally if you'd rather not. Please don't tell Sam I've sent this. Thank you, Lucy xxx.

TWENTY-SIX

SEPTEMBER 1999

Adra Roy is about to lose her patience. For a while, she's suspected that Taylor Love is spinning a line. Now, she's practically certain the woman was not a witness to a murder at all, but that she's somehow involved. Perhaps she is the real perpetrator. But Adra is well-trained in interview techniques. She knows not to give in to her frustration, not to be challenging or interrogatory just yet, despite the provocation. Despite Taylor's dramatic gestures, theatrical voices and her countless overblown expressions. Adra remains calm and professional:

AR – Tell me about Sam. We're putting all our resources into tracking him down and finding Evie… We need to know as much as possible.

TL – It was while Lucy was in Queen's Park with her friend Melody that I properly fell for Sam. I'd meet up with him during the day when I was looking after Evie. We'd go to his favourite restaurant – the

Brackenbury in Shepherd's Bush, do you know it? Really nice and with an open fire in the winter. It became *our thing.* Then, when Lucy moved out, I moved into number 37… Romantic love is the most powerful thing in the world when you're in the grip of it, don't you think?

At night, I'd cook and we'd open a bottle of wine and eat together and chat and he told me all about his work and about his background, which was kinda dysfunctional, like Lucy's. You need to know that… His parents had a horrendous divorce. His father was a real shit. Always cheating, then he moved out to be with an Italian woman… I can't remember her name… let's call her Donatella… Anyway, he'd badmouth the mother to Sam. Her name was Clemency, weirdly enough, because she was, apparently, an unforgiving bitch, a status-whore and a sociopath. And Clemency would come into Sam's bedroom at night and spout poison about the father. Families, hey!

Sam confided a *lot* about Lucy… He said that in the first year, the marriage was sort of perfect, Lucy acting out the dream-wife role, all supportive and fragrant – a bit nervy at times and unconfident – but within the realms of normal behaviour. Sam hadn't clocked at all that she was covering up for being batshit insane…

AR – He used these words about her?

TL – Well, yeah, he did. He said that she had a 'poor Sam… wonderful Sam' routine that he liked at first and that the early days were like something out of a Jane Austen novel. He was funny about it, in fact, making faces while he told me how he would read her poems, then she'd play for him on the cello. I mean! He had me in stitches…

AR – So, this is when your relationship started? I mean a sexual relationship?

TL – Yeah. One evening, I'd cooked and Evie was asleep and he said, out of nowhere, 'Oh, I got you something.' Earrings. Pretty. Moonstones and gold. From then on, the mood between us changed. It had to, didn't it? About a week later, I was wearing the earrings, and he said, 'Come here, let me look at them.' He lifted my hair, then he kissed my neck – and the next thing, well, I'll spare the details, but let's say on that first night we didn't get a whole lot of sleep.

AR – After that, did you move into Sam's bedroom?

TL – Yes, I did. I mean, we weren't going to have sex in the kitchen in front of Evie or anything. That would be weird.

AR – But you took her mother's place in the bedroom?

TL – Evie was *two,* Inspector Roy! She was perfectly happy, believe me. On Sunday mornings, we'd bring her into the bed and sing songs.

AR – Okay.

TL – I feel sick now… I mean he's a killer… but I totally fell for him. It was crazy, pheromones I guess, but our skins just adored each other. I was so wild for him that I was totally blinded to his bad side and blamed Lucy for everything. I thought she was so insecure and obsessive that she'd send anyone out of their minds. Then, with her drugs and her behaviour, I mean, the Munchausen's by proxy – I thought she was properly dangerous. Even when Sam behaved strangely, I thought it was Lucy's fault for winding him up.

AR – What do you mean by *behaved strangely*?

TL – Like sometimes, he could go very cold and then he'd suddenly explode in a terrible rage. It happened not too long ago… Lucy came to number 37 when everyone was out and she smashed a window in the kitchen. I know anybody would be angry about that, but Sam was totally consumed by it, he was like a great ball of fury, and he kicked a chair over, then stormed off to Queen's Park to confront Lucy. It was a foreshadowing, I guess.

TWENTY-SEVEN

LUCY

1999

It had been more than a week and I'd heard nothing from Rachel. Was she avoiding me? I'd write to her again soon.

Meanwhile, I was spending time with Evie and trying to ignore Taylor's ever-present watchful eye. *I will win this battle*, I told myself, *because I'm in the right and I'm strong now. Cold showers every day and fortitude meditations – I'm rewiring my brain.*

It was going well until yesterday. We were at the children's playground in Queen's Park; I was pushing Evie on a baby-swing and Taylor was sitting nearby on a bench, looking on vacantly. I called over, asking after Sam and she said, 'Oh, Sam's *thriving.*'

I pushed Evie's swing and snapped, 'You're not getting him, Taylor. I'm not letting it happen.'

'Lucy.' She made a patronising, oh-God-what-now face. 'I've no idea what you're talking about.'

'You know.'

Evie was giggling, waggling her legs up and down, totally oblivious.

'If you say crazy things like that, I'll feel obliged to tell Sam. That's not going to help you, is it?' She put her feet up on the bench and hugged her knees.

I left Evie swinging and ran to Taylor, hissing in her ear, 'Fuck off. I'm on to you. You can't win.'

She didn't reply, just smiled contemptuously. I wanted to scratch her eyes out. I wanted to gouge her face, wrench her hair out of her head, kick her mercilessly. Instead, I laughed flatly and went back to Evie as though nothing had happened, lifting her out of the swing and letting her run towards the slide.

That evening, Melody was out – she'd gone to the pub with her new colleagues. At home, I succumbed to half a bottle of wine and distracted myself with a Friends DVD. I was numb, not thinking of much in particular, when the front doorbell rang. I assumed Melody had forgotten her key and expected to hear her voice as I pressed the intercom button. But it wasn't her; it was Sam. 'It's me. Can you let me in?'

I buzzed him in and stood nervously at the top of the stairs. As he came up, he glanced at me with vacant eyes and a stern face. Sam, my Sam, handsome and funny, was veiled by hostility and loathing.

He brushed my cheek with a kiss, and we went into the flat. I turned off the TV and offered him a glass of wine.

'No thanks.'

We sat at the dining table, opposite each other.

'It's nice to see you,' I said softly – trying to reach into him.

'We should talk.' He looked down at his hands, spread out on the table, and was breathing unevenly.

'Sam?'

'I need to get this out.'

'Okay.' I was twisting my wedding ring round my finger. I stopped and folded my arms.

'Shit, I don't know how to say this. But you scared us today. I don't know what to do. Should I call the police? Taylor says not to – but I'm not sure.'

'What?' I stood up and stepped back. 'What has she told you?'

He slammed his fist on the table. 'Fucking stop talking nonsense, Lucy. You know why I'm here. You can't do this. You have to stop! Otherwise, it's the police.'

'Oh my God!' I was about to tell him that he was the crazy one if he thought an altercation in the children's playground warranted police intervention.

But he yelled, 'We *know* it was you! It's so fucking obvious. Smashing a window is a violent act – it takes brute force and a level of mindless rage. For God's sake...' He stood up now and was pacing back and forth.

I tried to process what he was saying, told myself to stay calm and be logical. When I eventually spoke, the words came out unnaturally slowly: 'Sam. I don't know what this is. But it isn't me. It's her. It's Taylor.'

He was pale with incomprehension. He put his head in his hands, and I thought for a moment he was weeping.

'I love our family,' he said. 'But I can't handle this. You know it. I know it. You left glass all over the floor; Evie could have seriously hurt herself. And how could I explain the slashed sofa to her? She's two! Please, please can we have a sensible conversation about it?'

I crouched against the wall and collapsed down to the floor. How could this be happening? 'No, Sam,' I said, my voice robotic and unnaturally slow. 'That isn't what happened. I've been nowhere near Russell Drive today. I swear. I swear on Evie's life.'

He looked up and shook his head. Ran his fingers through his hair, leaving it standing up on end. I had loved that, once.

'How can I believe you?' he said. 'Because, Lucy, it's bullshit. Isn't it?'

We stared at each other, our eyes shining with distress. 'Sam, I would never lie about such terrible things. This is like the drugs you found. When I said they weren't mine – I was telling the truth. Really. Except for one – the Valium. The rest I had no idea about. I have no idea where they came from. Sorry. That's wrong. I know exactly where they came from. Taylor put them there. It's the same now. It's Taylor. She smashed the window. She slashed the sofa. The woman is downright evil. She wants my life. She wants you. I swear it's the truth.'

He shrieked in a voice that I'd never heard before. 'No no no!' He stood up and threw his chair to the floor. 'Listen to me,' he hissed. 'Get help. You need it. I'll pay. But get help.' Then he left the flat, flying down the stairs desperate to leave, while I remained on the floor. I heard the door slam shut.

The following day I phoned in sick – and I was genuinely sick, jumping at any noise: a motorbike in the street; someone somewhere shouting; children playing football in the garden. I was in that shaky state when I sent Rachel Tang another email. Short and to the point, asking if she would meet me. A message pinged back straight away:

Yes. Happy to meet. After work this evening? Rx

The venue was her idea. A foreign correspondents' club in Paddington. I went up a long, narrow staircase to reach a reception desk, aware that I'd stepped into a different world – Sam's world. Black-and-white photos lined the walls, of journalists 'in the field' reporting on a news story – the Vietnam war, the 1989 revolutions in Eastern Europe. I was directed to a bar in a large wood-panelled room, and was surrounded by more photos. Tiananmen Square, Bosnia, the Berlin Wall. In the far corner, lazing in a banquette, was Rachel, wearing her scrappy leather jacket, a glass of whisky on the table in front of her. She didn't smile, just twitched the corner of her mouth as I sat down and ordered a white wine and bread.

'Thanks for meeting me, Rachel. I appreciate it.'

She raised an eyebrow. 'You're welcome. It's about Sam and Taylor, right?'

'I guess.' I didn't know where to start. 'I'm not living at home at the minute...'

'Yeah. I'm sorry about that.'

'Everything's kind of surreal. I thought you might be able to shed some light on what's going on with Sam. You're one of his best friends and...'

She leaned back, exhaled through slightly parted lips and contemplated the ceiling, like she was smoking a cigarette. Then she side-eyed me. 'I'm not comfortable about betraying a confidence. Then again... I guess you ought to know.'

'Know what?'

'Sam's not happy.'

I thought, *Well, thanks for nothing.*

But she went on, 'Obviously, you know he and I have a past?'

'I'm sorry?' I was blushing.

'Just thought I should get that out into the open before we discuss the current calamity... When Sam met you, out in the countryside wherever it was, he was like with me. You weren't aware?'

I remembered Sam's exact words when we met. *I want a proper relationship. Lately, I've been flitting.*

I'd quizzed him about the *flitting*. He'd said, *Someone here. Someone else there.* He was fed up with flitting. He'd not wanted to name the girls, and I suspected later that one of them was Rachel. But I didn't know. When we were married, I asked him specifically about her, and he said *Nah. Not my type. Too skinny. Too much hard work.* He'd lied.

'No,' I said weakly. 'I wasn't aware. When we met, Sam said he had a few casual girlfriends on the go. I didn't know you were one of them.'

'Harsh,' she said with a tight smile. 'I didn't know he had a whole all-you-can-eat buffet of girls.'

'Not a buffet exactly…'

She was unfazed, tapping her finger on the table and helping herself to bread. 'Anyway, darling, I wanted to get it off my chest because I suspected he hadn't told you. Or, in fact, that I still hold a little candle for him…'

I could see that she was hurting but that she'd never give up her tough girl act or resist a clever or funny remark.

'Thing is…' She surveyed me like I was an antique vase. 'I could understand it when he chose you. It made sense. Despite the buffet, he didn't want the whole *girl in every trouble spot* lifestyle that some reporters like. He wanted a mother for his children. Someone he could take care of. Bring home the bacon for. A bacon-eating English rose.'

My head was swimming with the metaphors. 'I'm an English bramble now,' I said. 'Prickly and destructive.'

'What's that you're drinking?'

'Sauvignon Blanc.'

'Let's get a bottle.' She stood up and went to the bar on the far side of the room, leaning on it with one elbow, like the queen of bars. When she came back, she said, 'I've ordered a plate of chips… Anyway, at the time it was revelation to me, but as I say, I could understand it – that he wanted the home-life, the reliable little wifey, no offence – and I accepted it. So, what the fuck is he doing with this Taylor girl? She's not making him happy that's for sure…'

I felt my earlier blush returning. 'So they are definitely together then?'

'Baby. Of course they are.' She glanced away. Someone she knew had come into the room, and she gave him a smoky look.

'You know for certain?'

'Yeah. This can't go beyond us. Paddington rules.'

'Okay. Paddington rules.' I couldn't believe that I was managing a controlled conversation. Amongst the roses and brambles in my head, green grenades were exploding.

'How long have you been married?' she said nonchalantly.

'Nearly four years.'

'Right. Well, Sam's been – I don't know – having doubts for about half that time, I guess. He comes out with me for a drink after work, and he confides a lot of stuff.'

'Why are you telling me?'

'Because it's best you know. I'd want to know if it were me. And there's another reason.'

'What?'

'You're his girl, Lucy. It's you he should be with, but it's become horrendous. If I don't tell you about it – you can't fix it.'

'Oh.' Tears welled up and I wiped them away. This bar was no place for crying. 'Talk me through it,' I said.

'That fucked-up dinner party for Sam's birthday kind of said it all. Sam just wanted you to be you. Your sweet self. But you were out of your head. You need to get a grip. He's emotionally stunted – doesn't know how to deal with you. And, that night, Taylor was such a bitch. Flaunting herself all over the shop. You didn't need to go apeshit, Lucy. You just needed to sit tight.'

Rachel confused me. That haughty world-weary tone. Her brazen sensuality. She was like a star from an old film-noir movie, ready to trade one-liners with Humphrey Bogart, all teasing and temptation and one step ahead – not the kind of girl you expect to give you agony-aunt advice about your marriage, especially when she's still in love with your husband. I took a slug of wine.

'I know it,' I said. 'But I can't do it. At least, I couldn't... I'm getting better.'

Our chips arrived and Rachel took one, holding it in her fingers, blowing on it to cool it down. 'He's bloody besotted with bloody Taylor at the minute. She's playing games – nice to him one minute, moody the next, twisting him around her little finger.' She popped the chip into her mouth.

'She's so much younger than me. And prettier.'

'As I say, he's not happy. It's not what he wants. Deep down.'

The bar was filling up. We'd been speaking in hushed voices, but the general hubbub was loud now, and my words came out too loud: 'You don't know the half of it, Rachel.'

'Yeah?'

'It's not a normal separation. I haven't moved out of the house voluntarily. Sam thinks I'm a danger to Evie. Has he mentioned that?'

She narrowed her dark eyes.

'Well. Kinda. Like he thinks you're neurotic. And I say to him – there's nothing wrong with a bit of neurotic from time to time. I can think of worse things. Like me. I'm worse. I binge and chuck up. That's worse.'

'You're bulimic?'

'Recreationally bulimic.' She shrugged it away.

'That's serious, Rachel. Do you get help?'

'Never mind me; we're doing you. My point is – you think that because you're neurotic, he'll stop loving you. You think that without him you'll be nothing. You'll die. And it's driving you crazy.'

'Is that what Sam says? That I'm an emotional basket case?'

'Nah. I just see it, is all. I have seeing eyes. I see you being a bit of a nutter, but I don't see you as a danger to Evie.'

'I'm not! Actually, that's not true... Maybe I have been lately...'

'Like how?'

'I've been knocking back Valium... which I bought online... illegally.'

She blew on her next chip. 'Well, that is very naughty, Lucy. But don't dwell on it. Stay focused on Taylor... I don't trust her.'

'With Evie?' I snapped.

'Oh – I'm sure she's fine with Evie. I've seen them together, she's lovely with Evie. But I don't trust her with Sam. She wants him to believe you're certifiable to make it easier to schloop him up. She wants the lot. You know – the lifestyle, the house, the arm candy.'

I hadn't expected this. I'd thought we'd have a short, awkward conversation, that I'd get straight to the point, and that Rachel would be bristly. But, as different as we were, I felt like we'd made some kind of connection.

'She did something really bad,' I said. 'Well, two things actually.'

'Oh?'

'The Valium I bought – I hid it away where Sam wouldn't find it. But Taylor found it and she... well, she supplemented it with a load of other prescription drugs, then told Sam where they were.'

I waited for her to be astounded, but she was quiet, looking up at the ceiling to think. It was getting warm in the bar, and she took off her jacket. I noticed then how thin and bony her arms were. I'd noticed before, I suppose, but I hadn't thought anything of it.

'That's utterly perverse,' she said. 'Deranged.'

'I know. But she did it.'

'You're sure?'

'Yes – it had to be her. Unless it was Sam. It wouldn't be Sam.'

'I guess not.' She wasn't as forceful as I'd have liked. 'What was the other thing?'

I poured the last of the wine into our glasses. 'Sam came to my flat the other day – where I'm living – in Queen's Park...' I said nervously. 'He was angry, literally shaking with rage and said someone had smashed the window in the French doors at number 37, and had broken in and slashed our sofa with a knife...'

'Which day was this?'

'Monday.'

'Oh my God. Sam was so weird at work today. Do you know what happened?'

'No. What?'

'We were in the edit suite, reviewing the Vietnam footage, and the editor just couldn't grasp something that Sam was telling him to do. Sam was snapping and sniping and angry, then he grabbed the guy by his hair and pulled his head right back and yelled, *I can't make it any clearer!* And he stormed out.'

'Oh my. That's assault.'

'Yep. The guy, Bennie, has made a formal complaint. HR is delving into it.'

'That's awful... I was going to say *it's so unlike Sam*, but...'

'But what? He didn't harm you, did he? When he came to your place?'

I sat up straight, feeling something shifting in my head, a cooling, like when I stood under the cold shower. I was thinking that, if things went wrong, if we ended up divorcing, I wanted Sam's perfidy on record: 'He was pretty scary,' I said. 'Yeah... I'm sorry, Rachel – I don't want to talk about it.'

'You're sure? The breaking-in thing – was he accusing you?'

'Yes. He said I'd smashed my way in as some sort of revenge.'

'Why are you going along with it, Lucy? Just go to the police.'

'I can't. Obviously. The drugs. The Valium. All of it... This is all about Taylor.'

'Sure. I get it.'

I put my elbow on the table and leaned my head on my hand and spoke sweetly like I was relating a fairy-tale. 'I've been imagining the scene. She phones him, he rushes home. She says – *Look what Lucy did.* He says – *She wouldn't. Not Lucy.* She says – *Get real, Sam! She only has to watch the house, see when it's empty, and smash the window. It's simple enough.*'

Rachel laughed. 'The way you put it, it's totally believable and totally unbelievable at the same time.'

'We both hate her. Will you talk to Sam for me? You could convince him Taylor's malevolent. I bet you could.'

She shook her head. 'Won't work, darling. He's starry-eyed about her. He'd be furious. That's all that would happen.'

'I think she's done this before,' I said. 'She works her way into families, targets the guy, flirts with him and gets what he wants. Whatever that is. I don't think it's about the lifestyle. I think you're wrong about that.'

'Oh?'

Suddenly, I realised how Rachel could be of practical use to me. 'I found out that she looked after some children for a couple who live in Kensington,' I said. 'The mother's name is something like Françine or Claudine and the father works at the BBC. Do you know any BBC guys with a French wife?'

'I don't think so. I can ask around.'

'Thank you.'

'I should go,' she said, picking up her jacket. 'But let's speak again soon. Oh, and I'm sorry about the pilchard joke. That was mean of me.'

'You're forgiven.'

Later, when I was back at Queen's Park, I received a message from her.

Hi Lucy, sorry everything is rotten. Sam has asked me to babysit Thursday night. I'll do that. Will snoop around at No 37 for you. Rx

TWENTY-EIGHT

EVIE

NOW

At the Paddington hotel, Evie is lying on her single bed, thinking of getting under the duvet and sleeping; it's only four in the afternoon and her room is alive with the rumble of traffic noise from the road outside, but she's so tired that her eyelids keep sinking shut. She's about to take off her jeans, snuggle down and give in to torpor when her phone rings and Adra Roy says: 'I found the phone number for Clemency Preston.'

Evie shakes her head, trying to wake up. 'Oh. Thank you.'

'It's pretty old,' continues Adra. 'But you never know...'

As soon as the call is over, Evie dials the number that she's just scrawled onto the back of her hand. The phone rings only twice before an elderly female voice says, 'Hello?'

Evie feels physically cold with nerves. 'Hello... Hello, I wonder, is this Clemency Preston?'

'No, it isn't. You have a wrong number...'

'Oh... I see... Please... can you help me? I was given this number for Clemency Preston... Do you know who that is and how I might find her?'

There's a long pause at the end of the line, then the voice says in a reluctant tone: 'She used to live here... but not anymore. Goodbye.'

'Please don't go! Do you know if she's still alive? And if she is, where she is now?'

There's another pause before the voice continues, now in an irritated manner: 'Well, it was very inconvenient when I bought the house. She'd given power of attorney over to someone and it was all very complicated... She'd moved out already, and the house was pretty rundown I have to say... She ended up in a care home, that's all I know... Name of Birchwood. Now goodbye.'

The woman ends the call, and Evie immediately puts the name Birchwood into Google, coming up with dozens of schools and medical practices and golf clubs. But it doesn't take long to land on Birchwood House, a care home specialising in dementia, situated just outside Chichester. Hadn't Adra Roy mentioned Chichester? Hadn't she visited Clemency there twenty years ago?'

Evie writes down the phone number of Birchwood House and still feels shivery as she sinks under the duvet, but she doesn't fall into sleep. Instead, she phones Antonio in Mexico City to tell him about Clemency. 'It's extraordinary,' she says. 'I may have found a real alive grandmother, though she probably has dementia. I'm suddenly feeling frightened about arranging to see her... After all, Mia took me away from all this. She thought it best to shield me from my birth relations. She must have had good reason, don't you think? I mean, she loved me and wanted the best for me... so...' Whenever she thinks of Mia, her head becomes muddled and the weight of grief overpowers her.

'I don't know,' Antonio says. 'You've gone all that way to discover your story, so I guess it would be strange not to see her.'

'I know. Of course, I will seek her out... I'm just having a moment of fear. I think it's because of the reaction I had when I went to Russell Drive... I felt a horrible emptiness, or maybe it was worse, a sort of revulsion...'

'It's understandable, it's natural to feel a visceral response, given what happened in that house. Your birth mother was killed there. That's a terrible thing.'

'Yes. But there was something else too... The fact that the house was an actual, physical challenge to everything I believed in... the truth of my life with Mia... the solidity of *us*. I don't want two mothers, Antonio! I want Mia...' Her voice is tremulous, her tiredness making her emotional, sending her towards hopelessness and self-pity. 'I'm sorry.'

'Hey. Don't be sorry. It's a lot to deal with.'

She laughs softly. 'Isn't it? A few weeks ago, I was such an ordinary girl with an ordinary life...!'

'You're far from ordinary, Evie...'

'You know what I mean.'

Wanting to escape the weight of it all, she asks about her colleagues at the coffee shop and wonders how Antonio is filling his time. He tells her about socialising with friends from the lab, about visiting a new restaurant near the apartment. 'Ordinary life is a sort of miracle,' Evie says at one point.

'It is,' he replies. 'When this is over, come home and be ordinary with me.'

She thinks of his marriage proposal, still unanswered. 'Love you,' she says.

After the phone call, she gets up from her bed and makes tea using the miniature plastic kettle provided by the hotel; then she helps herself to a plastic-wrapped shortbread biscuit and returns to the bed. It's understandable, she thinks, that finding a new grandmother is psychologically unsettling. Maybe it's easier to focus first on her father's friend Rachel Tang. The woman is a journalist, and journalists are supposed to deal in hard facts – and that's what Evie needs right now – some plain talking and specific revelations. With legs outstretched, she opens up her laptop again and Googles Rachel, finding three photos of her, two at an awards ceremony, one at some society party. She's surprised by how glamorous Rachel is: she's skinny and tall, a beauty with languid eyes and a faraway semi-smile. Evie adds the letters BBC to the search and finds that Rachel is currently presenting a politics show called *Westminster Now* on BBC Radio Four. She scrolls, trying to find contact details, and comes upon a general enquiry email address and a phone number for the channel. Trying not to think too hard, she swallows the last of the shortbread and makes the call.

She's put through to the *Westminster Now* voicemail and, slightly tripping over her words, she leaves her name, at least she says she is Evie Preston-Bliss, and gives her phone number, adding: 'I'd like to speak with Rachel Tang... Rachel, I hope you remember me and will call back.'

Leaning back on the headboard, Evie sips her tea and continues scrolling for more information about Rachel, but, almost immediately, the phone rings and she sees that the call is coming from the UK not Mexico, and that it's not Adra's number. She answers and listens to a woman's voice, velvety and slow, saying, 'Is that Evie? Is it really you?'

'Rachel?'

'Oh my God. Evie. I can't believe it... Give me a moment.' There's an audible slow inhale of breath and an even slower exhale. 'Evie... Is Sam... Is he with you?'

Now Evie has to control her breath. She hadn't expected that to be Rachel's first question. 'No,' she says. 'He's not.' She pauses. 'Can I meet up with you, Rachel?'

They make an arrangement for six-thirty that evening. Her body is emotionally exhausted. Evie sets the alarm, and nestles under the duvet, falling asleep as soon as her cheek is cradled by the white cotton pillow.

·   ·   ·

The bar that Rachel suggested is just two streets from the hotel; it's crowded and noisy and swathed in orange light from overhead lamps. Evie peers at all the animated heads; it's an afterwork crowd, upbeat young professionals from offices, and maybe staff from the hospital across the road. 'I'm easy to find,' Rachel had said. 'Chinese but extra tall and bony.' She missed out that she holds herself like the Queen of Sheba as she reclines slightly in her tall chair at the bar, sipping red wine, checking the room with an imperious face and knowing eyes.

Evie raises her hand, and their eyes meet. As she approaches, Rachel slips off her chair and opens her arms, beckoning, inviting a hug – Evie complies, finding that the reality of Rachel's hug is a slight brush of hands on her arm and her back. They sit at the bar and Evie notices that Rachel is gripping its edge; the nails on her fingers are bitten little stumps. A Queen of Sheba who's rough at the edges. She says, 'Evie Preston-Bliss. I can't believe it... Let's get you a drink, then you can tell me everything... What would you like?'

'I'll have the same as you...' Evie shuffles her shoulders out of her coat while Rachel attracts a barman – a skinny twenty-something guy with dark skin and bleached dandelion-blonde hair who looks like he's escaped the catwalk. He's busy with other customers, but has time for a quick nod and a grin in Rachel's direction. He finishes up and comes over: 'Wine? That's not like you.'

'Trying to be mellow,' Rachel says, drinking down the last of her red. 'I've a special guest. We're on the Cab Sav – the Margaret River.'

'Good choice.'

As he fills the glasses, Rachel looks Evie up and down. Appraising her. And as soon as he's gone, she raises her glass and says, 'It's hard to know where to start, Evie... How come you're here after all these years? Tell me everything. What happened to you?' Then: 'Tell me about Sam.'

Evie shakes her head, letting Rachel's expectations lie. 'No,' she says. 'I'm here because I want to hear about my father from *you*... What was he like – back then? When I was little?'

Rachel blinks slowly. 'Evie. You're the mystery... You're the girl who's come back from the dead after so many long years... I need to know what happened to you and Sam.' Her voice is low and slow and impatient.

Evie lets the noise of the bar take over. The guy with the yellow hair glances again at Rachel while he pours drinks three metres away. He likes her, Evie thinks, and it makes a sort of sense. Rachel is careworn and at least two decades older than him, but stunning all the same. Evie says: 'We both have mysteries, but I've come a long way – from Mexico – to discover yours. I'll just say this for now – I was raised by Melody King. But Rachel, I need you to go first.'

Rachel raises her eyebrows. 'Melody! Extraordinary... But I guess you're holding all the cards here. Go on then, ask your questions.'

'Like I said, I want to know what he was like back then. My father.'

'Sam. Dear Sam... People always said he was charming, but that's such a catch-all word – I don't like it. He was confident, certainly. Clever. Funny. A rebel. An adventurer... The world was more exciting when Sam was around, like the dial had been turned up a notch...' She's wearing a distressed leather jacket and she takes it off. Underneath, her look is bare. Just a khaki-coloured T-shirt and a gold bangle. 'And good-looking,' she continues. 'Blonde hair and dark eyes like you, olive skin like you... I kinda loved him...'

'What was my parents' relationship like?' She holds off from saying *birth* parents.

'Hmm.' Rachel sighs. 'Well, you know how it ended, Evie...'

'Of course. But earlier. Did it start well? Were they happy in the early days?'

'I thought so. Poor Lucy... I thought she was right for Sam... but they were both damaged people. Ultimately, Lucy bored Sam, and he couldn't forgive her for it.'

Rachel tells Evie about her parents' unhappy childhoods, explains the deterioration of their marriage.

Evie blocks out the noise of the bar, listening intensely. 'But how did it come to murder?' she asks.

Rachel leans in close, lowers her voice. 'Lucy became totally obsessed with your health, behaving strangely – taking you to the hospital all the time. Sam believed it was Munchausen's by proxy – that she was harming you on purpose.'

Evie's shocked. 'And did that fit with what you knew about Lucy?'

'No,' says Rachel. 'It didn't. But Sam was convinced, I know that. And there was definitely *something* wrong with Lucy. She was hooked on prescription drugs. She'd bought a ton of tranquillisers online...'

'Heavens.'

'Sam became angry about it all. At the same time, he was totally infatuated with the nanny.'

'Taylor Love?'

'Right. She wound him up... Made him more and more furious about Lucy...'

Evie reaches into her bag and pulls out the strip of photos that she has brought with her to England, the passport photos of the young woman, and she shows them to Rachel.

'Is this Taylor? I found the photos in Mia's bedroom.'

Rachel nods. 'Sure... That's her. God, it's so long ago – but that face is unforgettable... Pretty, right?'

Evie puts the photos away. 'But why murder?' she says. 'Educated people who have emotional problems, they go to therapy, maybe they get divorced... they don't kill.'

Rachel shrugs. 'Most murders aren't cool and calculated with a clear motive in mind... They're committed when emotions become uncontrollable. That's what happened with Sam. And blackmail was somehow involved. He told me in one of his emotional rants, at the end, that he wouldn't give in to blackmail. But when I asked what he meant, he shut me down.'

'Blackmail? Did you tell the police?'

'Of course. But I'm not sure they got anywhere with it...'

'But he definitely said it? That Lucy was blackmailing him?'

'No, it was unclear. Anyone could have been blackmailing him...' She pauses, crosses her legs to the other side, and says: 'Now it's your turn, Evie. What has Sam told you? I guess not the truth, or the whole of it, otherwise you wouldn't be here.'

'My father has told me nothing. I only found out about the murders a few weeks ago...'

Rachel raises her body erect, stiff with curiosity. 'What? How come? Now I'm more curious than ever. Tell me, Evie. Where is Sam?'

Evie shakes her head. 'No, not yet. I have more to ask. The police told me that Sam confessed to you... about killing Lucy... is that right? Did he? It bothers me that they never found her body... I mean, did she really die?'

The noise in the bar is now deafening and Rachel cups her mouth with her hand and speaks directly into Evie's ear in an urgent whispery voice: 'He told me, Evie. He stabbed her several times, in the chest and the neck, and after he'd done it, he was in a terrible state – of course he was. He told me he'd taken off with you – heading for the coast. I'm pretty sure Taylor was in the car with him. The idea was to get to Ireland and then escape somewhere. He was a good sailor. Maybe he was going to sail to France. He dumped your mother's body along the way. Somewhere remote. He said all that, then I never heard from him again.'

Evie closes her eyes and holds her head in her hands, trying to make the horrific words sink in. 'He told you? I mean actually told you?' she whispers shakily, beneath the din of the bar. 'The police said he texted... So, how could you know it was really him?'

'I'm sorry, Evie, but there's no doubt. The messages were pure anguish... from his phone of course, and there are certain Sam tics and quirks... his special words; they were all there.'

'Still... maybe...'

'It was totally convincing.'

'Do you still have it?'

'No. But the police have everything. They searched miles of countryside, every patch of woodland they could think of. But they never found her.' Rachel's voice drops. 'That's where Lucy is, Evie. Out there somewhere. It broke something in all of us. I haven't been back in the field since – can't face it.' She lifts her glass with a trembling hand. 'This helps.'

Evie stands, her legs unsteady. The weight of it – her mother's violent end, her father's darkness – is too much to bear. 'I need to sleep,' she manages. 'I'll call you.'

She walks out into the night without looking back, letting the cold air hit her face.

TWENTY-NINE

LUCY

1999

I had to see them together. Rachel had said Sam was *bloody besotted* and I wanted to see it for myself. So I took the tube to Little Venice on their date night, the night that Rachel was babysitting, intending to follow them when they left the house.

At Warwick Avenue tube, I lingered by a corner house a hundred metres from number 37. Taylor came out first and waited a couple of seconds on the steps. When Sam appeared, they walked side by side in the opposite direction from me. Sam offered his arm; she took it, and they were chatting and laughing. Taylor, I saw, was wearing a black shift dress; knee-length and beautifully cut; nothing like her old grungy floppy dresses. And heels – just high enough to be both sexy and chic. Her arms were bare, she must have been cold, and her hair was up in a messy bun. Even at that distance I could see her earrings – dangly and gold. She looked a million dollars.

I noticed that, despite her small size, and despite Sam's romantic offering of an arm, it was Taylor who was in charge. It was the way she moved – so alert and energised and confident.

This woman, I thought, needed no one; she was entirely self-sufficient. If she bestowed her attention on you, she was offering a special gift. I'd always known it – but only now could I put it into words.

Fixated, I followed them, backing into a bush when they turned slightly to check the traffic, and then crossed the road and went down into Formosa Street, where they entered The Orchard restaurant, a small and intimate Italian that Sam and I had visited many times. The thought that the waiters and the other diners would see Sam with Taylor in *our* place filled me with loathing. As they sat down at a table by the window, I scurried into the pub opposite the restaurant and watched from inside.

Sam was leaning across the table, gazing into her eyes. A waiter brought a bottle of wine. They raised a glass; then they were laughing, checking the menus, sharing little glances as they chose their food. His hand reached across the table, and her delicate hand reached back. Again, I noticed that her movements were so powerful. So assured and elegant. I felt awful, my entire body now wanting to get me out of there, and I left the pub in disgust, head bowed, hurrying back to Queen's Park and Melody.

At the flat, Mel gave me a hug and was sympathetic, though a little shocked at what I'd done. But, in truth, she was distracted by her new world at Tredenham Nurseries. There was a guy she kept mentioning – Oscar Meana. She said it like one word – Oscarmayana – making him sound like an option on a tapas menu and she was soon off on an enthusiastic monologue about him. *He's such an impressive person. He grew up in Mexico, but his mother's British and he came to the UK because he's interested in plants and the plants here are so different from the plants in Mexico. His mother speaks perfect Spanish, and Oscar's English isn't great. But he's learning so fast. He's so great. So kind and knowledgeable. His full name is Oscar Meana*

*Gill. Father's surname then mother's surname. That's the way
they do things in Mexico.*

I listened to her in a state of surrender. She was like
consoling music.

The following morning, I texted Rachel.

> How did the poking around go?

> Found in a kitchen drawer – a leaflet from the
> BBC creche. Looks like Taylor takes Evie there
> sometimes. Maybe Kensington Dad takes his
> kids there. I have a friend with a young son. I'll
> ask if she knows who the dad is. You might find
> the French wife. Rx

I asked her to text me straight away if she discovered a
name. Then I messaged Taylor, arranging to meet her and Evie
by the bandstand in Queen's Park. I saw her reply later, as I
stepped out of my cold shower. It read:

> Sam and I need a break and are going away. I'll
> bring Evie to stay with you.

I could scarcely believe it.

THIRTY

SEPTEMBER 1999

The moment has arrived for Adra Roy. She's had enough of her softly, softly approach and is ready to interrogate her witness with more vigour and precision. She's also had as much as she can take of Taylor's elaborate hand gestures, exaggerated expressions and melodramatic delivery. One moment, an intensely dramatic tone, the next an intimate, confiding whisper. It's all too histrionic.

Adra shifts in her seat, and speaks in her most formal, dispassionate voice:

AR – There's inconsistency here, Taylor… How did Sam go from being paranoid about Lucy to trusting her to look after Evie again? That's a dramatic shift. Almost unbelievable…

TL – It's not difficult, Adra! Lucy had her friend Melody staying with her. I tracked down Melody at her workplace, some garden centre called Tredenham Nurseries, and I asked her straight out. 'How's Lucy? Do you think it's safe to leave Evie with her for a few days? Will you keep an eye on her?' That sort of thing. Melody said Evie would be fine… So I started working on Sam, to convince him that it would be okay to go away for a couple of days. I guess my powers of persuasion are very strong – so he and I drove to a hotel by the sea. A romantic break! Somewhere in the west country.

AR – The name of the hotel?

TL – Umm. Sorry, it's not coming to me.

AR – The name of the town?

TL – Sorry. Nope. Very pretty. Sailing boats and a headland, and a lighthouse. Big terrace with a view. I could find out…

AR – Let's move on… Can you give me details, specific details that support your story? Support your contention that Sam killed Lucy and is on the run with Evie?

TL – I'm getting there, Adra. Getting there… So, it was while we were away that Sam started to talk about a future with me. And he said he'd gouge his own brain out before he'd pay Lucy a big divorce settlement or allow her to have custody of Evie. Then, he said, 'I wish she'd have a nasty accident. Fall in front of a bus or something.' He was laughing, like it was a joke, so I laughed and said, 'Yeah or put her finger in an electric socket.' And he said, 'Or fall down a manhole.' We kept at it, imagining more and more grotesque and bizarre endings for her – until I said a pig could fall on her head from a balcony and Sam replied with, 'There again, a kitchen knife through the throat might be the most satisfying. Nice and simple.' You know, dark humour. I feel awful now – I mean, dark humour was one of our bonds. But, looking back, he was telling me in all seriousness that he intended to kill her. He told me how and he told me why…

THIRTY-ONE

EVIE

NOW

After leaving Rachel Tang, Evie goes back to the hotel and sleeps heavily and dreamlessly, from ten at night until ten the next day. When she wakes, she finds that she has slept in the T-shirt she wore all yesterday and in her orange socks and that she failed to pull the brocade curtain across the sash window. Outside, the sky is black and purple and rain is falling heavily, looking like it might never stop. Sitting up, she looks around her little room at the scratched and worn oak desk, the lone upright chair with a tartan cushion, the dead spider scrunched up in the coving. She notices the faint smell of Brussel sprouts and can't quite believe that this is now her reality.

The en-suite bathroom is tiny with a plasticky shower and gale-force extractor fan, and she takes her shower in cool water, trying to wake up. She'd like to call Antonio – but it's four in the morning in Mexico so, when dressed in a fresh T-shirt and jeans, she pulls on a sweater and her black coat, steps down the narrow staircase and out into the street, in search of a coffee shop.

She doesn't have an umbrella, just a black beanie, so turns up the collar of her coat and runs from awning to awning – taking shelter when the rain becomes a bombardment and bounces off the pavements, running again when it lifts a little. Others are doing the same. It's cold and dark, and once again she thinks, *this is not my country. Not my city.* But, as she dips into a café, she finds people of all nationalities and ages taking shelter, drinking coffee, eating croissants, working on their laptops, idling on their phones: medics from the hospital across the road, college students, two dark-skinned young women who look like fashionistas. Everyone is caught up in an earthy steam brought on by the weather; she can, for once, see the charm and, as she joins the line for coffee and a pastry, she feels, for an instant, part of it all.

With her purchases, she finds a seat and discovers that the coffee's excellent – strong and rich and, starting to feel a little stronger, she takes a bite of her Danish pastry and checks her phone. A message from Rachel.

> Hope you're okay, Evie. I've been up half the bloody night. Why don't you know about Sam? All these years I've thought you were with him. All I can think about is how you were brought up by Melody King. She was so close to Lucy. Did she somehow get hold of you after the murders? Please talk to me soon.

Evie sips her coffee, eats her sweet Danish, tries to lose herself in the atmosphere of the café. After five minutes, she replies.

> Will do.

At eleven, she returns to her room, waits twenty minutes, then sits cross-legged on her bed and calls Antonio. It's nearly five-thirty in Mexico. 'Evie?' He sounds bleary.

'Are you awake?'

'Am now.'

'Sorry.'

'No worries. How are you? What's the latest?'

Evie tells him about Rachel Tang and how, even now, she seems captivated by Sam's charm. 'He confided in her when he killed my mother,' she says. 'Texted her and spelled out the awful details of the murder.' Her voice catches. 'Sometimes, I think that, because they never found Lucy's body, maybe she's still alive somewhere... But it's just wishful thinking, isn't it? I've lost two mothers, Antonio. Can you imagine that?'

'Oh, Evie,' Antonio says softly.

'Rachel painted this dark picture of Lucy. She said Lucy was addicted to drugs, and made me sick on purpose, because she liked the attention...'

'Munchausen's?'

'Yes. Shocking, isn't it?' Evie pauses. 'But it's all second-hand. It's all what she was told by others. By Sam and by Lucy. No outsider really knows what's going on inside someone else's marriage, do they?'

Evie sighs, stretches her legs and leans back into her pillows. In this moment she's deflated and tired. 'I keep returning to the same thoughts,' she says. 'All about Mama. I just want her here to answer my questions... If only she'd told me the truth, Antonio. If only she hadn't died taking these secrets with her.'

'I wish I was there,' Antonio says. 'I'd hold you so tight.'

'I wish that too... I miss you... I might go to Gloucestershire – to see where Mama grew up. To understand who she was before all the craziness happened. And there's this garden centre in London where she worked – Tredenham Nurseries. Someone there might remember her. I need reassurances that Mia was the person I remember – so loving and thoughtful and kind. I need to believe that my life was real.'

'She made your home into a sanctuary,' Antonio says. 'I felt it every time I visited – that absolute safety.'

'Will you do something for me?'

'Sure – what?'

'Do you remember the man with the silvery hair who came to Mia's funeral? I mentioned him before. Could you ask Ramona if she knows who he is? And maybe, if she doesn't know herself, she could ask around at the school? I think he may be the man who visited us when I was little – who brought me presents... I can't get him out of my head.'

'You're not thinking...?'

'That he's Sam Preston? It seems so implausible I know, but everything about this is implausible... Will you?'

'Yes, of course.'

She asks Antonio about life in Mexico: the food he's eating, the cat that comes in from next door, the soccer match that he plays on Saturday mornings and then they sign off.

Evie's mind returns to finding her grandmother. Summoning courage, she dials the number of the Birchwood House care home. She's scared that Clemency is no longer there, worried that her grandmother is dead. A woman named Debbie answers the call, and Evie asks nervously, 'Do you have a resident called Clemency Preston?'

THIRTY-TWO

LUCY

1999

I had five blissful days with Evie. It was glorious to know that Sam and Taylor were far away and for hours at a time I didn't think of them at all and when they did crash violently into my mind, I found myself wishing that they would never come back, would leave Evie and me to ourselves and our cocoon of happiness. Sam's betrayal was overwhelming and if he and Taylor simply disappeared from the face of the earth, I thought, my life would be so much improved. The idea was so powerful that it became a bodily sensation, a longing, and I felt it constantly as Evie and I went about our days doing our favourite things: the park, the science museum, the aquarium. I kissed and hugged her often, like it was the last chance I'd ever get, and I renewed the promise that I'd made to her as a newborn – that she'd always be loved and be safe, that her needs would always be more important than my own.

Our wondrous little holiday ended abruptly when Sam returned to London and came to Queen's Park to celebrate Evie's birthday. He arrived at the flat for afternoon tea and cake and as soon as I saw him, I could tell he was suppressing some sort of rage – he was stony-faced and had to force a smile when he picked Evie up and wished her happy birthday. As for Melody and me, he grunted a short, 'hello' with all the warmth of a razor blade, then gave Evie a present. The three of us watched as she tore off the paper. Inside was a little blue wooden sailing boat. 'I've been in Devon,' he said stiffly, 'where there are lots of boats like this. Would you like to go there one day, Evie?'

'On a boat?'

'Yes, darling, on a boat. Imagine Daddy has a boat and you and I could go on the sea.'

'Do this boat in the park,' Evie said.

'Yes – we can take it to the pond and sail it.' He sounded like someone who was never going to make it to the pond.

I brought in the cake with the candles and we sang happy birthday. Halfway through I noticed tears sliding down my husband's face. As he wiped them away, I tried to tell whether they were tears of anger or sadness; then Evie blew out the candles.

Melody cut the cake and Sam hissed in my ear, 'We need to talk. In private.'

'Hey, Evie, let's have some cake and stick some birthday stickers in your book,' Melody said, taking Evie on to her lap as I followed Sam out of the room, down the stairs and into the noisy street. 'We'll go to The Salusbury,' he said, pushing me along the pavement and into the pub. I couldn't tell what was going on. He bought us a lager each, and we found a table at the back near the wall. As we stared at each other, I thought he looked drawn and old, like he'd aged ten years.

I was waiting for him to start, but he seemed incapable. Until he came out with, 'God, Lucy. Things are bad.'

'Well, yes.'

'I can't fucking believe that I've been so stupid. It's not like me.'

A crowd of customers brushed past our table, talking loudly and trailing the whiff of ale. I wasn't sure that I'd heard him correctly. 'What?'

'I've been a fucking idiot. Taylor's played me for a monumental fool. And now we're fucked – both of us. You and me.' He leaned right back in his chair lips turned down, almost comically, his nostrils flaring.

'What are you saying, Sam? It's obvious that she's a devious cow – but...'

'She has the evidence – about you and the drugs. She has a computer printout. Orders and receipts.'

'It was only Valium – not the rest. Like I've told you. Not the rest of it. *She* bought it.'

'I know. She bought all of it, the total stash, and from your laptop, Luce.' He was speaking in a monotone, staring down at his lager.

'For fuck's sake, Sam. Look at me and show some respect.'

'Yeah, I'm sorry.' He didn't sound sorry.

I put my head in my hand while I tried to make sense of my emotions. At last, Taylor had revealed her true self. At last, Sam was seeing through her... but I didn't feel triumphant, not at all. I peeked back up. 'How can she have evidence? I don't get it. I haven't seen anything unusual on my laptop. I haven't paid for those drugs?'

'Oh, she's clever. She set up an email account in the name LBandEvie@yahoo.co.uk and bought the drugs from there. She showed me everything.'

'What? Is that possible?'

'It doesn't take a genius, Lucy. When you were out, God knows when, she took your laptop, set up an email account and bought drugs in your name.' His breathy, haughty tone suggested that, despite his anger, he was still in awe of Taylor – somehow seduced by her wiles, on top of all the rest.

'Paid how?' I said, panic rising.

'From some account she'd set up. Who cares?'

'And the drugs were sent where?'

'To Russell Drive.'

'Honestly. This can't be right.'

'You're not following me... Who picks up the mail in the mornings? It's usually her. Either you and I have left for work when it arrives – and on your days off, well, she got to the house before you were out of fucking bed.'

The loathing that we were sending back and forth across the table was horrendous. No romantic reconciliation. No forgiveness. Just fierce honest repugnance.

'And that's only the half of it...' He gripped his empty glass like he wanted to throw it at my head.

'What?'

'She's done it to me too.' His dark eyes were flashing and glinting like jet.

'What do you mean?'

'Fuck it, Luce. She's... she's...' Tears rolled down his cheeks. 'She's totally deceived me. I can't think of a way out.'

'Tell me! Tell me what else she's done.'

'I'm getting another drink.' He wiped his face and went to the bar, coming back with two full glasses, handing me one with his left hand. He wasn't wearing his wedding ring. I only noticed it then.

'She had my trust. Totally. But she wants money because of the drugs and... That's what all this is about. She wants a lot of it... in cash.'

'Sweet Jesus...'

'I'm probably going to give it to her.'

'Why? What did she do to you?' I leaned forward. 'Sam – you need to tell me the whole story. What happened in Devon?'

THIRTY-THREE

LUCY

1999

It had started out all butterflies and rainbows. A rented Porsche, driven with reckless speed down to the south Devon coast where they arrived at a luxury hotel on a cliff, with a pool and a panoramic view of the sea. Taylor had swum a hundred lengths each day and they'd sipped vodka Martinis in the evening as the sun set. They'd lain side by side on loungers as he told her that he'd never been so happy and it had been a long time coming, but he would divorce me. He wasn't sure that he'd ever truly loved me; he'd made the biggest mistake of his life in marrying me... ('It's true Lucy, I messed up totally'. He didn't say sorry). Taylor had consoled him, and Sam had gazed at her, thinking *she's so innocent and waif-like. So sweet and caring.*

'Sam,' I said. 'You're a fucking moron.'

On the third night, she'd said, 'Sam... any chance of *a little favour?*'

'Sure,' he'd said. 'Name it.'

'It's a bit of an ask. But if you and I are, like, together – I want to feel like I'm your equal. Do you get that?'

'Of course. It's not the nineteenth century.' He'd laughed affectionately.

'I knew you'd understand.' They chinked Martini glasses and she pointed out a beautiful sailing boat coming towards the shore. 'What's it worth, a boat like that?'

'That's a beauty. A schooner like that – anything between £300,000 and a million.'

'Worth it, though.'

'Yes. I'd like something like that. One day.'

'One day.' She'd raised her glass again. 'In the meantime... I was thinking – a little advance...'

She wanted £20,000. As a gesture, and that kind of soured the mood.

Over the following twenty-four hours, the conversation had gone back and forth. 'You're so rich, it makes me uncomfortable,' she'd said. 'I don't want to feel like I'm on the game, sleeping with you for trinkets.'

He went for a long walk, alone, on the beach at midnight. Infuriated. How could she be so grasping? So unreasonable? It hurt him like a mortal wound because he was in love.

He'd walked some more, barefoot, letting the cold sea lap at his feet. Tried to see it from her point of view. The itinerant nanny, dependant on him every time they ate out, went away, did anything that involved money. He'd liked it. It made him feel masculine and protective. But it was 1999 and women liked to feel independent... After walking for an hour, he persuaded himself that Taylor was right.

He'd returned to the room, ready to compromise. To offer £10,000. 'As a down payment on our future.'

'Yuck, Sam,' she said with no hesitation. 'That's neither one thing or the other. I'm looking for something that says commitment.'

He fled to the beach and slept there, cold and troubled.

Returning to the room at dawn, he found her in bed with a champagne breakfast on a tray. All innocence and admiration.

'Love you!' she said. 'Love you so much for sleeping on the beach... I adore the craziness!'

Half of him wanted to sweep her up and give her the full £20,000, but he tried to reason with her. 'Giving you £20,000 feels like I'm buying you. Like it's a slave market.'

'Poor Sam.' She giggled.

'Taylor, how can we resolve this thing? Seriously.'

'Seriously?'

'Yes.'

She got up from the bed, tiptoeing prettily across the room, and reached for his laptop. 'Sam Preston,' she said. 'Whoever would have thought that you're a paedo... It took me a while to come to terms with it. I'm pretty traumatised by it actually.' While she was talking, she twisted her hair up on to the top of her head, and secured it with a pen.

'Not funny,' he said.

'No. Not funny at all. I've found 672 indecent, hardcore images of children accessed by you. That's not good, is it?'

'What!' He looked over her shoulder at the screen. 'Oh, my fucking Christ. What the fuck have you downloaded?'

'Not me. You,' she said coyly. 'And all of it backed up with your family photos – so "losing" your computer won't help.'

Sam seemed like a broken animal, explaining it all to me, his head shaking, his eyes full of terror.

THIRTY-FOUR

SEPTEMBER 1999

AR – We need to pick up the pace, Taylor. If Sam is out there with Evie, I need more specific information…

TL – Okay then. How about this? In Devon, Sam told me he had this thing about luxury boats. You know, sleek classic yachts, the sort of thing you'd find in an old film with Cary Grant and Katherine Hepburn or someone. Sipping champagne and sunsets and all that. We laughed about it and Sam said he'd like to buy a luxury sailing boat for us and we thought up names for it – Sam suggested *The Slip* because we'd be giving ordinary life the slip and I said *Seventh Heaven* because he and I had been in Seventh Heaven with our crazy nights mixing sex and cocaine… oops, I shouldn't have said that, should I?

AR – Stick to the pertinent facts, Taylor.

TL – Well, I just thought you should know… He may well be trying to get her out of the country by boat… I remember, he made a joke about taking Lucy out on *The Slip,* and her *accidentally* slipping and falling into the sea one night, like Natalie Wood. So boats were definitely on his mind...

AR – Does he have access to a boat?

TL – Sorry, don't know about that...

AR – Okay... Before we move on, was there anything else about this holiday that is relevant, directly relevant, to the murder?

TL – Something significant did happen actually; something truly disturbing in retrospect. One afternoon, Sam went out for a walk along the beach and I stayed behind in the room... As soon as I was on my own, I saw his laptop sitting on the coffee table and I felt overcome with curiosity, you know how you do sometimes? And I picked it up and started poking around. I'm pretty good with technology and have an instinct for where people hide things – it's one of my talents! And you know what I found?

AR – Obviously not Taylor.

TL – Only child pornography! I mean, what the hell? That blew my mind... Sam Preston, *the* Sam Preston, had child pornography on his laptop. I mean, I knew he was somebody who liked to transgress, who'd lived outside normal boundaries, but this was beyond the pale by anyone's standards. I felt sick. Totally violated in fact. So I put the laptop back on the coffee table, and just sat up on the bed and waited for him to come back from his walk. My head was exploding... When he came back in, all smiley and sexy, I just confronted him with it. I couldn't believe his reaction, he blew up in anger with *me* for looking at his laptop. I mean, of the crimes here, I couldn't see that mine was the problem...

He made a big effort to explain it – he said it was there because of research he'd done for a TV report that, in the end, never happened. I said, 'So, why on earth is it still on your laptop?' He made some excuse, like it was still possible that he'd go ahead with the story and it was evidence on some sort of slavery group that he'd found involving a British paedophile group living in Thailand now, or some-thing like that. And he said, anyway he was going to hand it over to the police when he had more to consolidate the story… But he looked rattled and I realised that he wasn't telling me everything… so I pressed him on it. And you know what he said? It was pretty astonishing.

AR – Do continue, Taylor…

TL – He said that sweet little Lucy Bliss had done the same as me, had gone looking into the dark corners of his laptop and had found the same material. And you see the significance of that, Inspector Roy?

AR – Go on…

TL – Well, I'm surprised you can't work it out yourself, but still. If Lucy had made copies from Sam's computer, it gave her power over him, didn't it? She'd be able to use it against him in a divorce, to get custody of Evie and whatever else she wanted. I mean, who'd believe Sam's excuse? I don't believe it, do you? Not now. And it explains everything – like the depth of his anger towards Lucy and why he lost it and attacked her like he did. He was prone to rages anyway, and in those circumstances, triggered like he was, he just lost it and he killed her…

AR – Okay, Taylor… we need to move on. Tell us what happened when you came back to London. Tell us about the day in question and the death of Lucy… Take us through it.

TL – I can't say this more strongly, Adra. I'm helping you as much as I possibly can. I really want you to save Evie. And to find Lucy's body... You need to put Sam Preston behind bars. So yeah, here goes... the day in question.

THIRTY-FIVE

LUCY

1999

The Salusbury road pub had filled up with young people – media types – and was noisy. I leaned in so that I didn't have to shout, and was eyeball to eyeball with Sam. 'How do I know you're telling the truth? Was it really her who downloaded the images? Or was it you?'

'You know it wasn't me. Paedophilia, Lucy!' He looked utterly stunned.

'Really? How can I know? Everything I thought about you turned out to be a lie. I thought you wanted me as I was, your beloved homebody who'd raise your children. Your anchor. Instead, you wanted *her*. I was stupid, wasn't I?'

'For God's sake. Don't be ridiculous.'

'Oh yeah, I'm ridiculous. Really ridiculous.'

I bit my thumb until it hurt, knowing that I was on the point of hysteria, that I had to rein myself in. Sam, too, was trying to calm himself, sitting back and taking breaths.

'Luce, let's not go off subject,' he said. 'We need to deal with Taylor. We need to get her out of our lives.'

'I repeat – how do I know it was her and not you who downloaded those images?'

'Of course you know. She planted those drugs in your drawer and now she's done this... She's not normal.'

'I'm not so sure now,' I said. 'What if it was you? I mean, you're the one trying to take Evie from me... You're the one who wanted me out of the house. I'm dead sure you know how to get hold of all those drugs.' We were locked in a bubble of mutual loathing and, in my case, unbearable pain, a fire in my heart, hating and loving him at the same time. A large guy holding two beers jogged our table as he squeezed past and my drink began to topple. Sam reached out and caught it. Sharp as anything. In that instant, he had total control.

'Sorry, mate,' the guy said.

'No worries.' Sam grinned at him – alive and shiny – then faced me, once more angry. I seemed to be seeing him from a distance now, with a steady, alienated gaze. I watched as he rolled up his shirt sleeves, put his elbows on the table, slowed his breathing again, then offered me his hands to hold. My revulsion was overwhelming, but I couldn't bear to believe in it.

'Lucy,' he said, 'I'm really sorry. I am. I've been so stupid... but honestly, darling—'

'Don't call me darling.'

'I'm not a monster.' He softened his voice. 'You know that. You know me... This is what happened. A while back – maybe a year, eighteen months, something like that – I'd thought about doing a story about child abuse. And I downloaded a couple of images for research—'

'Research? Really?'

'Yes. And you know what – I thought *I can't do this.* I've covered everything in my time. War. Rape. Ethnic cleansing. But when I started looking into paedophilia, I feared for my own sanity – there's only so much human depravity that one person can take. I couldn't handle it... I thought of Evie.'

I sat back, folding my arms, watching him, inspecting every little element of him – those long fingers, those dark eyes, and I caught the smell of him, or imagined I did. A dark, foresty, hunterish smell. 'Okay,' I said eventually, in despair. 'I believe you.'

'Taylor's a conwoman. That's it. Short and simple. She did the same thing with each of us. She took the germ of something that she found on our laptops, and she worked it up into something she could blackmail us with... I don't think we have a choice. We have to pay her off.'

'Or go to the police?' The thought of paying her was sickening.

'But we can't, can we?' Anger was rising again in his voice. 'The first thing that will happen is bloody child protection. And Taylor's bloody clever... and she's ruthless. Those allegations against me. Even if we put up the best fight, people would always wonder. I can't live with that, Lucy. I *won't* live with that.'

I thought about it – of the drugs in my drawer and the end of my career, and of my overwhelming desire for this nightmare to come to an end. 'Okay,' I said eventually. 'So £20,000...'

'It's not £20,000 anymore,' he interrupted, looking at me as though I was naïve. 'It's £100,000. There's no way she'd settle for twenty.'

'My God. That's astronomical... and wouldn't she come back for more?'

'I dunno.'

'You know what,' I said. 'I don't think she would. I think she just moves on – like, to another country and another con... I think she's totally professional and we were totally fools. We welcomed her in.'

'Yeah.'

I had never known pain like it. Looking at Sam, seeing him as my dearest love, and my worst enemy at the same time. His betrayal burning inside me as we held it together just long enough to make a deal... agreeing that Taylor would never be alone with Evie again, and together we would do everything it took to get rid of the woman. She was monstrous, maybe a psychopath, and Sam had convinced himself that she loved him. I'd done something far worse and convinced myself that she loved Evie.

NOW

Yes, Clemency is alive.

Within twenty-four hours, Evie is leaving Chichester train station and walking ten minutes along wide residential streets until she finds Birchwood House care home, a vast red-brick sprawl of a building surrounded by well-tended gardens. Partly lofty and old – Evie guesses nineteenth century – the rest of the care home is a random network of modern extensions, one of which has a square-box conservatory at its end and she sees three ancient women in there, sitting at angles in armchairs, mouths open; each gazing at their own chosen part of a discoloured window. One of the ladies is wearing a pink cloth bucket hat.

At reception, Evie is greeted with a thin smile by a young woman in a shiny navy uniform; she wears a badge which says *Naomi*. Naomi has a stye, red and bulbous, on her left eye and she's distracted by it, poking at its outer corner. 'Sorry can you say that again? You've come from where?'

'I'm visiting from Mexico. My grandmother is a resident here. Clemency Preston. I spoke to someone on the phone...'

'Did you speak to Debbie? You'd have to speak to Debbie.'

'Yes, I did.'

'I didn't know Clemency had a granddaughter.'

'Yes, she does... So, may I see her?'

'You know her dementia is severe? Mostly likely, she won't have a clue what's going on?'

'Debbie explained.'

'Can you write in the visitors' book then?'

Naomi is closing her eye now and looks like she might cry. She hands Evie a pen. As she writes her name, *Evie Segura,* she finds herself hoping for a miracle. That Clemency will have an astounding moment of clarity and will be able to answer her questions.

'Follow me then.'

Naomi leads the way along a wide corridor with high walls and a terracotta tiled floor; they turn right and Naomi taps a security pass on the wall which releases two heavyweight metal doors, and now they are in one of the extensions – the ceilings are lower, the floor's a uniform rubber-grey and two cluttered cleaning trolleys rest at the side, their cloths and brushes smelling of bleach and putrescence. Clemency's room is at the far end. Her door is open – attempts at homeliness have been made: a thick brown carpet and woodland scenes hung on the wall, and a painting of a cat in a meadow. Clemency sits stiffly in an armchair by the bed, gazing at the window just as the women in the conservatory had done. She's wearing a smart cashmere sweater and woollen trousers, polished tan loafers, and she's holding a teddy bear.

'Clemency,' Naomi says gently and with irritation. 'Clemency, Edie is here. Your granddaughter has come to see you.'

'Evie, I'm Evie.'

Clemency turns her head and looks vaguely at the two women as though she's waiting for more information. Evie registers her wide-spaced brown eyes and her high forehead and the way in which she holds her chin, firmly and high. She moves closer and sits on the bed, just a few feet away. 'I'm your granddaughter. Do you remember me?'

'Who is she? What did she say?' Clemency speaks like an aristocrat, a splinter of ice in her voice.

'I'll leave you two together,' Naomi replies. Then to Evie, 'Just press the buzzer when you want to leave, and someone will come fetch you... Bye bye, Clemency – you have a lovely time now, darling.'

'Not her darling!' Clemency barks as Naomi slips backwards and shuts the door.

'No,' says Evie. 'You're not her darling... I'm Evie. You knew me when I was a little girl. I'm Sam's daughter.'

'Sam Sam the butcher man. Washed his face in a frying pan.'

Evie sits still and wonders what to say next. She notices that somebody is looking after her grandmother's fingernails, which are painted pink, and that she wears crimson lipstick and glistening eyeshadow. But no brows. Her eyebrows have faded away almost to nothing, exposing a pale bony ridge across her forehead.

'Does Sam ever come to see you?'

'Ha! I saw him yesterday. Or was it Thursday?'

'Yes? He came *here*?' Evie leans forward.

'Where do you think? They don't let me out, you know. Not ever. It's forbidden. They have guards, you know.' Clemency has metallic eyes.

'Tell me about Sam... Does he live nearby?'

'Oh no. Sam likes the seaside. That's where he lives. I can't remember where. Bournemouth, I expect. Or the south of France – that's it. St Tropez. Cap Ferrat. Antibes...' She closes her eyes and holds the bear to her chest and then she's singing in perfect French. At least it sounds perfect – but Evie knows little of the language... it's a pretty tune and she makes out something about *tous les garçons et les filles* and *les yeux* and *la main*. Clemency forgets the words and begins to hum.

'Sam,' Evie repeats. 'Sam comes here? He comes to see you?'

Clemency glares. 'Who are you in that big coat?' She slaps the bear's head on the arm of the chair.

'I'm Evie. I'm Sam's daughter.'

'Sam doesn't have a daughter! Who are you?'

Evie backtracks. 'Tell me about Sam.'

'Always off to France. Never telling me when he's coming back. He was here yesterday. Or was it Thursday? He was out there!' She waves the bear at the window. 'Climbing... climbing... you know with the green on. The leaves. And dawdling upside down. I told him, come home for tea. Fuck you, Mother. You bitch. You slut. Sam Sam the butcher man...' She starts to shake.

'I understand. I understand.' Evie reaches for her bag. 'I brought something for you...' She'd bought a box of chocolates at a specialist shop in Paddington. Velvety truffles sitting in tiny pink paper cups. 'Do you like chocolates?'

Clemency turns her head and looks out of the window again and Evie places the chocolates on the bed. They sit in silence for five minutes or so, then Evie asks what Sam was like as a child. This time, Clemency becomes quite lucid. He was a charming boy, apparently, with a lot of friends, but he'd been expelled from school because he was too fond of fighting. 'Fond of fighting,' she repeats dreamily. 'A very physical child. We didn't know what to do with him.' Then she drifts off into a long reverie about the clothes she dressed him in as a baby, her own clothes, the times she wore Chanel and Yves St Laurent, all the different hairstyles she'd had. Eventually, Evie presses the green buzzer on the wall. She stands and places her hand over Clemency's: 'I'm going now. Thank you for seeing me, Clemency. I'm glad we met.'

The touch makes Clemency start and fix Evie with angry eyes. 'Forget, Sam!' she shouts. 'He's no good. Only ever did one decent thing. He snatched you away from mad Lucy Locket. Clobbered her to death, though, didn't he? He told me all about *that!*'

Evie steps back in shock. 'When? When did he tell you?'

'Wouldn't you like to know, little miss, coming here in your big coat, asking questions! You're not Evie! You're nothing like her!'

Naomi appears. 'Enough now, Clemency,' she says. 'Cup of tea coming up in five minutes and a biscuit – oh look, your granddaughter brought you chocolates. Aren't you lucky?'

As Clemency repeats over and over 'nothing like her!', Naomi escorts Evie out of the room, back along the corridor and through the secured doors.

'She said her son came to see her,' Evie says.

'She says all sorts of things. You just have to go along with it.'

'It's not true then?'

'Nah. He's scarpered, the son. That's what they do, the selfish ones... When the old ladies go downhill.'

'Do you know anything about him?'

Naomi squeezes behind the reception desk and squints at Evie, suspicion in both her eyes – the good and the bad. 'Thought you said you were her granddaughter.'

'I am. But I've been away a long time. In Mexico. I don't know what became of her son – my father.'

'Well, he hasn't been here, that's all I can tell you. Whatever she says. And that's in all three years she's been here. Now, just sign out in the book please.'

On the train, Evie thinks of the venom and enthusiasm with

which Clemency had spat out her words: *clobbered her to death*. Like she truly believed her son to be a killer and took some perverted pleasure from it.

As the train reaches the London suburbs and she watches terraced houses with patchwork gardens slip by, it strikes Evie that maybe this story is not as preposterous as she'd imagined. Maybe it is simply an account of a violent man who killed his wife, an event as ordinary and disturbing as everyday life.

THIRTY-SEVEN

LUCY

1999

Taylor told Sam that she was going away for a few days. 'Just to give you time to get the cash together.'

He'd asked the obvious question, face to face: 'If we pay you – how do we know you won't come back for more?'

She'd laughed. 'You can't know. But I'm telling you, I won't be back. I know posh people like you; you think you can control everything. You'll burst your entitled little brains trying to think up some trap for me. No – in and out – that's how I work. It's in my interest and that's your guarantee.' She'd blown him a kiss as she left number 37, pulling a large pink suitcase-on-wheels.

'I think you hallucinated that kiss,' I said. 'You've been hallucinating a lot of things lately.'

Sam gave me a scornful look, which quickly turned to pleading as he said, once more, that he wanted me to come back to Number 37. I didn't show my distress. My utter confusion. I said no; I told him that I needed to keep my distance, and I insisted that Evie stay in Queen's Park with me and Melody. So Sam was living in our plush palatial flat by himself, wallowing in his anger, spending time online, disinvesting here and there and rounding up his cash. We had a joint bank account. I checked it and saw he'd transferred £350,000 into it, not £100,000. I didn't question it.

There was a French mother who came into the BBC crèche. Wife of a producer – she was called Émilie. Not Françine or Claudine. Rachel laughed. 'French names kill me. So sugar-sweet schoolgirl!' She gave me Émilie's number.

'Is she rich?'

'Loaded. Big art auction house family. Mansion in Kensington.'

A quick phone call, and ten minutes later I dropped Evie with Sam, took the tube to Kensington and found my way to Phillimore Gardens. Émilie's house was way grander than ours, a white stucco pile that would suit an ambassador or an Arab prince. The front door was answered by a maid in uniform who showed me through to a sitting room the size of a small swimming pool with formal furniture, statues, a grand piano and a dozen large artworks on the walls; they were probably all by famous artists, but I recognised only one – a swimming pool painting by David Hockney.

Émilie was sitting bolt upright on a yellow brocade sofa, ankles crossed. Tailored shift dress. Just so hair and nails. Dark claret-coloured lips. She was stick-like and brittle, like an insect queen and signalled with a tiny finger that I should sit in the chair opposite. I put my rucksack on the floor beside a table made from gleaming apple-green resin.

'So,' she said, barely moving. 'This woman. This nanny. What do you know about her?'

'I came here to ask you the same thing.'

'Yes. But I wish to hear from you first.' Evidently, Émilie was accustomed to giving orders.

'Okay. She's been working for us, my husband and I, for a few months and…'

I couldn't think what to say. Émilie folded her hands on her lap, her claret lips held tight, threatening to scowl. She blinked slowly. 'Are you trying to say that this woman is not what she seemed to be at first?'

'Yes. Exactly.'

'You pay her in cash, yes? And you employed her because she earned your trust? In effect, she had no references, yes?'

'Yes. All that.'

'We have all done this in our lives,' Émilie continued, 'based our actions on trust rather than technicalities. I suppose it comes from a sort of self-regard, thinking that we have good judgement and are clever… But we weren't, were we? Because now she would like some money from you?' Her expression was a little puzzled – I could see her sizing up my T-shirt and jeans and old rucksack.

'Oh God…' I made my desperation clear and Emilié pushed a little box of tissues in a silver box across the table towards me, thinking I might cry. But I was past that. I just wanted to make an impression. 'She did it to you too?' I whimpered. 'How much did you give her?'

She stood up and walked round to the back of the sofa as though she'd been given a stage direction and faced me, her twig hands splayed on the yellow brocade. 'This is in complete confidence, you understand. I am telling you only because you are suffering. I am a compassionate person as well as gullible. I gave her £250,000.'

'Oh my. All at once? Or did she ask repeatedly for money?'

'All at once, as you put it. Eighteen months ago. I have heard nothing since. My husband cannot know. Nobody can know.'

I looked at the family photos in gold frames on top of the

piano. Identical twin boys with proud eyes and puffed-out chests. 'How old are your children?'

'Now they are five. And yours?'

'My daughter has just turned three.' Neither of us wanted to say our children's names.

'Can I ask...?'

'No.' A clipped little utterance. 'I cannot articulate it. But she created a nauseating allegation against me, fabricated evidence that would take my boys from me forever. Here, in this house, her name was Chloë Farmer. When I met her, by chance – but, in reality, not by chance at all – I'd thought *a pretty name for a pretty girl*. I was enchanted by her. Maybe I liked it that her Christian name was French.'

'You think you were targeted? That she had researched you?'

'Certainly. I believe that she found us via the crèche at the BBC. The staff there, they chit-chat. She'd collected some other child, joined in the gossip about who were the rich parents with the spoiled children. From there – simple.'

'My child has been in that crèche,' I said. 'Not often. But enough, I suppose.'

A lonely silence filled the stupid over-adorned room. Émilie didn't offer me anything – not even a glass of water – and I knew she wanted me to leave, but I wasn't ready. I blurted out: 'If it happened to you, then it happens all over again with us – that's evidence, isn't it? We can go to the police. Surely.'

She shook her head. 'No. Never. We go to the police and even if we are successful, which is unlikely, one day my boys would know about the disgusting accusations she made against me. Accusations that I cannot disprove. I will not have that. I simply share this to reassure you that if you pay, she *will* go. She strikes. She moves on.'

She turned her back to me and faced three vast windows,

curtained in silver satin. In different circumstances, I would have found her melodramatics funny.

'Thank you,' I said. 'Goodbye.'

The maid was waiting at the front door.

On my way back to Queen's Park, I collected Evie from Sam. He'd been drinking while looking after her, but I said nothing. Who was I to judge? I simply wanted to pick her up and leave as quickly as I could, but Sam followed me towards the flat door and as I went to open it, he murmured in my ear, angry but not wanting Evie to hear him, 'The woman is pure evil, Lu. Why don't we just get rid of her? We could do it, you and I. It wouldn't be hard. And we'd be doing the world a favour.'

'Stop it, Sam,' I said. 'We pay Taylor the money. Stop talking like an idiot.'

THIRTY-EIGHT

SEPTEMBER 1999

TL – The journey back from Devon was a nightmare. Sam was out of his mind… He was saying, 'Lucy's fucked up my life. She's put Evie in danger. She's a fucking danger to herself. I won't have her taking me to the cleaners in the courts. I won't have her taking Evie. She's pinned me down. I'm trapped.' Like that. Over and over. At one point I feared for my life he was driving so fast. Like 120 miles an hour or something. Actually, he might have been drinking; I don't think he was focused on being legal. I mean, the child porn and all that.

When we got home, I told him, 'You need to calm down, Sam. I can't be in the house with you when you're like this.' And I went away for a few nights.

AR – Where did you go?

TL – I checked into one of those little hotels where you just get a tiny single bed and a shower room and not much in the way of natural light.

AR – The name of this hotel?

TL – Dumb name. Buzz Hotel. It's in the East End. Aldgate. Around there.

AR – What did you do there? During the day?

TL – Let me think. I got up late. Didn't fancy the help-yourself Buzz Breakfast. Congealed eggs under a metal cover and charred bacon – totally gross – brain tissue and gristle. So I went to a café to read a book.

AR – What book?

TL – Haha! Is this book group now? You want to know what I was reading! That's really funny. Well, I'm not a Jane Austen type, Inspector Roy. As it happens, I was reading something philosophical. The works of Montaigne. You didn't expect that, did you?

AR – Which works of Montaigne?

TL – Ooo, this is getting surreal. I'm the proud owner of a 1958 edition of the *Complete Essays*. Let me tell you, I've learned a whole lot about human nature. It's my special subject.

AR – After this very elevated reading, what did you do next?

TL – I visited some of the sights of London. I went to St Paul's Cathedral and walked around and just kind of looked at stuff. They're building that bridge over the Thames down there and that new Tate gallery. Very fascinating, I thought.

AR – Did you meet anyone? See anyone you knew?

TL – No. Not once, but that's because I don't know anyone. I'm new to London. I think you know that already, don't you? I'm from Brazil and I've been travelling in Europe. Like, I've been to Ibiza and Spain and Portugal and stuff. Then I went down to South Africa. Then here.

AR – When did you arrive in this country?

TL – Late January.

AR – And you've made no friends since January?

TL – None. Apart from lovely Lucy. That's why I was spending time by myself.

AR – Will anyone at the hotel be able to verify your whereabouts that day and evening?

TL – I walked past the reception desk a few times, but I can't remember anyone that I said hello to or anything like that. No harming in asking around, though.

AR – Can you remember the name of the street? Where it was exactly.

TL – Nope. Sorry. Somewhere in Aldgate. I don't know that area and I was just wandering around like an old donkey.

AR – When did you go back to Russell Drive?

TL – Not until the third day. I thought Sam might have calmed down by then, but I couldn't have been more wrong about that because that's when he killed her, on that third day. I shouldn't have left him alone; that's what I think now.

THIRTY-NINE

LUCY

1999

I woke every morning with the adrenaline already pumping. Obsessing about Taylor, about Sam. Fixating on his betrayal, remembering the beauty and romance of our early days. *How could you do that, Sam? How could you throw away the most wonderful thing in the world?* I'd take my morning latte to the terrace and attempt to tend to the pots of plants, trying to emulate Melody. I'd watched her work, squatting down low as she dead-headed geraniums or planted daisies, and I'd envied her state of peace, her total involvement.

But, in no time, my thoughts would return to Sam, with all the power of a riptide dragging me into the ocean. There was no point resisting and once more that voice would be back in my head: *How could he hurt me so much? How could he destroy Evie's life along with mine, all for the sake of a charming little psychopath?* More than once, my thoughts turned to Sam's first love, Willow Kelly and his confession that the crueller Willow became, the more infatuated with her he was. *Damaged kids do that. They can't accept the truth and try to fix things emotionally.*

Whatever it takes. I understood it. After all, I'm damaged myself.

When Sam phoned, I struggled to keep my emotions under control. He was selling equities, he said. Amassing enough money for us to go far away and start a new life. But I didn't believe him. My trust was utterly gone and, for all his talk of a new future, he didn't once apologise to me for his relationship with Taylor; he didn't once say that he loved me or that he didn't still love her; he didn't even express concern for Evie.

We didn't know where Taylor was staying, and she never answered her phone. She listened to messages, though, and replied when she felt like it. Whenever she called, Sam phoned me afterwards in order to rant. *I've been so stupid. I was taken in entirely and I blame myself. But she'd been so convincing, so...* It was obvious that, true to form, the worse she became, the more he was under her spell.

One day, Sam called to say that Taylor was growing impatient. 'I'll give her the cash tomorrow evening,' he said. 'It will be a relief. Once it's done, come home, darling. I need you here. I need our old simplicity.'

That might have seemed sweet if there wasn't a bitter tone to his voice, a barely suppressed resentment, and he quickly reverted to his favourite subject: 'Taylor's fucking clever, isn't she?' he said in a weird breathless voice. He sounded sleep deprived. 'I mean, she worked it all out. Got us both exactly where she wanted us... I can't bear to think of her face, that innocent beauty.'

He may as well have stabbed me through the heart.

'That photo album,' he went on. 'The one she made for my birthday? It's not here. She took it. Why would she do that?'

'What do you want, Sam?' I said desperately. 'A pendant with a lock of her hair inside?'

'No. No. That's not it. But I thought we should have

pictures of her... in case everything goes wrong, in case we end up with the police.'

'That's why she took the album. Obviously.'

I didn't tell him about the passport photos that I'd retrieved from Taylor's bag. 'We can't end up with the police, Sam,' I said. 'We can't disprove Taylor's allegations. We'd go to prison. It would destroy Evie's childhood. It could destroy her life...'

'Are our passports up do date? Mine is. But what about yours and Evie's?'

'What's that got to do with anything?'

'Just tell me.' He was shouting now. Aggressive. 'Are they up to date?'

'Yes. They are. I have them with me in Queen's Park.'

His voice slipped down a register and was calmer. 'Good. Okay then, I'll pay her tonight.'

While this was unfolding, Melody was in Gloucestershire, seeing her mother. She phoned to ask if I'd been able to arrange more parking permits for her van, for when she came back to London. I laughed out loud – it was surreal to be thinking of parking permits.

'God, Mel,' I said. 'I've been so distracted, I haven't done it yet.'

'I'm sorry to be banging on about them.'

'No, it's important. Listen, I'll sort them out. When are you back?'

'Tomorrow. I'm helping Mum out in the garden – I'll finish off in the morning, then head for London.'

'I don't think I'll be able to get Queen's Park permits in time, but we have some at Russell Drive. Could you park there for a few days?'

'No worries. You all right? You sound strange.'

'Yes.' I paused. She had no idea, she was in blessed ignorance of the blackmail and Taylor's perfidy. I let the pause run – then was surprised at the words that came out of my mouth: 'Actually, I am a bit scared,' I said. 'I'm worried about Sam.'

'What's happened?'

'He wants me to move back into Russell Drive, but he sounds, I don't know, threatening and aggressive.'

'Lu? He's not likely to be violent, is he?'

'He's capable of it,' I whispered.

'God! You mean in the past he... did something?'

'Yes.' My voice was tiny now. It was an act. I was lying. A whole new scenario was playing out in my head in which Sam and I were heading for divorce and I had to do everything possible in order to protect my daughter, to keep her happy and safe. In that moment, I didn't care what it took.

Shortly after, Rachel Tang rang. 'Hey sweetheart. What's new?' I could practically see a cigarette in her hand and a single malt on a table. I didn't know how to respond to her airy tone.

'Taylor's gone,' I said seriously. 'She's moved out.'

She took a long draw on her cigarette. 'Oh.' She was thinking. 'And how's Sam?'

'Really, Rachel? That's your question?'

'Sorry, sweetheart. It's just that he came into the office today and he was kind of thrashing about and angry with everyone... Did *she* leave *him*? Or did he chuck her out?'

'I don't know. And I don't care anymore.'

'God, I'm sorry. You sound awful...' Rachel said.

'I feel awful. Of course I do.' Then I added, 'Sam, when he's in that sort of mood... well, he's scary, isn't he?'

'No. I've never thought of him as scary. He has high passions.'

'High passions...' I laughed sarcastically.

'You're not really afraid of him, are you? I mean, not physically afraid?'

'Yes, I am, Rachel. Bloody terrified. I worry what he might do to Evie or me. He's so enraged about it all.'

As I ended the call, I felt guilty, but less helpless. I was done being helpless.

I started to dream of a different future in which Taylor had fled the country and Sam and I were divorced. I'd rescue Evie from Little Venice and rich Londoners. Maybe return to Gloucestershire, to the green and gentle countryside. I imagined the two of us walking hand in hand through a field of docile sheep and the sun shining down. We'd have a little terraced cottage; she'd go to a village school, and I'd make friends with the other mothers – women with no ambitions to write newspaper columns or claw their way into publishing or architecture; women who might paint but never presume that their sloppy art conveys a fascinating personality. These women would prefer to talk about gardens, baking, and ups and downs at the school. I'd play the cello again.

In the afternoon, I took Evie to Russell Drive. I wanted to see Sam before he met Taylor to pay her off, fearing that he'd buckle at the last minute, that he would plead pathetically with her like he did with me. I suspected that all the hundreds of thousands of pounds he'd transferred to his current account was for *their* lives together, not ours.

I rang the bell to the flat and heard Sam before I saw him – pacing the hallway with a clattering step. As we entered, he began talking manically, piling on thought after thought. 'Everything is in place now,' he said as we went down the stairs into the kitchen. 'We'll pick up and start again. We have so many options. With Taylor's toxic influence out of the way, Evie will thrive – fuck knows the effect Taylor's had on her. The three of us will be happier than we've ever been. It's about the future now. God, I can't sleep for thinking about Taylor; how she's twisted my emotions...'

He fell back into the sofa, his long legs sprawled wide, and picked up Evie, plonking her on his lap, bouncing her up and down vigorously. She thought it was a game.

'Waltzing Matilda! Waltzing Matilda! Who'll come a waltzing Matilda with me...'

Evie shrieked, 'Wooshing A Tilda!'

'Do you know about kangaroos, Evie?' Sam said.

'Sam. You're being weird.'

He looked into my eyes. 'I've sussed it. We destroy Taylor, pick up and start over in Australia. There are great schools in Sydney. We'll be near the beach. Have a pool. *Whad'ya say, darlin.*' That last bit was said in a mangled Australian accent. 'Come here.' He patted the sofa. 'Family hug?' He narrowed his eyes like he was suggesting a dare.

I remained standing. 'There's the small matter of work permits.'

'Oh, we'll think of something.' He lifted Evie up and the two of them rubbed noses.

There was something so hollow and fake about his words. Was he planning to leave the country with Evie and then hook up with Taylor in Australia? Did he think I'd just accept that? Sam was a mess. I needed to bring him down to earth.

'I'm worried about this evening,' I said. 'The transaction with Taylor needs to be clear-headed and businesslike. *Here's your money. Now fuck off.* Can you manage that?'

'Yeah, yeah...' He was only half listening.

'Keep it short. You tell her, if she ever comes back, we'll unleash the hounds of hell.'

He laughed at *hounds of hell* and twirled Evie's hair around his finger. 'Yes, Lucy dearest. Whatever that means…'

'Just say it. Then get her out of here. Don't do anything stupid. Call me as soon as it's over.'

'Yeah yeah…'

'Promise me, Sam.'

'I promise, Lucy.' He sighed a big fake sigh and rolled his eyes.

'I'll be waiting for the call,' I said as I took my daughter in my arms and left.

FORTY

LUCY

1999

Taylor was due at Russell Drive at seven, but seven o'clock came and went. Quarter past seven, half past seven, and still there was no call from Sam.

I called his mobile. No answer, So I dialled the landline, which rang and rang. At ten to eight, I poured a glass of Sauvignon Blanc and tried to think straight, but my mind kept returning to the idea that he hadn't gone through with it, hadn't paid her. I imagined that, right now, he was pleading like his life depended on it. *Come away with me to Oz. We'll have a massive house, a beautiful boat, hot and hold running staff...*

I circled the kitchenette looking for comfort food, seizing upon a packet of cheese and onion crisps, which I tore open and scoffed. Fifteen long minutes later, I tried Sam's phone again. He didn't pick up, and my tolerance for waiting evaporated. I crept into Evie's bedroom, scooped her up from her cot, wrapped her in a blanket and called a cab.

At number 37, I let myself in from the street and rang the

bell by the inside door. Nothing. So I rapped on it like a lunatic, calling out Sam's name.

I heard footsteps on the wooden floor inside, and the sound of the latch. The door opened slowly, the chain lock still fastened. Through the crack, Taylor's face appeared, flushed and sweaty, but as pretty as ever, a tendril of wavy hair falling across her left eye. She did her wonky smile. 'Hello, Lucy. How are you?' I felt sick.

Evie in my arms, all sleepy and floppy, said with a beaming smile, 'Taylor.'

'Hello, little chou chou.' She was talking sweetly, pretending everything was normal.

'Where's Sam?'

'Oh, he's right here... We weren't expecting you. Do you want to come in?'

I called out again, 'Sam!'

The sound that returned my call was muffled and indistinct – a low moan.

'What's wrong?' I said, confused. 'Let me in, Taylor. Do it now.'

'Sure, no problem.'

Deftly, she unfastened the chain.

Sam was on the floor halfway down the hall, lying on his side, his back to me almost foetal. He moaned again, low and faint like a wounded animal, and I edged forward, clutching Evie's head to my neck. As I reached him, I saw a kitchen knife. Sticking out of his chest.

I froze, holding Evie too hard.

'Oh my God, Sam...' My words were barely audible, nausea rising.

I had to get Evie away, and I forced myself to step over his body, carrying her through to the sitting room. 'Stay here, sweetheart,' I whispered, laying her on the sofa.

'Daddy,' she murmured, turning towards the cushions. She

put her thumb in her mouth and dozed off.

Back in the hallway, I crouched down, stroking Sam's forehead with my hand, touching the knife, not knowing whether to pull it out or leave it.

'Sam... Sam... Oh my God.'

He looked vacantly into my eyes. I felt the pulse in his neck; it was fast but faint. His lips parted and closed again.

'Oh God, Sam... Don't speak. I'm calling an ambulance. Just hang on in there...'

His lips parted again, and he whispered so faintly that it was barely audible. 'Taylor.'

Was he calling for *her*? 'What?' I said. 'What?'

She was still leaning against the door, contemplative but cool, like an elegant spectator at an art installation.

'Sam, it's Lucy. I'm here, darling.' I held my face close to his.

He whispered again: 'Taylor. I want Taylor...'

I stood up on shaky legs thinking that I might pass out and turned to her. 'What happened?'

She shrugged. 'It was self-defence, Lucy. He was trying to rape me.'

'What? I don't believe you.'

'I'm telling the truth... He was trying to take me away from you, wanted us to go somewhere together, like Australia... You know that's what he wants – to get me and Evie and to get you out of his life. But I said no way and you know what he's like when he's angry? He came for me, and he was forcing me up against the wall... I was terrified...'

I looked down at Sam, still lying there, still breathing. A smudge of blood was seeping into his grey T-shirt and on to the floorboards. I tried to think logically.

'You're lying, Taylor. You just happened to have a kitchen knife in your hand at the time?... I'm calling an ambulance.'

My phone rang inside my bag. I ignored it and crouched down to stroke Sam's forehead, which was cold and damp. 'The ambulance will be here soon,' I said. This time, his eyes seemed to focus, but not on me; he was looking across at Taylor and he mouthed a single word: 'Please...' My phone rang again. I took it out and looked. It was Melody. Fuck. She needed the parking permits for her van. I took the call, walking on weak legs to the sitting room where Evie was sleeping.

'Hey, Lu.' She sounded breezy.

'I'm at number 37,' I mumbled. 'Are you here?'

'Right outside. How are things with Sam?'

'I can't talk. Listen, I'll come out with the permits. Evie's here – can you take her back to Queen's Park? It's just... I can't explain... can you take her?'

I found the permits in a desk in the sitting room, then came out carrying Evie. Taylor hadn't moved; she was still leaning nonchalantly against the door, seemingly enjoying the drama.

'Melody's outside. I'm taking Evie to her...' I was ready to fall into Melody's arms and ask her to call the ambulance.

But Taylor said: 'If you say anything about Sam, I'm pinning this on you. It won't be hard. I've cleaned the knife – no fingerprints of mine on the knife, just yours – and there's the history – your jealousy and your derangement, the slashed sofa and all that... You understand? You say anything at all to Melody and you're going to prison for a long time, Lucy. And that's Evie's life destroyed...'

I saw Sam's chest moving, the knife moving with it. Maybe the injury wasn't serious – maybe we could patch him up without the police getting involved...

'I'll be right back.' Hugging Evie, I left. 'You're going with Melody, darling,' I said. 'She'll look after you.' I kissed the top of her head.

Melody was at the front gate and the van was right there in front of the building.

'Everything all right?' she said.

'Daddy hurt,' Evie said sleepily.

Melody looked at me, questions in her eyes.

'He's fine,' I lied. 'He stumbled.'

'Sure you're okay? Are you safe? I don't like leaving you.'

I handed Evie over without meeting Melody's eyes. 'Yes, yes. I'll explain later.'

Melody, in her oversized fleece, took Evie who snuggled into her like she was a teddy bear. I spotted a black cab coming towards us; yellow light on and called out. 'Taxi!'

'Lucy, look at me,' Melody said gently. 'You seem strange.'

'I'm fine,' I said, hurrying back to the house. I was scared of collapsing, right there in the street.

Taylor was sitting on the floor now, looking at Sam in a studious way, like she was about to take notes. I noticed that his leg was in a different position, more bent at the knee; then I saw it move a fraction, a slight quiver. I looked at my wounded husband, but as he gazed at Taylor, I was overwhelmed by pain and the compassion wouldn't come.

Taylor stood up and headed down to the kitchen. 'Well, I'll get my money and I'll be going... It was nice to see you, Lucy. Good luck with all this.'

I followed her. 'No, wait. Don't go...'

'Sorry, I have plans.' She picked up several piles of bank notes that were on the kitchen table and looked around for her bag.

'Taylor. Stay here... We need to attend to his wound. Sort him out.'

'Oh, Lucy... Why would I do that?'

We stopped talking then because Sam called out again. 'Come here! Help me!'

FORTY-ONE

SEPTEMBER 1999

TL – Sam was in a total rage about Lucy. Losing his mind! Yelling and cursing. I knew she was in danger, and I tried to warn her, Inspector Roy. Did she listen? No. She was too stupid for that. But, honestly, I tried to save her…

AR – How did you warn her? In person?

TL – I phoned her. Three times. You can check my phone.

AR – Yes, we will be doing that. Speed it up, Taylor! Tell us about the murder. Give us some facts.

TL – Sure! No problem! So, all hell broke loose on Wednesday. I went to Russell Drive – about one in the afternoon – to see Sam. To try to talk sense into him. But he was whacko by then. Got crazy heavy with me. Promised me the world. 'Come with me to Australia, Taylor! We'll take Evie. You'll have anything you've ever wanted… Fancy your own business? I could set you up in fashion or food…' I said, 'No way – but if you love me so much, you can give me some cash. A hundred thousand to set up in business somewhere like Brazil. Away from you.' He went berserk. Came at me, pushing and shoving, and he picked up a knife!

AR – The knife that he later used on Lucy? The same one?

TL – Yes, a Sabatier. He was coming at me with it but was interrupted by the bell ringing and Lucy arriving. He still had it in his hand as he went upstairs to let Lucy in.

AR – You stayed in the kitchen? You didn't try to warn Lucy?

TL – I was in shock! At least, at first. But then I heard them tearing each other to pieces. Sam was shouting, 'I'm taking Evie!' Lucy was sobbing, yelling, 'I'll kill you first! You've ruined my life!'

At that point, I ran up the stairs and when I got there… okay, I need to breathe… this is harrowing stuff… So, Sam was shouting, and the knife was dangling in his right hand. I mean, he was holding it loosely. Lucy grabbed it, went for his chest, and she drew blood. But Sam was ten times stronger than her, and he snatched it right back… That's when he did it… He stabbed her deep in her chest and she fell to the floor, almost like in slow motion, kind of drifting across the hallway as she went down… Sam went crazy – kicking her over and over, stabbing her again. He seized an umbrella from the stand and started whacking and clobbering her with it – but she must have been dead already. He was in a frenzy.

AR – Are you okay, Taylor? For the record, Miss Love has her head in her arms and is face down on the table.

TL – I'm fucking traumatised, Adra! He killed her! Lucy was lying there, and she was full-on dead. Her eyes were bulging like ping-pong balls, goggling up at the ceiling, and her mouth was hanging open. And Sam was blocking my way, so I couldn't run out of the front door.

FORTY-TWO

EVIE

NOW

Flecks of snow spin in the air outside the window and Evie sits at a bar stool, watching the steely faces of passers-by in puffa coats and woolly hats, dipping their heads into the wind. Nobody had told her that, on days like these, London is bitter and icy.

She sips her Caffè Nero hot chocolate, then examines her phone. She's researching Bernard Wu, the brother of Jackson. Bernard, she thinks, is like her – collateral damage in this horror show. Maybe, like her, he has turned detective. Has uncovered buried truths. She wants to meet him.

Ignoring the clatter and buzz of the café, she examines a profile, published in *Kult,* – a fancy architecture and design magazine. Once a banker, Bernard's now a philanthropist. A big-cheese patron of the arts, with his own foundation. He's pictured in a grand home with high ceilings and pale walls covered in art works, some of them enormous, abstract and textural; others historical portraits. She spots two of her favourite artists – Agnes Martin, Ethan Cook.

In the photo, Bernard sits stiffly at one end of a baby blue, silk-covered sofa. His feet perfectly aligned. Looking straight ahead. At the other end, is his partner Kendis Williams, head in perfect profile, chin raised, as he gazes affectionally at Bernard, one arm resting on a small white dog, the other holding a wine glass.

Did Bernard curate this photo? Or Kendis? The composition is perfect. And the colours. The men's clothes connect beautifully to the baby blue: Bernard's ultra-marine shirt and cerise slippers; Kendis's nude-pink T-shirt and mud-grey jeans. Crazy, but they seem to have considered their skin tones. Pale Bernard in strong colours, deep-dark Kendis in neutral tones, balanced by the claret-red of his wine.

Bernard, she reads, made his money from banking and now travels the world for his charity. He has homes in London, Hong Kong and New York. There's a younger sister, Sisi, an artist. Her work is pictured separately – a jumbled, bulbous little ceramic. A male body with the internal organs exposed.

Evie scrolls, finding the website for Bernard's foundation and a phone number. Maybe the way to speak to him will be through their shared love of art. Leaning towards the window, she makes the call. 'I'd like to speak to Bernard Wu. Is he around?' She's ridiculously nervous.

'Putting you through.'

'Bernard Wu's office.'

'Hello. My name's Evie Segura. I'm visiting the UK from Mexico; I'm researching some of the artists in Bernard Wu's collection – I wonder, would it be possible to talk to him about the works? I'd like to see them if that was possible.' She's trying not to sound desperate.

'Who's the research for? Are you an undergraduate?' The woman sounds dismissive.

'Oh no. It's for a PhD... Possibly a book...' She's surprised by her effortless lie.

'Could you put your request in an email?'

'Is he in London now? Will he see my email today?'

'Not sure.'

'Thank you. I'm only in the UK for a short time and—'

'I'll do what I can,' says the woman abruptly.

Evie hangs up and dashes off her email, saying she's particularly interested in Bernard's Ethan Cook woven canvas. She signs off as Evelina Segura.

To her amazement, he replies almost immediately.

'If you want to see the art, you'd better come now. I'm flying to Hong Kong tonight.' In a plain, businesslike way, he states his address.

The specks of snow have given way to darkness and a blizzard of grey sleet. Evie's taxi turns into an empty cobbled street, shaded by tall buildings on either side – warehouses converted into apartments. She glimpses the river and realises that she's in the old docks. Dickensian London scrubbed clean. Bernard's apartment is at the top of Cannon Wharf, a vast brick building with swanky glass door. When she steps out of the lift at the fifth floor, Bernard is waiting – holding open the door to the flat. He seems older than his photo in *Kult*, and larger. No handshake or introduction, just: 'I can give you ten minutes; but I'm afraid we're rather pressed for time.'

'I understand.'

The palatial living room has huge square windows overlooking the Thames. It's like a gallery artwork, ancient and modern, everywhere. Bernard's partner, Kendis, reclines on one of a pair of blue sofas. He smiles and says hi, but doesn't get up to greet her. A Jack Russell, patters across the room, tail wagging, jumping up and down, bouncing off Evie's legs.

'Push her away. She's a nuisance,' Bernard says.

'Oh, I like dogs.' She tries to pat it, but it's like patting a whirlwind.

'Here, Sukie,' Kendis says breezily, although it's obvious the dog doesn't obey commands. Bernard picks it up and drops it in Kendis's lap. He glances at his watch. 'So, the art.'

'May I look at the other works before the Ethan Cook? I'd like to think of it in this context. It's happy in the room.'

Bernard regards her more closely, frowning. 'Yes, you're right. It is happy in the room.'

Kendis sends her an encouraging half-smile from the sofa.

She's struck by the way in which the art has been hung. The modern works are interspersed with Renaissance paintings – a *Madonna and Child*, *The Visitation of Elizabeth*, some secular portraits. The room itself, she realises, is an exceptional artwork. She asks questions – *Why is this painting next to this one? I don't know this artist – Who is it? Did Bernard do the hanging himself?*

His answers are short. Yes, he did the hanging himself, with Kendis's help. Hanging is an art form. The way an alteration can shift the whole experience, can cause the eye to move in different patterns, see different elements in the individual pieces.

Evie spots Sisi's ceramic, separate from the rest. 'Can you tell me about your sister's work?'

'No,' Bernard says. 'That's personal.'

She nods and turns to an Agnes Martin painting. Perfectly proportioned pale-yellow stripes across the canvas.

'You know about Agnes Martin?' Bernard asks.

'Yes. She created such sensitive works, on the face of it simple, but connecting to the heart.'

'Could she have achieved it without her emotional terrors?'

'I don't know,' says Evie. 'Schizophrenia is terrifying.'

'Part of me wants to live her life. Alone in the Arizona desert.' Bernard says this with utmost seriousness.

'And you have this sense of...' she hesitates, trying to find the perfect words.

'It's not healing...' Bernard says.

'No. Is consolation a better word?'

'It is... Form and structure – they are God given...'

Bernard and Evie are their own cocoon. Suddenly, Evie feels sick at her deception. She takes a step back and looks to Kendis. His expression is open and honest, and a curl of shame rises from her stomach.

'Bernard,' she says. 'There's something else... I'm sorry... I should have told you at the start – but I have another name. I'm Evie Preston-Bliss – the daughter of Lucy and Sam who disappeared on the night that your brother was murdered...'

Bernard instantly turns his back. Moves robotically towards Kendis, placing his hands on the back of the sofa.

'I'm sorry,' Evie says.

'What does this mean?' Bernard asks without turning to face her. 'Do you know what happened that night? Do you know who killed him?'

'No. At least, not yet...'

His voice lowers into an angry hiss. 'Get her out of here, Kendis. Get her out.'

Kendis removes the dog from his lap and taps the back of Bernard's hand, then approaches Evie, not unkindly, with the words, 'Come on... I'll see you out.'

'Goodbye, Bernard.'

He doesn't reply and she leaves with Kendis, who says he'll come down in the lift. They descend in silence, then he follows her out of the building into the street.

'You disappeared back then,' he says. 'What do you know?'

'I was taken to Mexico by a friend of my birth-mother, of Lucy Bliss. I only recently found out about the murders. I know practically nothing. But I'm trying to find out...'

'Why did you come here? To us?'

'I don't know. I *am* sorry. Genuinely. I thought I might have something to offer Bernard. – but I don't. Or that he might have something to offer me.'

They're backed up against the wall of the building, a failed attempt to get out of the wind, and Kendis says: 'His family was destroyed that day... Do you want to hear about it? Or are you a voyeur?'

'I'm not a voyeur. And yes – I would like to hear.' She draws her coat around her and sees that Kendis, wearing nothing more protective than a designer T-shirt, doesn't care about the cold.

'Bernard's family... they were almost too good to be true. Striving immigrant family, parents opened a restaurant – not far from here... in Whitechapel. Incredible work ethic which they passed on to the three children. Bernard went into banking with a determination to succeed and provide for his parents in their old age – and to use his money for good... which he does. He's a good man.'

'I can see that...'

'Jackson became a lawyer. He was a gentle, conscientious young guy – not ambitious like Bernard. All he wanted was to marry, settle down, be a father. Very simple. He was engaged to be married when it happened... And Sisi – Cynthia – she went into medicine – was in her second year of a medical degree when Jackson was killed... What happened to her was almost as bad a shock as Jackson's murder...'

Evie bows her head, gazes at the stone pavement.

'You want to hear?'

'Yes.'

'Her body gave way as well as her mind. She developed early-onset rheumatoid arthritis at twenty-two and dropped out of medicine. Bernard would say *to become an artist,* but that's not the truth. She rarely produces anything – she isn't talented or trained. Her life is... well... just say it's chaotic... Bernard supports her of course – but money can't save her.'

'Bernard's the strong one...'

'In a way. He tries to lose himself in art, as you've seen.'

'And his parents?'

'His mother died a few years after the murder – cancer – and his father went to Hong Kong to be close to the extended family. Can you imagine, as they raised those children, how proud they were, how optimistic about the future – security and grandchildren? Jackson's death destroyed everything. Maybe it would have been different if it was a peaceful death – a kind of force majeure. But a murder, a human act, and a violent death – it was too much.'

Evie looks up. 'I am truly sorry to have done this – I've savagely reopened a wound and done more damage...'

'You have your own story,' Kendis says.

'I do. But it's only half-formed. I'm trying to figure it out.'

Kendis pulls himself straight. 'Don't write to Bernard again.'

'I won't.'

A blast of wind sweeps down the street sending debris cavorting into the air. Kendis hugs his hands into his armpits. 'If you discover anything that would be useful rather than cruel – come to me, not him. I'll send an email so you have my address.'

FORTY-THREE

LUCY

1999

Sam called out again: 'Taylor, come here! I need you!'

I'd been standing by the kitchen island, ready to go to him, but now my legs gave way and I collapsed to the floor. Those words broke me, and I began to sob.

'Go to him, Taylor – you have to help him...'

'He's beyond help, Lucy, in so many ways...' She laughed dryly.

'I can't do this on my own,' I whispered from the floor. 'We need to get that knife out and bandage him up. I need your help.'

Tucking a tendril of hair behind her ear, she said, 'Poor Lucy. You're delusional... Now, I've got my money and I'm out of this hellhole. All that' – she waved her long fingers towards the stairs – 'is *your* problem.'

She walked around the room; plucking two photos from the fridge, putting them into her bag and started walking towards the stairs.

'Wait,' I said. 'Just tell me this. Tell me that you were lying – he didn't try to rape you.'

She turned to me with a pitying expression. 'Oh, Lucy... Your Sam really is a filthy violent predator you know.'

'No...'

She sat on the stairs. 'Let me take you through it... When I got here earlier, he was ranting and raving in his normal way – wanting me back, despite everything. I told him that all I wanted was my payment and out – and he went totally berserk. Had his hand round my throat, pushed me up against the wall. I thought he was going to kill me. Really! So I did what I've done a million times before... I lied to him... I persuaded him to let me speak and he took his hand off my neck, and I said a few nice words... something like, *Sam, what we have is amazing. I've never known anything like it... Just give me a few hours to think. Please. You know how much I'm in love with you...* He backed off, tears in his eyes, and sat down at the table, kinda shocked at what he'd just done, and that's when I seized the knife and dashed for the stairs, not even stopping for my money, and ran up... but he caught up with me in the hallway, grabbed my arm, and I just turned and I did it, I stabbed him in his chest. Honestly, I don't think he's too badly hurt – you can patch him up. It'll be fine.'

'You're crazy,' I hissed from the floor.

'Oh, one more thing...' She reached into her canvas bag, pulled out a notebook and pen, and tore off a sheet of paper. 'If you want to give me more money,' she said, 'use this number. But you've only got a couple of hours, then I'm dumping the phone... You never know – I might help you with Sam, for a little extra payment.' She left the paper on the stair, stood up, and left.

Sam called her name again as she passed him, then I heard a clatter, something falling over. Slowly, I dragged myself up from

the kitchen floor. I'd made a decision, I'd call the ambulance... My phone was upstairs, in the hallway.

My legs were so weak. I had both hands on the banister,
taking my time over every step; concentrating on not collapsing
again. In the hallway, I saw that Sam had moved a little closer to
the door. He'd knocked over the umbrella stand and there was a
smear of blood across the floorboards. I knelt down and ran my
fingers through his beautiful hair. I traced his face with my
finger, softly along the bridge of his nose, then across his cheekbones, while he closed his eyes as though taking a break from
struggling, as if he wished to be asleep.

I knelt down, wanting one last moment of our old love.
Then I lay down beside him, my head against his back, my arms
around his body, hating him but loving him too. One last
moment of intimacy before I made the emergency call. But as
soon as I closed my eyes, I felt Sam shudder and writhe and
shout something guttural and incoherent as he twisted his body
towards me and spat aggressively into my face. He flung an arm
across me with sudden strength, gripping and squeezing my
neck. As everything became black, my final thought was this:
*Melody, please keep your promise, take Evie away, keep her safe.
Give her a new life. Give her peace.*

FORTY-FOUR

SEPTEMBER 1999

AR – Are you okay, Taylor? Would you like a cup of tea?

TL – Oh, thank you for asking. Yes, that would be perfect. Black, no sugar.

Adra and Sinead leave the interview room and as soon as the door is shut, Sinead says, 'She's a piece of work! How do we break through this? She's lying, I'm certain of it – but we don't have anything concrete yet, do we?'

'No... But she'll slip up. She's bound to. She's a game-player through and through, and way too sure of her abilities. The question is, why is she lying? To what end? She's so keen to incriminate Sam – but was she involved too? She appears to want us to find Lucy's body, and yet she'll go on flights of fancy rather than get to the point. Why? That's the question. What are we missing?'

As they make their way to the kitchen, they discuss the forensics and the need to get the results as soon as possible, to check the DNA on the blood on the knife, the T-shirt and the strands of hair. Lucy's mother is somewhere in the West Country – she'll be good for a match. Adra makes three teas, and as they return to the interview room, she says, 'The timings are odd. If we can show them to be wrong, that would be a way through... A charge of perverting the course of justice there as a start. Maybe we'll end up with accessory to murder... Assisting an offence...'

Adra opens the door, enters the bare little cell and places the three mugs of tea on the table.

AR – So Taylor, you witnessed Sam stabbing and battering Lucy – you witnessed the killing?

TL – I did yes. I've seen a lot of violence in my life, but nothing like that.

AR – Did you try to stop him?

TL – God no. I'd have ended up dead myself.

AR – And all this happened in the hallway at the front door approximately twenty-eight hours ago, is that correct?

TL – Yes.

AR – Why have you come to us only now? That's a long time.

TL – Well, there was no way that Sam was going to let me contact you right then, was there? And I thought that if I'd made a run for it, he'd kill me too. So I went along with him, with everything he told me to do, until I could escape.

AR – What did he tell you to do?

TL – He kept me right with him the whole time, pulled me down to the kitchen where he found black sacks and duct tape, then he forced me back up the stairs with him and we somehow got Lucy's body into the sacks and dragged it down to the kitchen, and left it near the back door. Sam had me help him scrub the floor all around the hallway with bleach and put the umbrella back in the stand – you'll find my finger-prints on that. Then it was back downstairs, to finish wrapping up Lucy.

Adra sits right back in her chair, eyebrows raised. What audacity this girl has! What monumental self-confidence. Because, in Adra's assessment, she's fabricating – but how much? It's hard to tell what's true, and what's utter nonsense.

AR – That's a day ago, Taylor. What happened between then and now?

TL – I should tell you something – when we were down there in the kitchen, Sam told me that one morning, he'd come into the kitchen and caught Lucy grinding pills with a pestle and mortar, and that Evie's beaker full of orange juice was sitting on the counter, right next to her. That was how she'd been doing it – adding drugs to her daughter's orange juice. I was shocked. I mean, Lucy could have killed her own child—

AR – Can you return to the chain of events, Taylor? You were in the kitchen and Sam was *finishing wrapping up Lucy?*

TL – Yes, and at one point, I helped him. I had to, he had such power over me. And that's when I had the idea to cut off a chunk of Lucy's hair, so that when I could get away and speak to you, to the police, I could show that I was telling the truth. You can get DNA from it, can't you?

AR – What do you think this proves, Taylor?

TL – I guess it doesn't absolutely prove anything. But it fits with what I'm saying, doesn't it?

AR – How did you get Lucy's hair while Sam was with you?

TL – I distracted Sam. I said, 'I really need a drink. Do you have any wine in the fridge?'

AR – Honestly? You're taping up a dead body and you suggest a glass of wine?

TL – Well, if you've never been in that situation, you can't begin to imagine what it's like. And it worked. He looked inside the fridge, and, in that moment, I cut the hair off and stuffed it down my bra by pretending to scratch an itch… Which was ironic, because in no time at all it really was itchy down my cleavage. Don't ever stuff human hair down your bra, that's my advice. And that's when I cut off that bit of her yellow T-shirt, with the blood on it. I put that down my bra as well. There will be a lot of my DNA on it, I guess.

So, Sam poured the wine, and we drank it at the kitchen table. Like in the old days. Sam even made a joke, something like, 'Well, this is unexpected.' One of those classic British understatements.

I joked back, 'Yes, life is full of little surprises…' but I was thinking – how the fuck do I get out of here? I didn't want to antagonise Sam, obviously, so I just made conversation. I asked him what he was going to do with Lucy. Sam said he'd borrow a car from a friend and would drive it to the external gate that leads to the communal garden, and get her body into the car from there. At night. And that's what happened.

AR – The name of this friend?

TL – He didn't say. But later there was a car outside, and the keys were in an envelope that someone had dropped through the letter box.

AR – And you moved the body later that night? Last night?

TL – Correct. The time went really slowly in the kitchen. Lucy was all sealed up ready to go and we'd done another clean with bleach. But I purposely left some little smears behind, so you'll find them with a bit of luck. Just little bits of Lucy's blood. And I noticed a piece of Lucy's fingernail and left it in a corner, you'll find that, I hope.

Around eight, we got hungry, and I made a fennel salad with olives and lime and fried salmon. The sort of thing that Sam liked to eat. I drank some more, but he stayed sober, because of the night ahead.

AR – You weren't inclined to stay sober yourself?

TL – Nope. I wished I could get paralytic. Believe me, in that situation you'd be the same! I guess it was around two or three in the morning, when he said we should get Lucy's body across the communal garden and into the car and I thought – this is my chance to get away! But it didn't work out like that. He made me come with him through the street, gripping my arm like a vice. It hurt real bad! Actually, he had a knife stuck in my side while we walked. Surreal. We were pretending to be love birds, but he was jabbing me with a kitchen knife!

AR – So you reached the car. Where was it parked?

TL – A few streets away. By that pub, The Warwick Arms, no CCTV around there – that's what Sam said. He'd checked. Everything seemed pre-meditated, to be honest.

AR – Did you get the number plate?

TL – No, that was a mistake. I was so busy not being stabbed I forgot to look.

AR – Quite an oversight, Taylor.

TL – Wasn't it!

AR – Describe the car, please.

TL – I'm no good with cars. All I can say is that it was black and old and scruffy.

AR – Big or small? Saloon or hatchback?

TL – Don't know what saloon or hatchback even is. And I'd say medium-sized. I do know it had central door-locking, because he locked the doors. Is that helpful?

AR – Mildly.

TL – So he drove it round, it wasn't far. Three or four minutes? And backed the car into the passageway. Then we crept across the garden to number 37. He'd left the kitchen doors unlocked, so we could get in easily. Lucy was all packed up by the back door – like a parcel for collection and we each took an end, and we carried her across the garden.

FORTY-FIVE

LUCY

1999

Sam's eyes narrowed with hate or anguish, I couldn't tell which, and I could feel his grip on my neck weakening; his long fingers losing their strength, and it was easy for me to grab his wrist and pull it away. I looked at his handsome, tormented face and all I felt was despair. 'Sam,' I said imploringly. 'Don't do this...' I slid backwards across the floor, until my back was against the wall. 'I'm calling an ambulance... I'm doing it now. Help will be here very soon. Stay still... I love you...'

I watched in silence as he fell into heaviness, softening onto the floor, his legs apart at an unnatural angle, his face now set into an incongruous expression of mild surprise, his eyes gazing upwards at nothing at all. I was frozen, maybe for seconds, maybe longer; then I felt my own body melt into a state of total impassiveness, the realisation radiating through me that Sam was dead. I crawled towards him, touched his chest close to the knife and felt no movement. I put my cheek to his mouth and felt no breath and when I gently rested two fingers on the side of his neck, there was no pulse. I pulled out the knife and placed it on the floor. Then, my head totally numb, I lay down and put my arm softly around him.

'Oh dear, this is very bad for you, Lucy...'

I looked up and saw Taylor sitting on the stairs up to the bedrooms watching as if she was in the theatre. She was enjoying this.

I'd thought she'd left the flat. But she'd watched the whole thing. Not bothered about my survival. Indifferent to Sam's death.

'Come downstairs,' she said.

I forced myself up onto my knees and leaned over to close Sam's eyes. Seeing those dark irises for the last time, running my fingers through his thick blonde hair, now damp with his sweat. My final words to him had been *I love you*. But his final coherent word had been *Taylor*.

'Come on.' She held out her hand to me and, without understanding why, I took it as she led me downstairs to the kitchen.

'Lie down. Lie on the sofa and I'll fetch some water.'

As she handed me the glass of water, she started talking of the new life that I might have now that Sam was gone. An escape overseas. Just me and Evie.

She laid it out with clinical precision. The police would find my DNA everywhere – on Sam, on the knife, on the floor. Melody would have to testify that I was here at number 37 at the time of the murder. As for motive, what a fool I'd been! 'Raging about Sam's betrayal to the entire world, slashing the sofa like a mad person!' She knelt in front of me and took my hand. I brushed it away. 'Poor Evie,' she said, 'alone, her mother in prison for the murder of her father. She wouldn't stand a chance.' As for Taylor, she'd be long gone having moved out of the house. Every angle covered.

'You need to be strong, Lucy,' she said. 'Come on, don't let Sam destroy you. That's what it will be when you're in prison, just the conclusion of the suffering he caused you. He was gaslighting you all the time, you realise that? He totally went along with it when I bought those drugs, and it was Sam who hid them in your drawer. He was a nasty, controlling man, Lucy. Leave all that toxicity behind, start over somewhere new. That would be best for everyone – but most of all for Evie.'

She wanted money, of course. A huge payment, and for that she'd take charge of my escape; she'd get rid of Sam's body – make it look like he'd murdered me and then disappeared into the sunset. That sort of thing happened all the time – men killing their wives. It wasn't even very newsworthy. 'The perfect endgame,' she said, her eyes shining with the thrill of it.

She sat down next to me on the sofa now, leaning back and stretching out her bare legs so that her biker boots rested on the coffee table. 'Money... I'm all about the money. I know there's a ton of it in your joint account with Sam, far more than he paid me. Trust me, Lucy. This could work out really well for both of us.'

Later, at the Queen's Park flat, I went to bed and I slept and slept.

Melody assumed that I was unwell and when I eventually awoke, at nine-thirty the following morning, she offered to make me porridge. She thought I was being melodramatic when I said, 'If anything happens to me, you'll look after Evie?'

'Sure I'd love to. I'd love her to bits and devote the rest of my days to her... But you're not dying, Lu. You've just caught the flu or something...'

I was grateful, not just for her big heart and her friendship, but for everything that she was. Solid. Dependable. Positive.

. . .

When I visited Russell Drive, I found that Taylor had put Sam's body into black sacks and tied it up with green plastic string. Despite being so tiny, she'd managed to drag it or push it downstairs to the kitchen, ready to be moved across the garden – and now it was a huge, fat parcel of God knows what... decomposing flesh? Disintegrating organs? Whatever it was, it was not Sam.

I moved around the flat like a zombie, wandering from room to room, stroking surfaces, sitting in my favourite places, looking at myself in mirrors – contemplating my wrecked life. Nothing seemed real.

The murder weapon had disappeared – Taylor had hidden it somewhere, knowing it had Sam's blood on the blade and my fingerprints on the handle. I searched for it, half-heartedly and in vain, while the truth settled over me. I could surrender myself to the police and destroy Evie's life, or disappear and give her a chance of happiness. It didn't feel like a choice. I would follow Taylor's instructions.

Two days after the murder, I asked Melody to look after Evie while I went to Russell Drive on the pretext of 'trying to patch things up with Sam – one last chance – I may stay overnight.'

'Sure,' Mel said, eyeing me up quizzically. 'But are you up to it?' I'd spent most of the time in my room, wrapped up in bed. She still thought I had the flu.

'Yeah,' I responded. 'I'm fine.' As I left, I picked up the key to her van from its resting place in a bowl by the front door.

At the flat, Taylor was in a state of high excitement, her cheeks flushed, her movements quick. 'Final preparations,' she said excitedly. She had Sam's phone in her hand. 'Take a look.' She passed the phone across to me and I saw that she'd composed a message from Sam confessing to my murder. It was pitch perfect. Agonised. Detailed. Sounding like Sam. 'I'll send it to Rachel Tang,' she said. 'Once we've got rid of the body and you're out of the country.'

She waved her hands at me to show off a pair of pale cream latex gloves. 'Here, prick your finger. We need blood.' She handed me a sewing needle and I did as she asked, then watched her smear my blood into several corners and cracks in the hallway. She made more marks at the bottom of the kitchen stairs, and another close to the French doors. 'Just specks,' she said, 'like he tried to clean up but left traces behind.'

I was hunched over the kitchen island, my head in my hands, and I barely heard her coming towards me, barely registered the grip on my shoulder until I felt a sharp pain shoot across my back, fast like the strike of a match.

'It was the easiest way, Lucy, look...' She showed me the knife she'd used – the one that had killed Sam. It was glistening red at its tip. 'Done, it's over...' she said. 'The best way, like ripping off a plaster.'

The moment felt like a turning point. Sam's blood gone. Replaced by mine. I was the murder victim now. 'Am I injured?' I said.

'Didn't go deep. Take your T-shirt off and I'll inspect the damage... All fine, Lucy, all fine. Don't panic. There's a trickle of blood at one side, just let me wipe the knife over it...'

I took off the yellow T-shirt and noted the spots of blood along the rip. Taylor smeared the knife across my bare back.

'Have to be careful,' she said as she placed the knife next to the sink. 'Don't want to ruin my forensic work. I replaced your fingerprints with Sam's – before I packaged him up, obviously.'

She sat down, as relaxed as a child on a playdate, and started playing Snake on her phone.

'I want it over and done with,' I said, reaching for the knitted blanket we kept on the sofa, wanting to cover myself up.

'Yeah well. It will be soon.' She pointed to a packet of crisps on the table. 'Help yourself. I'm going out to collect bricks from that skip next door. To weigh him down.' She glanced across at the body in the sacks. 'Give me the key to the van.'

When she returned, she was lively, wanting to chat. 'I guess I'll stay in Europe when this is over,' she said. 'I speak a little Spanish and Portuguese. I picked up some French when I worked in Kensington.'

'I went to see Émilie,' I said. 'At her mansion.'

She roared with laughter. 'What a trussed up chicken that woman was! And what a secret! Turned out that her husband wasn't the father of the twin boys. I was only there a week before I realised something was up – fragrant Émilie had had a lover in the building trade. Nice guy actually, good-looking, called Julius. Unusual for a plasterer, but there we go. Anyway, I helped myself to strands of hair from a selection of hair-brushes – got the tests – and jackpot! The boys were Julius's kids, not Mark's or Tim's or whatever his name was... Now, what shall we do next? How about tearing some of your hair out?'

'No – leave my hair out of it.' I thought about it. 'I have a chip in my fingernail. You can have a sliver of nail.'

I bit the end of my nail off and gave it to her. She cleaned it at the sink, went upstairs to rub it in Sam's dirty clothes – 'prime DNA!' – returning to drop it by the back door. Then we lay at each end of the sofa, drifting in and out of sleep.

Her phone's alarm went off just after midnight. 'Let's get on with it,' she said, standing up and stretching dramatically. 'I'll take the van round to the gate.'

I dressed myself in a big fleece, a jacket and walking boots and tried to collect my thoughts. I'd endure these few hours of hell, whatever it took; I'd be tough. I went to the mirror and pulled my hair back into a workmanlike ponytail, fixing it with a rubber band.

Taylor knocked on the French doors and I went down to let her in.

'It's all quiet out there. We're going to be fine,' she said.

It was a half-moon night, a gloomy mix of silver and darkness. I noted the enormity of the London plane trees that guarded the perimeter of the communal garden and our route across it. Only three lights were on in the grand houses, and they were soft lights, distant and high.

Taylor picked up her crossbody bag, put several knives inside including the bloodied one, and handed me latex gloves 'in case we need to grab the walls and door and stuff... I'll throw the bloody knife in a bush.' Then we held the body by the straps, half lifting and half dragging it through the private section of garden to the communal part, stopping once to regain our strength.

We took up the straps again and stumbled across the main lawn, heading for a rhododendron bush where we crouched down to catch our breath – our focus was suddenly interrupted by a distant noise. A cough. A dog appeared out of the dark, a cute pale-coloured dog, a labradoodle, walking this way and that, its fur catching the moonlight, its snout sniffing the length of the black sack, its tail wagging. I recognised it immediately. Taylor put her hand over her mouth. I think she was giggling. I pushed the dog away.

From the other side of the garden, came a shout: 'Rupert! Rupert! Rupert!' It was my neighbour, Jackson.

Taylor's shoulders were heaving as she tried to stifle her laughter. I shushed her, slapped Rupert across his nose and gave him a hard shove. A loud whistle now, and it was clear that Jackson was closer, only metres away. Rupert was still obsessed with the body, so I slapped him harder still and this time he ran off. For a second, I thought we'd be okay – but Jackson's voice was now coming from the other side of the bush.

'Come here, Rupert, time to go in.'

Rupert bounded back to the body, as excited as an airport dog catching a whiff of cocaine. I saw Taylor reach into her cross-body bag, just as Jackson appeared and stopped short at the sight of us.

'What the f...!' he said, almost under his breath, as Taylor launched herself at his ankles, trying to bring him down.

'Push him. Push him!' she said urgently, but I did nothing. I froze, while Jackson fell to the ground, calling for help. Rupert was jumping back and forth like we were playing a game.

Taylor had a kitchen knife in her hand – the knife that she'd used on Sam. Suddenly, she was astride the man, stabbing him in the chest. Over and over. He tried to shout again, but he couldn't get a sound out, and his body pulsated while his eyes rolled around in their sockets. Then he was still. Rupert was growling now, but it kept its distance. I backed away from the bush, in shock.

'Well, isn't this just what we wanted?' Taylor was heaving, blood splattered across her face.

I crawled back towards Jackson's body. He'd only been walking his dog, an ordinary end to an ordinary day. Now he lay dead. I started to weep. Beside me, the dog was whimpering. Taylor grabbed his collar, her hands slick with blood.

I looked at her face, alert and alive, flushed with exhilaration.

'I can't go on,' I sputtered. 'We need to call the police.' Taylor gave me an arch, despairing look.

The dog started wriggling under her grip. 'Shall I kill it?' She pushed the knife into its fur.

'No! For God's sake.'

She threw the knife into the bush. 'I'm sorry, Rupert darling. This evening has turned out a bit peculiar for you, hasn't it?' It was the gentle voice she'd always used with Evie.

My body was trembling, and I thought I might vomit. Taylor whispered in the dark. 'Nothing needs to change... We leave the body here. The knife has this guy's blood on it and yours. Everything still fits.'

That phrase stopped my crying, suddenly like a blow to the face. *Everything still fits.* I wondered if she might kill me once she had her money. She was capable of it. For my own sake, I didn't care. I truly didn't. But for Evie...

'We should take the dog with us,' Taylor said. 'He might start barking if we leave him... and anyway he'll be nice company.' She took a knife from her bag and sliced off a length of plastic rope from the lattice around Sam's body, using it to tie Rupert's collar to a branch of the bush. It started to rain, big cold beads on the back of my neck.

'Come on, Lucy, you have to finish this. You have no choice...'

She was right... I hated her for it, but I blindly followed her commands as we hauled Sam's body to the next rhododendron bush, then to the gate and, with a final effort, into the waiting van. 'I'll go back for Rupert,' she said, 'you stay here.'

'I'm coming with you.' I didn't trust her with the dog.

I ran with her back across the garden and watched as she pushed the body further into the bush and moved the earth around with the toe of her shoe, removing footprints, while saying, 'The rain's a good omen.'

I hoped that it was washing away my depravity.

It pelted down for an hour or more, easing up as we reached Gloucestershire in the early hours. I guided Taylor along familiar streets, until we reached the final stretch – a twisting, muddy, potholed lane that ran through Radley Woods for half a mile, ending at a car park by the disused canal.

'I'll bring Rupert,' I said. 'He needs to get out of the car.'

I tied him to a tree and Taylor opened up the back of the van, then we dragged the body a hundred metres or so to the edge of the water – which was thick and black beneath us – a totally lost place, thoroughly ignored by time.

We worked quickly, running back and forth to the van, collecting black sacks filled with bricks, and then a large lawn-mower. We used Stanley knives and plastic rope to knot the bags to the twine around the body. Out of nowhere, I realised that I was still wearing my wedding ring under a latex glove, and the thought of it appalled me. I pulled at the glove and yanked off the ring, passing it to Taylor – 'stick this in a bag.' She took it and carried on her work with the weighted sacks. Finally, we knelt on the wet stone at the edge of the canal and pushed the whole lot in. There was no great sound, no obvious big splash. It was more like the blink of an eye, a flash of darkness, barely perceived.

FORTY-SIX

SEPTEMBER 1999

TL – She was heavy as fuck. I'd have thought she'd be lighter – she wasn't fat or anything. Sam still had his knife, that's why I was obeying orders, helping get the body across the garden. We were taking a rest by this big bush – when Sam says, 'Fucking hell, what's that?' This voice calls out, 'Rupert! Rupert!' We both had to suppress our laughter. You know how people do at funerals? Something about death really triggers it. Then this adorable dog appears. I can describe the dog better than the car. It was about so high, floppy ears, straw-coloured fur, a bit of a curl in it, cute collar – really nice.

So, it's sniffing round Lucy, and Sam's going, 'Bugger off, Rupert. Go on!' I felt like I was going to laugh too loud, and I realised, Sam had put something in my wine. Maybe that's why I was being so inappropriate, don't you think? My head was kind of woozy and happy. Like cocaine, but sleepy… So, the guy comes looking for his dog, and Sam grabs him and shoves the knife in. Can I have a minute? I'm feeling terrible again.

AR – For the record, Taylor has once again slumped forward, her head in her arms, her face to the table. She is trembling. I'd like to press on, Taylor. A drink of water?

TL – Thank you. Yes.

AR – You're flushed. Were you laughing?

TL – God no, Inspector Roy! I'm traumatised. How many times do I have to say it? I think I have PTSD.

AR – Did you see where the knife went in?

TL – Yeah. In his chest. Three or four times. Like this…

AR – Wasn't that your chance to run?

TL – As I said, there was something in my drink and I was mentally unbalanced; like it was all happening at a distance and was nothing to do with me.

AR – But you remembered the stabbing pretty precisely.

TL – It was a murder, Adra. Anyone would remember that. I definitely remember Sam throwing the knife into the bush… The knife you found.

AR – So we will find his fingerprints on it?

TL – Yeah, probably. You should definitely check.

AR – What happened next?

TL – Pretty straightforward. We got Lucy into the trunk, the boot, of the car, and we took Rupert.

First, we went round to the flat in Queen's Park, to pick up Evie. We had the key, because it had been in Lucy's handbag, and we snuck in. I guess the friend, Melody, was a deep sleeper because she didn't stir. And Evie came quietly from her cot, as sweet as ever, and hugged her daddy, and we got back into the car. Surely Melody has called you? I mean, she woke up this morning to find Evie gone. Have you spoken to her already?

AR – Don't worry, Taylor. Melody is very much on our radar. Can you tell us what route you took?

TL – I'm not from the UK, as you know. So I couldn't commit towns to memory or anything. But we were on the M1 for a bit going north. Does that help?

AR – For how long?

TL – Half an hour. Something like that. Then he turned off and took little roads. He was trying to keep it twisty. I was in the car with him for about two hours.

AR – We need more information on Sam's movements. That is our most pressing requirement. This is urgent, Taylor. If Sam's out there with Evie, we need to find him.

TL – So, where was I? Sam was pootling along country lanes. We were twisting and turning for ages. Then, get this, he stopped in the middle of nowhere, and said – really angrily – 'Get out! And take the dog.' I thought – why's he letting me go now, after all this! But I didn't hang around. I figured that all the talk of a future life together was a fantasy, but he didn't want to kill me either because he was still in love with me. He'd just been buying time. So I ran and ran, even though my body felt like a dead elephant, and, in no time, I was in these dark woods.

AR – What about Evie?

TL – There was no way he was going to let me take Evie, so I just ran and got to the police as quickly as I could.

FORTY-SEVEN

EVIE

NOW

Several times now, Evie has revisited Russell Drive and the surrounding roads – Warwick Avenue, Randolph Crescent and Formosa Street – imagining Lucy and Melody here, picturing Lucy confiding to Melody that she's scared of Sam. Urging Melody to protect Evie should the worse thing happen. She's been struck by the contrast between the claustrophobia of her parents' dangerous marriage and the wide, airy spaces in their opulent neighbourhood. She's thought of Melody leaving for Mexico. Never returning. Her ashes scattered so far away from her homeland.

Today, she's venturing further afield, to another expensive part of north London a few miles from number 37. White mansions line the road, rising up from pretty, well-tended gardens and she reaches out her hand towards a long evergreen bush so that, as she walks, her palm brushes the leaves. She tries to appreciate the silver sunshine and pale sky, and to feel the chilly breeze on her face. This is England and, in this moment, she is part of it. Turning a corner, she sees her destination –

Tredenham Nurseries, where Mia had worked. Her instincts have brought her here. It's just possible, she thinks, that someone will remember Melody King.

The entrance is marked by two stone pillars and a path lined with miniature trees in pots, and as she walks towards it, Evie's uneasy. She knows that she's causing chaos by digging up the past. How might this affect Bernard Wu? She thinks of him moving so quietly and seriously about his apartment, of his restrained voice and careful words. Her impression was of someone living a devotional life, like a monk or a craftsman; and in that way he reminded Evie of Mia. She, too, was living a life of service and care. But, as she enters the nursery, she knows she must continue in her quest. It's not just her curiosity at play. Or her personal journey. It's also a profound sense of justice.

Soon, she's walking the paths that separate wooden plant tables. Trailing her fingers through wispy ferns, she pretends to read about plants for shady areas, viburnum and pheasant grass and glances sideways to examine the place. It's huge and packed with greenery, but few customers – just a couple of tiny women in expensive fake furs, strolling around, picking up pots of daffodils and tulips, turning them left and right, squinting at them in the sunlight. Three workers in mud-coloured uniforms are pushing trolleys and attending to plants. Inside a greenhouse café, small groups of people are inspecting delicate lunches, dogs lying at their feet. Dogs everywhere, in fact.

Evie watches two women in uniforms chatting nearby. Wiping a bead of sweat from her forehead, she takes a breath, and approaches them. 'May I ask something?'

'Sure. Go ahead.' A young bright-faced woman beams broadly.

'I'm trying to track down someone who used to work here.'

The second worker, older and frowning, takes an interest.

'It's a long time ago I'm afraid. Twenty years. Her name's Melody King.'

They look at each other. 'Melody?' the young one says. 'Melody is one of the owners. But she's not Melody King; she's Melody Carter. Is that who you mean?'

Evie can't think straight. 'Could Melody Carter be the same person as Melody King?' she asks.

The older woman is wearing a badge that reads *Denise*. Squinting at Evie, she says, 'I guess she may have been King before she married... Melody's an unusual name.'

'Is it?' Evie doesn't know about British names.

'Melody's not at this site anymore,' Denise says. 'Hasn't been based here for about five years...'

In her state of confusion, Evie manages to ask, 'Could I have her email address? Would that be okay?'

'I can't give that out,' says Denise. 'But I can send her an email if you want. To give her your details.'

'Thank you.' She follows the two women into an office that smells of wood and earth. Seed packets, fertilisers and garden tools are on show – hundreds of them packed into the space. Denise logs on to a computer beside the till. 'Who shall I say wants to contact her?'

'Evie. Evie Segura. No, sorry. Evie Preston-Bliss.'

'Email address?'

Evie tells her, thanks Denise and leaves, half running past the mansions and towards the tube. At the end of her journey, she emerges into a crowded street in Paddington and walks briskly towards her hotel, checking her phone as she dodges commuters coming the other way. Melody Carter. She's emailed already.

A rush of possibilities hits Evie. One of them – beyond bizarre – is that Melody Carter is in fact Lucy Bliss. Her real mother.

FORTY-EIGHT

LUCY

1999

Halfway back to London we took a detour and dropped off Rupert in the grounds of a golf club. He bounded away and into a bunker where he started scrabbling in the stand and running in circles.

We returned to the motorway, Taylor at the wheel, high with excitement, me drifting in and out of a stupor, like I was drunk. Driving fast, over eighty, she started humming a tune then, tapping her fingers on the steering wheel. She said softly, 'He gone forever, deep sleep in stagnant water, eternal rift from little daughter...'

I dragged myself into consciousness. 'Stop it...'

She smiled. 'Oh, you're awake.'

'Of course I'm awake.'

'I've had an idea,' she said. 'I can help you some more. For more money...'

I didn't respond.

'Listen,' she went on, 'It's worth a lot. I'd say another £100,000...'

I ignored her, closing my eyes.

'How about this? I leave it a day or so, so you can take Evie out of the country, then I go to the police and tell them a story... You listening?'

I looked at her wearily, and she continued: 'While you get Evie to France – you're driving her in big Mel's van, right? – I'll sit tight, then turn up at a police station saying I know all about the missing woman and her daughter. I'll have a ton of evidence with me – that yellow T-shirt of yours with the blood, I'll take some of your hair, that sort of thing... And I'll tell them that I witnessed the murder. I actually witnessed Sam killing you. Or as good as. Say, I found him with your dead body, and he confessed everything. How about that?'

My numb head struggled to take in her words. 'I don't understand...'

'It's pretty straightforward, Lucy. I'll have tremendous fun... I'll go to town on how crazy you are. All the drugs. The hospital trips. Munchausen's by proxy. You were a danger to Evie, and Sam was anxious and angry, and he snapped in the middle of an argument. Yeah, I can pull that off... No problem. I'll take £50,000 up front, and the rest when you're safely in South America or Ulan Bator or somewhere crazy.'

'Who *are* you?' I mumbled.

'Wouldn't you like to know!' She laughed and swerved to overtake a lorry.

'Seriously, Taylor. Who *are* you?'

'I'm just a girl who likes games,' she said. 'Especially when the stakes are high.'

'Do you care about no one? About all the pain you cause?'

'I don't care about stupid, self-obsessed adults,' she said with a flick of her hair. 'Especially the smug, rich ones... Fleecing those bastards is a public service. It's profoundly satisfying. But I'm not a total monster. I wouldn't hurt cute animals. And I genuinely like Evie.'

I thought of the garden and how she'd wanted to kill Rupert. Of Jackson, and how she'd stabbed him simply for being in the way. As for Evie... I couldn't bear to think about Taylor's time with Evie. 'You disgust me,' I said.

FORTY-NINE

SEPTEMBER 1999

AR – A six-hour gap between the time you left Sam's car, and you dialling 999 from London. That's frankly bizarre, Taylor.

TL – Because of the drugs he'd slipped me, I fell asleep in that wood. Look – I've still got mud on my leg. Rupert ran off. I suppose he'll turn up in some animal shelter... When I woke up, I hitched a lift to a station and got the train back to London. I thought, I need more sleep before I can talk to anyone, and I might as well do that on the train.

AR – Which station did you come from?

TL – Oh God – I can't remember. I was so tired and drugged. Nobody in my condition would have remembered...

AR – Okay, that's enough. I'm stopping this interview.

TL – Ooo that's rather sudden, Inspector Roy. Can I go now?

AR – No, Taylor, you can't. This account of yours is frankly outlandish. I have enough evidence here to charge you with perverting the course of justice…

TL – Outlandish! You work for the police in London and you think *this* is outlandish… Like more outlandish than all the other murders and stabbings out there?

AR – That's enough, Taylor. I would like to take a DNA swab, and for a nurse to take a blood sample. I would also like to take possession of your passport. An officer will accompany you to your hotel to fetch it.

TL – Amazing… You're going to look like idiots you know? Lucy's body is out there and you're not believing me!

AR – As I was saying…

TL – All right already… I have my passport in my bag. Here you are. Can I have the blood sample taken here? I don't have to go to a doctor's office or anything?

AR – Yes – the blood sample will be taken here.

TL – It's just that I think I need to go to hospital… Look. It needs stitches…

Adra watches as Taylor Love stands up, lifts her dress and shows the officers her stomach. A long, fresh open wound snakes across her right side.

Adra has become accustomed to the brazenness of this young woman, to her self-confidence and shamelessness. Nonetheless, she's surprised by what she sees. The girl has been in pain throughout the interview.

AR – My God, Taylor, what happened? An officer will accompany you to the hospital. It's five minutes away. In the meantime, would you mind standing up and putting your arms and feet apart. Sinead, will you frisk, Taylor?

TL – That's going to be very painful and I'm not carrying weapons! I'm not a criminal! You have to believe me, you know. Lucy's body is out there in a ditch somewhere, probably in a wood – the rodents will be at it by now.

AR – We're doing everything we can to find her. Now, we'll find an officer to go with you to St Mary's, then you will return here for further questioning.

FIFTY

LUCY

1999

On the street in Queen's Park, we said goodbye. She fixed me with those bright green eyes and performed her wonky smile. 'Good luck in your new life, Lucy. It's been fun.'

'Goodbye, Taylor.'

I watched her walk towards the tube, a picture of innocence: flimsy skirt flapping around her skinny legs, her tiny form so childlike. She turned the corner, and I hoped with all my being that I would never see her again.

Exhausted and aching, I returned to the flat, rehearsing the conversation that I was about to have with Melody. I was ready to tell her everything and, at the same time, was distressed about burdening her with terrible truths.

I found her lying on the sofa eating muesli from a bowl while Evie played with coloured bricks on the floor.

'God, you look awful,' she said, looking confused at my incongruous outfit and walking boots. 'How was it?'

'What?'

'What do you think? How did it go with Sam?'

'Come to my bedroom.' I led her away by the hand, Evie paying no attention.

'What is it? What's up?' She sat on the edge of the bed, her big blunt fingers spread out on the duvet.

'I don't know where to start.' I sat with her, leaning my head on her shoulder, taking a long breath and beginning my story – Taylor had killed Sam, maybe it was in self-defence, it was hard to know. But there was no way she was going to be charged with murder. She'd made sure that all the evidence pointed to me, not her.

The words spilled out, gathering speed: 'I should have called an ambulance for Sam. I know it. I should have gone to the police and told them everything – about the canal, and Taylor, and Jackson's murder... I deserve prison, Mel, and I'm ready for it. But Evie...' My voice shook. 'I can't do it to Evie.'

She folded herself in two, staring at the floor. I looked at her mass of wavy red hair, and I waited. When she looked up, she said, 'This... it's just too much. I need time to think.' Her eyes were bloodshot, her skin pallid. Like she'd been suddenly struck with a fever.

While she tried to process my confessions, I played with Evie in the sitting room. We took out her miniature wooden village, tiny houses, people, shops and a railway, and arranged a perfect little world across the carpet, inventing families and lives and stories until Melody beckoned me from the bedroom. I went to her.

'For as long as I can remember, you've been a helpless, hopeless victim of life,' she said as we lay on the bed. 'First that situation with your father. You blame yourself, but you were a child, Lu. Just twelve years old. And the only child of an awful, unloving couple. Your father always putting you down. Your mother, so petty and self-absorbed. It was a terrible start in life... Your mother pretty much killed your father...'

I didn't want it, but I started to weep. 'Oh Mel,' I said quietly. 'I can't bear to think about it.'

'After your dad died, you couldn't speak. Do you remember that? You went weeks without speaking?'

'I can't help it. I'm still sick with guilt... But it's no excuse for what's happening now.'

She made me sit forward while she puffed up the pillows behind my head. 'Hear me out,' she said, settling back beside me. 'It's not an excuse – but it's an explanation... There are things I've never said which I want to say... Your marriage was fucked up from the start, Lu, and you didn't know it. You were too damaged to tell which way was up... and you fell head-over-heels for Sam even though it was obvious to anyone sane that he was so entitled and narcissistic – and never nice to you. Not really. Making jokes at your expense, putting you down like your father did – only with humour and charm. You couldn't see it. You just became more cowed, more unsure of yourself. It was hard to watch...'

'That doesn't mean he deserved to die!'

'I know. But he *is* dead. That's just a fact. And *you* didn't kill him, Lu... I can't let you take responsibility for a murder you didn't commit just because you're falling apart... The consequences for Evie are unthinkable. It's best that you just get out of here. Escape to some far-off country... and let Taylor do her work – let her make up the scenario that Sam killed you. She may be evil – but she's clever. She'll do it really well.'

I took one of the puffed-up pillows and hugged it to my chest. 'Do you really think that nobody would believe me? That I'd pay the price, not Taylor?'

'I'm sure of it. You had motive and opportunity and there's the forensic evidence. And your personality, your damaged character... people will totally believe it's you. You see what I'm saying, Lu?' She held my arm and stared into my eyes.

'Yes,' I said. I desperately wanted to take Evie thousands of miles away and to start over. I wanted everyone to believe that I was dead. 'Maybe Mexico?'

My baby appeared at the bedroom door. '*Mummy.*'

'Nothing to worry about, sweetheart. Come here.' I stroked her hair. 'We're going on a holiday,' I said gently.

'With Daddy?'

'No. Just us.'

'There be seaside?'

'Yes. We'll find seaside.'

Mel helped me put a few clothes into a Sainsbury's carrier bag – everything else was to be left behind: my make-up, my toothbrush, my jewellery and my phone. Then we packed for Evie, most of her clothes and toys, filling a large rucksack. I took Evie's passport although I was hoping not to use it to leave the UK or enter France, hoping she'd be safely asleep out of sight wrapped in blankets in the van.

Melody gave me her own passport, gravely and in silence, like part of a ritual, and I took it to the bathroom where, with a pair of kitchen scissors, I cut a thick fringe to cover my forehead, long enough to reach my eyelashes, and fashioned the rest of my hair into a rough bob. I used tongs to add messy waves, then I made up some big smoky eyes. In her passport photo, Mel was wearing a roll neck sweater – she went to her bedroom and found the same sweater, which I put on. Together we compared my new look with her passport photo. It was possible for me to pass as her. Highly possible, I thought, but not a certainty. I could only hope.

Then, I reached into a back corner of a bedroom drawer and found the passport photos of Taylor that had been in the bag that Persephone had given me. I'd take them too. They could be useful one day.

I returned to the sitting room and Evie looked up with widened eyes. 'New hairstyle,' I said. 'Could you oversee Evie's lunch?' I asked Mel. 'There's something I have to do before I go. It's going to take a while. Maybe an hour or so.'

'Lu?'

'What.'

'If you're going to Mexico – I want to give you Oscar Meana's address.'

'The guy from work?'

'Yes. He's gone back to Mexico to work in a botanic garden. I won't see him again. I don't want to. I liked him, but he didn't like me back – not in the same way. He's a wonderful guy – beautiful hair... heart-breaking smile... Look him up. He lives in a nice area in Mexico City, near Frida Kahlo's house.'

She tore a page from a notebook and copied down the address.

And then I wrote everything down in a long letter to Evie. The whole terrible truth. And when I finished, I sealed it in the rose jewellery box. One day she may need to understand what happened here, but not yet. Not for many years.

From here on, I'd give myself to my daughter. Help her build the confidence and courage I never had. I would support the two of us by teaching little children. I would have a kitchen garden.

FIFTY-ONE
EVIE

NOW

Evie stops dead, moves away from the tide of people in the street, leans against the window of a newsagent and reads the message:

I knew this day would come, Evie. Are you here in England?

That's all. No embellishments. Just a phone number.

She can't get to the hotel fast enough and pushes through the revolving door before sitting heavily on the closest armchair; it's by the check-in desk under a huge painting of Big Ben, and the Houses of Parliament. Breathing out to calm herself, she taps the number into her phone – her brain is filled with the crazy idea that this is Lucy Bliss, that she's about to speak to her birth mother, the mother who left her behind all those years ago.

A woman answers, her voice trembling with emotion. She sounds a little like Mia – her vowels and intonations are similar as she says, 'Evie, at last. Where are you?'

Their call is short. Evie says that Mia died suddenly two months ago and the woman, with shock in her voice, explains in staccato sentences that she wants to see Evie as soon as she can. She could come to London right now, or Evie could come to Stroud where the woman lives, close to where she grew up.

'I'll come to Stroud,' Evie says.

She dashes to her hotel room, picks up a few overnight things, and runs with her suitcase back to Paddington station – jumping onto a train just as the whistle blows. Before long, the train is out of London and is hurtling through the English countryside. Fields and trees and cows slip by, and clusters of brick houses with sloping roofs and chimney pots. Everything seems small, the colours cold and cloudy. She registers the patterns of this world then closes her eyes, her mind racing.

At Stroud station, teenagers are drinking from cans, bouncing around, jostling each other, speaking too loudly, until a friend arrives and they to turn leave the station. As they part, Evie notices a woman coming towards her, a mass of red hair close in colour to Mia's, though wavy where Mia's was straight, and a long fringe covering her forehead, just as Mia's had done; pale skin like Mia's and a freckled face. But she's wider and generally bigger than Mia and has a longer stride; her clothes are workmanlike and baggy – an ill-fitting pair of jeans tugged into country boots; a chunky green sweater. There's an air of generosity about her, in her movements and her eyes.

'Evie?'

They stand at a slight distance, taking each other in and Evie discovers that this is not Lucy Bliss after all.

'My mother told me her English surname was King,' Evie says. 'And I found your passport in her belongings... So I believed that she wasn't my real mother at all... That our lives had been a lie...'

'Oh. I'm sorry, darling. That must have been horrible.'

'It's only now, seeing you, and how it's you in the passport, not her. It's only now that I really know... I was imagining all sorts of wild things... I thought maybe she'd become you, and you became her...' She wipes her eye.

'Yes, sweetie. She was your mother. Mia was Lucy.'

They stand in silence for a second or two, then Melody takes the bag and they walk to the car, a battered green Land Rover – two white retriever dogs are turning circles in the back and jostle to greet her, their tails flapping wildly.

'Okay, Brewster. Come on, Bob. Settle down,' Melody commands.

'They're adorable.'

'Well, sometimes.'

On the twenty-minute drive along narrow country lanes, there is a tacit agreement that they will not talk yet about the central subject, the history that binds them. Instead, Evie remarks on the strangeness of the countryside that she's seen from the train and is now flickering in front of her in the beam of headlights. 'There's such order to it! Like in an eighteenth-century painting.' The landscape and its history that had seemed alien, was starting to draw her in.

They turn right, and follow a gravel driveway, parking in front of a house that reminds Evie of English costume dramas and Jane Austen. Melody goes to the back of the vehicle, lets the dogs out and lifts Evie's case, as Evie protests, 'Oh no. Let me...'

A stumpy bulldog of a man emerges from the house, marching bow-legged to the vehicle and taking the case.

'Evie, Jim – Jim, Evie,' Melody says. They shake hands and Jim leads the way inside.

Evie is settled into her room, which is under the eaves and homely, then she joins Melody in the kitchen. A beef stew is cooking in a pot on top of a heavy-duty range. 'I forgot to ask if you're vegetarian?' Melody says, as she gives it a stir.

'Oh no, not at all.' In truth, she's trying to cut out meat.

'Normally, at this time of year when it's colder, I drink red wine. But your mother and I had a history of white. Especially a glass of Sauvignon Blanc after work. Would you like one? It might be a good way to toast her?'

'Yes, please.' Evie's surprised. Mia was teetotal.

Melody pours the wine and gives a glass to Evie. 'To Lucy,' Melody says.

'To Mia,' says Evie.

'Come through to the sitting room and we can chat while the stew is cooking.' Melody picks up a plate of sourdough bread, oil and olives, and leads the way. The room is long and narrow with an uneven low ceiling. In a large brick fireplace, a fire is burning. The dogs are sleepy, lying on a rug and soaking up the warmth. Melody and Evie step over them to reach two antique armchairs, either side of the fireplace, and the bread is placed on a small table. It's all a little precarious.

'Jim's going to give us some time,' Melody says. 'He's having supper in his shed.'

'Oh – not because of me!'

'Supper in his shed is his favourite thing. He has a lathe.' She says this firmly, then leans back in her chair assessing Evie again. 'You have your mother's expression,' she says. 'And your father's colouring.'

Evie's heart flickers. 'You knew my father?'

'A little.'

'I want to know everything. About him. And what happened.'

'I'll tell you all I know, Evie. But why don't you tell me about Lucy first?'

'I don't know what to say. Were you in touch with her? She never mentioned you to me, I'm afraid. She didn't like talking about her life before she came to Mexico.'

Melody leans forward to stoke the fire. 'She wrote a few

times at the beginning – but she didn't tell me your address, and I wasn't able to write back. I have some loving reports about you – how you were getting along at school, and the holidays that you took with your Mum – that sort of thing. You have an interest in art, is that right?'

'Yes. I studied Fine Arts.'

'Tell me about your earliest memories, Evie. Do you remember anything before Mexico?'

'Not really. I visited Russell Drive a few days ago and wondered if I'd remember anything – but I didn't. I mean I felt a sort of familiarity and I imagined myself there – but that was it.'

'You saw the inside?'

'Yes, I went with the police...'

Melody shifts in her chair. 'You've been in touch with the police?'

'Yes. It was only when Mia died that I found the press cuttings about the disappearances in 1999 – I had nowhere else to start...'

'Have they interviewed you? I mean, you were a central part of the story...'

'Not formally. Not yet. They will, though. Sometime in the next few days.'

'Right.' Melody leans sideways, her head in her hand, one big leg crossed over the other widely so that the bottom of her slippered foot is almost in the fire. 'Anyway – go on. Tell me about your life.'

Evie smiles at Melody, like she's known her forever, and experiences a softness, an intimation of safety as she starts her story: 'When I was little, I was so happy alone with Mia – just the two of us in our little apartment in Mexico City. I used to like playing in the kitchen, lots of drawing and painting, and running around in the yard outside. She and I were quite isolated from the world – we didn't have many friends. I knew I was different. At school, I was the English kid who spoke two languages. Who didn't have a father. Mia was sensitive to all that... I have quite an idealistic view of her from that time. She radiated a sort of calmness.'

'Did she?' Melody reaches down to stroke one of her dogs, looking at Evie with a puzzled eye.

'Yes. She was always calm – but when I was older, I realised that she had to work at it. She meditated twice a day you know. She said *finding peace* was the most important thing in life.'

'Ah.' Brewster or Bob places his head on Melody's knee, and she strokes him while he closes his eyes.

'Wasn't she always like that?'

'No. She was very different once. I'm pleased she found some peace.'

'I think so. But she was never happy in an ebullient way, if you know what I mean. She didn't walk into a room buzzing with joy.'

'Did she have a man in her life? She didn't mention anyone in her letters.'

'When I was small, there was a guy called Oscar who came around a lot and helped out with fixing things and took us on outings. I think there was something there...'

'Oscar Meana Gill?'

'I'm not sure. You know him?'

'Maybe. Did he have a mass of bushy black hair? Really wild hair?'

'Yes, he did.'

'A big bear. And tall?'

'Yes! I think his hair turned white. And that he came to Mia's funeral. I went through a phase of imagining that he was my father... How did you know him?'

'He worked in London a long time ago. At Tredenham. I liked him very much... Before I met Jim.'

'Mia saw him for a few years and then he just disappeared from our lives... Except one day, years later, he came to visit with his wife and two little children.'

'Ah.' She pushes the dog away and reaches for the bread.

'Do you have children?' Evie asks.

'Yes. Gracie is in her first year of university and Ross is seventeen. He lives close by in a community for young people with learning difficulties. It's sad that your mother never met them.'

'So you were close?'

'We were. Since school. I was her best friend... I'll tell you all about it; don't worry. But you carry on, Evie. I want to know what happened next with your mum.'

'She became a teacher. Of little children. Four- and five-year-olds. She was good at it. But, apart from work, her life was kind of narrow. People thought she lived like a nun. She had her books and her garden—'

'She gardened?'

'Gardening was part of the zen thing she had going on. She found it consoling.'

'That pleases me.' The big dog who'd been enjoying Melody's attention puts his paws on her lap and tries to scramble up into her chair. She laughs. 'No, Brewster, you silly sausage...' He turns away unperturbed and lies on the rug with Bob.

Evie drinks the last of her wine. Although she has many questions for Melody, she is grateful for the opportunity to go first. To pay a proper tribute to her mother before she delves into the poisonous circumstances of her disappearance all those years ago. Before she asks about her father. Once these questions are in the open, the purity of Mia's Mexican story will be lost.

'I rebelled as a teenager,' she says. 'I went off the rails for a while. Drank a lot. Stayed out all night. One time, I left home to be with a boy and stayed away for three days.'

'Gosh. How did Lucy react?'

'Mia, I think of her as Mia. She was calm... it infuriated me! But I'm grateful for it now... I mean, she might have called the police or something and she didn't. She said that she'd known where I was, in her bones, and knew I'd be back within the week.'

Melody has her mouth full of bread, and chews and swallows as quickly as she can. 'My oh my! They say people don't change – but your mother did. There was a time when something like that would have made her hysterical. Now, let me fetch you a top-up.' She stands up, pushes her fringe of curly hair away from her face, and strides to the kitchen, followed by the dogs. Evie gets up to inspect family photographs on a shelf. Wedding pictures – Melody towers over Jim, but they look alike in their twin smiles and joy. There are several photos of small children – wrapped up warm, running in fields, playing on cold, windy beaches.

Melody returns with the dogs, pours the wine and settles back into her chair.

'Would you like to tell me what your mother said to you? About why you left the UK? And about your father? There's no need if you'd rather not...'

'I'd like to talk about it,' Evie says nervously. 'But only if you give me your version afterwards.'

'Yes. Of course, sweetheart.' There's deep tenderness in her voice.

'She told me that her parents were dead.' Evie's quiet voice reflects her doubts. She's wondering if anything about her mother's account was true. 'She said her relationship with my father had been brief – but would never name him or talk about him... which was hard to take. Did you know that when she came to Mexico, she chose the surname Segura – which means safety or refuge?'

Melody, deep in thought, shakes her head. The fire is barely glowing now. She stands and reaches for tongs, placing two fresh logs carefully across the embers, then she says, 'I have something for you, Evie. A jewellery box that your mother gave me for safekeeping. It contains a letter for you, and you alone.'

FIFTY-TWO

SEPTEMBER 1999

Taylor Love is in the back of a police car on the way to the hospital, weighing her options. The streets of Paddington are not busy. She'd prefer them to be busy.

It's raining a slow drizzle, and the few pedestrians are not rushing. A woman in a black niqab inspects vegetables outside a grocery store; a young man under an awning talks on his phone; two blonde-haired women amble along the pavement arm-in-arm. Taylor is remote from them all. She's never identified with civilians.

As they pass an entrance to the tube, she imagines disappearing down there and into the underground tunnels. If only she could get out of the car. But the doors are locked. She's checked.

In the front, are two officers – an overweight white man with a bald patch on the back of his head, circular like a bulls-eye, and a short black woman who looks not old enough to be out of school. Teenager's driving while Mr Blobby gazes out of the window. Taylor hopes that when they reach the hospital, the driver will stay in the car. She could escape from Blobby. No problem.

She reflects on her performance at the police station. She'd got carried away, had overacted. Still, the T-shirt with Lucy's blood – that should have done the job. Surely, the police will believe that Lucy's dead. Surely, Lucy will pay up the extra cash. And if not, well nothing ventured, nothing gained.

She'd been right to wound herself beforehand, to have that reason to leave before they took a DNA swab or detained her on some pretext. She laughs out loud, remembering her theatricals in the interview room. She'd loved the shocked eyes of the policewoman, Adra and her sidekick, dopey Sinead.

The police car stops on a narrow street that curves up to the main entrance of St Mary's. 'I'll wait,' Blobby says, his voice a dull thump. Teenager shrugs, leaves the car and opens Taylor's door. 'Let's go.' Taylor gives her best flirty smile, but the officer doesn't respond, just sticks to Taylor's side, whisking her through the reception area to the lifts. They go up to the fourth floor and, as they exit, Taylor assesses the wide corridors, the porters pushing trolleys, the brisk-walking medics in scrubs. A running girl chased by a running police officer? That's not possible right now.

They report to a reception area and wait in adjacent plastic seats. Taylor says, 'This is fun,' and turns on another winning smile.

This time, the officer smiles back. 'Shouldn't be long.'

This is good. Teenager seems unaware of Taylor's significance in a murder case. Unconcerned.

'Busy day?' Taylor asks sweetly.

'Pretty routine. Getting to the end of my shift.'

'Got a good evening planned?'

She never finds out because a female nurse comes to a door and reads out her name from a clipboard. She gets up and follows the woman into an office. Teenager stays in the waiting area. She's texting someone.

'Take a seat,' the nurse says. 'Should be with you in a few minutes.' She disappears through an internal door.

Taylor looks round again. It's not an office after all. It's a second reception room – and there's a corridor to her right. She can't believe her luck. Quietly, she gets to her feet, walks down the corridor. She speeds up and hums a tune: *I want to break free!* Coming to a little crossroads of corridors, she turns left. Somehow, left looks more promising than right, and fifty metres later, she pushes heavy swing doors and finds that they open on to a concrete staircase. Everything is perfect. The gods are smiling.

Taylor runs daintily down four floors and is now face to face with a fire-door. One almighty push on the metal handle and, in a rush of cool air, she's outside in an alleyway and is running towards a road. No one's around. She spots the police car 200 metres to her left; Blobby leans against it, looking into space. She turns quickly right, hoping he doesn't see her. But, as she reaches the next corner, she hears 'Hey! Hey!' She's now at the steps into the tube station and she races down. Oh, the exhilaration! She's practically weeping with joy.

Her preparation has been perfect – she has her ticket ready. Surely, Blobby won't catch her? He's in no fit state to leap the barrier and it will hold him up to demand that it be opened. She's soon in the tunnels, heading for the Bakerloo line. A train thunders in and Taylor is on it, panting as she sits down and watches the doors close. As the train pulls out of the station, she sees Blobby huffing and puffing onto the platform. Exquisite timing!

Seven stops later, she disembarks at Charing Cross. Her stomach wound throbs a little, but it's nothing that she can't take.

FIFTY-THREE

EVIE

NOW

Evie takes the jewellery box onto her lap, wiggles the key into place and turns the lock. Inside is a white envelope, fat with its contents, sealed with sticky tape. In her mother's handwriting, in blue pen, it says *For Evie, if she wishes it*. Evie puts the box on the floor, holds the envelope, squeezing it slightly, feeling the roughness of the paper, committing it to memory.

'It's the whole story.' Melody strokes one of the dogs. 'Your mother wrote it on the night that she fled the country with you.'

'*Do I wish it?* Why does she ask?'

Melody sinks her fingers into the soft fur around the dog's neck. 'It was written twenty years ago. You were practically a baby, and she had no idea whether you should know the truth one day... She wrote this, just in case she died before she'd told you.'

'... and then it happened. She died.'

'Yes.'

'And why did she give the letter to you? Why not bring it to Mexico?'

'She thought she might be arrested when leaving the country and didn't want it falling into the hands of the police. Didn't want it to end up in a court of law... and there was a psychological reason too. She wanted to leave this story in Europe, far away from her new life, that was part of it. You must choose whether or not to open it. Evie...'

Evie laughs gently. 'I can hear in your voice that you think I shouldn't do it. But why not? It's my history. And my mother wrote it. For me.'

'How old are you? Twenty-five, twenty-six? Don't you think she would have told you what happened by now if she wanted you to know?'

'I don't know... Not necessarily. I mean – she never told me about this letter. She never said – *I wrote you a letter once, but I don't think you should open it.*' Evie holds the envelope against her cheek.

'That's true.'

'I feel lonely without a past.'

'You may be lonelier with one.'

FIFTY-FOUR

SEPTEMBER 1999

Three hundred metres along the Strand, and Taylor enters the left luggage store. It takes only a few minutes to retrieve her suitcase and enter the Palace Hotel, padding along a claret-coloured carpet, heading for the fancy *powder room*. She sits down on a velvet padded stool and takes one last look at herself in the mirror. She does soft loving face. Hurt but resilient face. Deep empathy face. Goodbye Taylor Love, what a minx you were!

She opens the suitcase and, five minutes later, the girl in the powder room is a different creature. This young woman wears a black T-shirt, black leather jacket, and grey ripped jeans. Her hair is shoved into a scruffy camouflage beanie, pulled low over her forehead. She wears the same boots as Taylor Love – she's not giving up the boots! Leaning over the sink, she washes off her make-up with soapy water, then strides out.

This girl has a swinging boyish gait. This girl chews gum and makes up raps. *He gone forever, deep sleep in stagnant water, eternal rift from little daughter.* Lucy had hated that! But she'll do better, she'll saccharise the poetry to suit the next lonely mother she befriends. She loves new beginnings – new games.

At Charing Cross, she catches the Dover train and opens up a book. A travel guide to Australia. Bright skies and red earth, flashy white smiles and beach culture. It will be a whole new colour-palette after grey, wet England. A different world. But she'll find the same Lucy-and-Sam types, she's sure of it. Neurotic, screwed-up women and vain, gullible men. They're in every country, the dopes.

The train heaves over an old bridge crossing the Thames. She looks each way – at parliament, at the shiny City towers. It's the centre of the world here; she may come back one day. A hit or two in Australia, then back here. The tattered buildings of south London slip by, but she's barely paying attention. Instead, her mind is returning to that moment in the woods – the thud and splash of Sam's body, and those ridiculous tied-on weights. She's a killer now, courtesy of Sam Preston. What a piece of work he'd been!

All the little cruelties directed at Lucy: the demeaning actions on his birthday – eyes lighting up at everything Taylor did – the meal, the photo album – followed by cold glances at Lucy who was disintegrating at the far end of the table. Later, when Sam accused Lucy of smothering Evie in the bed – well, it was obvious that he was exaggerating and distorting. Taking pleasure in breaking his already broken wife.

Taylor had loved making Lucy the common enemy. And it had been so easy to slip Evie fragments of rotten food, mixed in with her milk or her orange juice. Beans left in an open can, raw sausage. Every time, Evie had gone green and spewed up. And Sam had lapped up the idea that Lucy was harming Evie. Had revelled in the power it gave him... What a manipulator he was!

Had he left the knife under Evie's cot that first day? She'd forgotten to ask...

The train has moved beyond the city now and picks up speed as it whips through open fields and into dark ravines. Not long to go. She'll sit on deck of the ship and gaze at the sea, let the wet salt air permeate her hair and skin.

'Tickets!'

The ticket collector is a black guy, greying hair, large, lidded eyes, a belly. 'Dover Priory. Off on an adventure, young lady?' he says.

She grins as she retrieves the ticket from her rucksack and hands it over. He shambles off, giving her a quick wink, before calling out again 'tickets!' She has this effect on people. She doesn't even need to say anything – they are drawn to her, want to be liked by her. It's always been this way. She's always been the popular girl.

She's supremely confident that her skills will be invaluable in Australia. In the most expensive Sydney suburbs – Bellevue Hill, Vaucluse, Mosman and Bronte. There will be kids' clubs and nurseries and swimming classes to investigate and, in no time at all, she'll befriend a young woman who is struggling in some way, desperate for an ally. Her guard down.

She returns the train ticket to her bag and registers a gleam of gold. It's her one souvenir. Her trophy. Lucy's wedding ring – slipped into a pocket on the night at the canal. She leaves it at the bottom of the bag and takes out her new passport.

Rylie Cox. Great name. She runs it around her head. Rylie Cox. Like Taylor Love, Rylie will be untouchable and uncatchable. The thought comes into her mind not as a certainty, but as a dare.

FIFTY-FIVE

EVIE

NOW

'Remember that your mother wrote the letter at a terrible moment in her life,' Melody says. 'If you read it, you may never forgive her.'

The walls of the little room are painted deep mulberry red. There are bookshelves and trinkets; photos and paintings; dark beams and rugs the colour of blackcurrant jam. The light is soft and golden, and Evie feels like she's wrapped up in a warm blanket as she speaks the dreadful words: 'She killed him, didn't she? Sam Preston was violent, and she killed him in self-defence.'

'No. It's not as straightforward as that... The nanny, Taylor Love, was the killer, I'm practically certain of it. And Lucy didn't attack the unfortunate young man in the garden. Jackson Wu. She wasn't capable of it... That was the nanny too. But Lucy's actions were... unconventional. She was a damaged young woman who witnessed a murder and made an unusual decision about what to do next.'

'You lied, didn't you? To the police?'

'Yes, I did. For Lucy and for you – so that you could have a new life – and I'll never be certain that I did the right thing.' Melody sighs. 'You had a peaceful life with your mother and remember her with love. The letter may wreck that memory, Evie. Why don't you sleep on it? There's no need to decide right now.'

Evie agrees. She will sleep on it.

The following day, she's on the train heading back to London, listening to ambient music on her AirPods, watching the now-familiar fields, woods and villages passing by and contemplating the heavy grey sky with a sort of acceptance.

She has a section of four seats to herself and the envelope is lying on the blue plastic table in front of her. Melody had asked at breakfast, 'Have you made a decision?' and Evie had slowly stirred the porridge in her bowl and said enigmatically, 'I'm still thinking.' But deep down she knew what she was going to do. In the end, this wasn't about her alone. As things stood, the survivors of the whole, sickening episode, were still suffering; still living with the absence of answers. The figure of Jackson Wu was like a ghost at the far edge of the story. His family deserved to be moved to the centre. She thought of Bernard Wu and Kendis Williams, of Bernard's sister Sisi in Glastonbury and his father in Hong Kong. They deserved to know the truth. As for Sam's surviving family – she'd like Clemency to be told, whatever that might mean, whatever her ability or wish to comprehend.

She thinks of Mia in the kitchen in Mexico City, quietly cooking or reading. Mia in the courtyard, tending her plants. Mia the teacher of little children. Melody had thought that the horrors in these pages would contaminate such memories, but Evie disagrees.

She thinks of that day, just a few weeks ago, when the

purple jacaranda trees were in bloom and she'd dodged the traffic on her way to see her mother, knowing that she had a decision to make about her future with Antonio, and that Mia would offer wise counsel. She can see Mia, in her blue dress, picking up her straw hat, smiling at Evie and saying, 'Do you have everything you need?'

Those final words have a different meaning now. This letter is the '*everything you need.*'

It will deliver her from secrets. Will reveal who she really is. Who her mother was, and her father too. In reading, Evie will be more complete. More equipped to take her next steps in life.

'There's something else,' says Mia's voice as Evie sees her again – not entering the house as she had done in reality but sitting back down at the table in the courtyard, where the bread and olives and wine are set out on a patterned cloth. 'I had to make a choice, darling. Go to prison, as was just – or run away with you.' She looks Evie squarely in the eye. 'I chose escape and a life of sacrifice and atonement so that you could flourish. You're an adult now, darling; my job is done. Read the letter. Read it to the end and then make your big decision; choose your truest path.'

Evie is about to pick up the envelope when her phone vibrates in her pocket. It's a message from Melody:

> I have this video of you and your mother – it's very sweet, do take a look.

Evie watches as a young woman, not a much older than herself, runs around the garden at Russell Drive and in hand with a tiny, fair-haired child wrapped up warm on a cold day. The little girl's cheeks are flushed and her eyes bright. 'I try to protect her from all the dangers in the world,' Lucy says to the person behind the camera. 'But she has such a curious soul.' Mia and Lucy, Lucy and Mia. As the train rattles through a tunnel, the two personifications of her mother at last become one in Evie's heart. She picks up the fat envelope from the table, peels back the yellowing sticky tape, and takes out the pages.

For the next half hour, Evie is back with her mother, hearing her mother's words not from the ether or from inside her own head, but from real words written on real, tangible paper. 'I fell in love with your father,' she reads, 'because he was clever and funny and charming, and he was my rescuer, taking me away from my family home.' She learns that Geraldine was responsible for the death of Lucy's father, and of Lucy's disastrous upbringing. 'But my childhood does not excuse my actions in these past few months,' Lucy writes. 'Sam was killed by Taylor Love. But I held him in my arms while he was wounded and still alive. I didn't call the ambulance. Maybe he died because of me, just as my father died because of my mother's inaction. I will never know.'

Lucy tells Evie that she is determined to raise a strong and confident girl who will never surrender to the power of a controlling man. Will never give into contortions in her head that make good things seem bad and bad things seem good. Will have a clear moral code. 'I suspect that if you are reading this, then I am dead,' continues Lucy, 'So it falls to you, Evie, to decide whether to hand this letter to the police. As I write, I think that would be the right thing to do. If you are free now, then it's time to bring Taylor Love to justice.

'If, as you read this, the police still have no idea what happened – then you may wish to let them know that I paid Taylor to convince the police that I was dead, that maybe you were too, and that Sam was the culprit. She and I dropped Sam's body into a section of disused canal deep in Radley woods near my old home in Gloucestershire. Right by the little stone bridge.

'This is what I know about Taylor: I'm certain that her real name is something altogether different and that she's a rootless and self-created woman who grew up all around the world. She plays life as a game, seeing people as resources for her entertainment, her manipulations and her desire for wealth. She has no empathy and her biggest fear is boredom – so she's a psychopath, I guess. But it would be wrong to reduce her to a label, a psychological type. This woman is extraordinary for other reasons. She's deeply intelligent and possesses a sensuality that I have never seen before. But she's not infallible, Evie. I did not bring her to justice, but maybe you will.'

The train picks up speed and the paper shakes in Evie's hand as she reads to the end, then starts again at the beginning and re-reads.

At last, her big decision is made. She knows what she will do. This evening, she will phone Antonio and tell him that she's not yet ready for marriage and has decided to stay in Europe. Her truest path is clear now – she'll get to know this heavy, cold place; its landscape, its history and its people.

Her visit to England has made her realise that there was always a European side to her that was suppressed in Mexico, that was calling to her through art and art history. She has an idea about a link between art and healing, about studying such subjects and making a career of them, and she hopes that Antonio will be patient. Will understand that she needs to explore, and be curious. And she'll tell him of another, more immediate, intention.

Evie reaches into her bag, pulls out the photographs of Taylor Love and examines them, finding that they are as clear as she remembered, believing that they will be useful to Adra Roy – surely this face is on a database somewhere. There's a chance, at least. She will hand the photos over to the policewoman along with Lucy's detailed and incriminating letter. Evie's resolved now to stay close the investigation; she'll pester and provoke Adra to deliver justice.

The train pulls into Victoria and Evie does up the buttons on her black wool coat, picks up her bag and disembarks. The cold air doesn't bother her, and she almost feels at home as she makes her way through the London crowds, walking purposefully towards the tube, each step feeling more certain. She's heading for Paddington and the police station there.

A LETTER FROM THE AUTHOR

If you enjoyed *What the Nanny Said* and would like to join other readers in keeping in touch, stay in the loop with my new releases by signing up to my email newsletter here.

www.stormpublishing.co/lara-finch

If you could spare a few moments to leave a review, that would be hugely appreciated. Even a short review can make all the difference in encouraging a reader to discover my books for the first time. Thank you so much! Review here.

I've loved writing Lucy Bliss, not least because I'm fascinated by the power that dangerous people have and I wanted to explore how they manipulate, deceive and control those around them. When I grew to know the wealthy community of Little Venice, I thought – what a great setting for my dangerous person to cause her havoc! I sat down at my laptop with the intention of writing a tight, twisty and suspenseful novel that brought those elements together. I do hope you liked the result!

Very best wishes,

Lara

ACKNOWLEDGEMENTS

A heartfelt thank you to my family – Tom, Carol, James, Kate, Harry, Freddie and Molly.

Thank you too, my dear friends – Tom, Jim and Jeni.

I'm especially grateful to Sophie, who has listened to my literary dilemmas with patience, and has advised me with intelligence, skill and enthusiasm.

Finally, thank you everyone at Storm, in particular Claire Bord who has worked so brilliantly on this book. And also my agent Jon Wood, who brought it out of the darkness into the light.

Printed in Dunstable, United Kingdom

66389835R10181